TRI-SYST

THE
JAKE CUTTER
CONSPIRACY

R. Kyle Hannah

Jumpmaster Press™
Birmingham, Alabama

Cover Illustration by Dimitri Walker

Library Cataloging Data

Names: Hannah, Kyle, R. (Richard Kyle Hannah) 1967-

Title: The Jake Cutter Conspiracy / R. Kyle Hannah

5.25 in. × 8 in. (13.34 cm × 20.33 cm)

Description: Jumpmaster Press digital eBook edition | Jumpmaster Press Trade paperback edition | Alabama: Jumpmaster Press, 2018. P.O Box 1774 Alabaster, AL 35007 info@jumpmasterpress.com

Summary: How far would you go to clear your name? A tale of survival and revenge.

Identifiers: ISBN-13: 978-1-949184-09-9 (ebk.) | 978-1-949184-08-2 (trade)

1. Science Fiction 2. Action/Adventure 3. Space Opera 4. Aliens 5. Adventure 6. Conspiracy 7. General Fiction

Printed in the United States of America

For more information on R.Kyle Hannah
www.rkylehannah.com

TRI-SYSTEM AUTHORITY
Book One

THE
JAKE CUTTER
CONSPIRACY

R. Kyle Hannah

Leah,
All the best!

Also Available from R. Kyle Hannah:

Time Assassins
Assassin's Gambit
Assassin's End
To Aid and Protect

I'd like to thank everyone who has come out to the conventions over the last couple of years to meet me. This book is dedicated to you!

Chapter One

What's with the shot *across the bow?*

The order to shut down the engines still echoed from the communications terminal as the ship rocked from the warning shot. Jake Cutter stood at the engineering console and steadied his portly body by grabbing the edge of the panel. Another flash of light, another mini explosion outside the cockpit window rocked the freighter and Jake began punching buttons in earnest. His lazy, carefree attitude turned to increasing panic with each explosion outside the cockpit canopy. He felt his knees tremble as his fingers flew over the controls, shutting down the engines. He touched another set of switches, cutting the repulser shields.

They wouldn't do much against a TSA ship anyway, he thought.

Distracted by the anticipation of another warning shot, Jake's sweat slicked fingers flipped one too many switches and the ship plunged into darkness.

"Great." He shook his head. He blindly reached for

the master switch, found it by touch, and froze. *Did I get the engines offline before the master switch was tripped? If I didn't and I turn that switch...* He did not want to get blown out of the universe. Jake stood in the middle of a triangle of seats, the control center of the ship. A single pilot seat sat forward, with consoles for engineering and communication to the rear right and rear left, respectively.

With a deep sigh, he removed his hand from the control panel, turned his back to the stars winking beyond the cockpit canopy, and stood silently in the dark cockpit. A chill slid across his skin as the cold of space crept into his dormant freighter. *Gonna need to reactivate life support soon.*

Jake Cutter, a freelance freighter captain, was two days out of the Zar'got system, his hold full of crates that read "Perishable: Protein Packs". His ship, the *Fortuna*, had no weapons, only meteor reflector shields, and no value other than it served as Jake's livelihood. He had no idea why the Tri-System Police would want to board him.

That T'Traxi merchant did seem a bit nervous, he thought as he stood in the darkness. A flash of anger warmed him despite the chill. *If he planted contraband on my ship...*

He heard magnetic grapples engage his freighter and felt a tremor move through the ship as the TSA locked on. He glanced out of the cockpit canopy and saw the bow of the police picket grow larger as it tugged him in. His freighter shuddered as the ships docked. Jake felt vibrations through his feet as the hatch opened and men boarded his ship. He heard footsteps echo through his dormant ship, followed by gruff voices muffled by police armor. He took a deep breath and raised his hands as the cockpit door opened. Two Tri-System officers entered with weapons raised.

"Freeze!" one of the men ordered as bright light filled the cockpit. Jake squinted against it but said nothing.

Peering passed the light, Jake saw that both officers wore the black armored uniform of the Tri-System Authority Police Force. The laser proof armor lay atop form fitting neoprene body suits. Flexible plastic, that provided environment protection, but little armor, covered the joints and neck. Illumination strips sat on either side of the reflective visors that covered their faces. Jake's brown eyes narrowed against the light and he caught his reflection in the mirrored visors. Nervous sweat trickled from his brown hair, sliding down his face.

Great. I look guilty of something. This is not going to be pleasant.

Another armored officer appeared behind the two in the cockpit. His visor had turned transparent and he wore the stripes of a Sergeant on the chest of his armor. He strolled into the cockpit, looked around in disgust and made a show of slowly taking off his gloves. He slapped them against his left palm and sighed disdainfully.

"Name and manifest, citizen." He sounded bored.

Jake slowly lowered his hands, his voice almost

cracked. "I'll need to reactivate the power, for the lights."

The officer waved a dismissive hand. "Fine. Be quick about it."

Jake turned his back to the Sergeant and, using the light from the officer's helmets, found the master switch he had turned off in his near panic. He offered a prayer to a long-forgotten deity, hoping that he turned the engines off before the main power. He closed his eyes and flipped the switch. A low hum filled the ship as the lights came to life. The life support system engaged and Jake felt a current of warm air brush across his sweaty face. The engines, thankfully, stayed dormant. He slowly exhaled the breath he did not realize he'd been holding.

He turned back to face the officers, a polite smile on his face. "Now, what can I do for you?"

"Name and manifest," the Sergeant repeated.

"Right." Jake nodded and moved slowly to the communication on the other side of the control center. He punched up the manifest list and backed out of the way. The Sergeant moved past him to read the screen. Jake kept his hands visible to the other officers as he spoke to the Sergeant's back. "I'm Jake Cutter, Captain of the Freighter *Fortuna*. I have perishable protein packs bound for the Blu'clic moon, Mirohm."

The Sergeant studied the manifest list for a moment before he straightened. He turned, faced Jake, and stared at the freighter captain. "Perishable protein packs," he repeated, as if tasting each word. "Well, Captain," he said with a disbelieving smile, "I'd like to see these perishable protein packs."

Jake returned the same disbelieving smile. Something wasn't quite right and he felt a cold tingle tickle his spine. "Of course," he said, waving a hand toward the door leading to the bulk of the freighter. "Right this way."

Jake felt the *Fortuna* shiver as the TSA Picket released his freighter. He flipped two switches, activating the lateral cameras he had installed to watch merchants as they loaded or unloaded his ship. The external cameras showed the picket retracting the magnetic grapples and slowly moving away. Jake waited until he couldn't tell the ship from the stars before he powered up the engines and resumed his course.

He sat down heavily in the pilot's chair and ran a hand through his short, brown hair. His hands still shook a little from the intrusion. He took a moment to breathe deeply, slowing his racing heart. Calmer, he leaned forward and double checked his course. Satisfied, he pushed the throttle forward and the *Fortuna*'s engine's flared. Two hours of his life wasted and he had to make up that delay if he wanted to arrive on time.

What were they looking for? he thought for the hundredth time.

He turned his head to stare through the open cockpit door toward the cargo hold. The police search had been systematic and deliberate. The officers had moved from crate to crate, verifying every item on the manifest. Not that unusual, so he had been told, but Jake found the whole affair gut-wrenching. This time, it was his ship being searched, not some stranger reciting a story. Even though he had nothing to hide, the fear that something was amiss gave him the shakes.

The police left as abruptly as they appeared. No apology, no explanation. Jake stood and left the cockpit. He replayed the search in his mind as he headed for the cargo hold to verify everything was secure. He rummaged through the hold, examining every crate and, in a flash of paranoia, he double checked to make sure nothing had been planted on his ship. He had been warned of that trick, too.

Jake returned to the cockpit and tried putting all of it out of his mind. The adrenaline overload waning, he dropped his body into the pilot's chair. The navi-computer read-out showed eight hours to Mirohm. His eyelids felt like they weighed a ton each. He closed his eyes and let the blackness of sleep take him.

"You're late."

Jake stopped at the sound of the voice. He stood halfway down the *Fortuna's* ramp; shy of the shadow of the ship and the afternoon sun. He stared daggers at the green-skinned Klan'do merchant standing at the base of the ramp. Four other Klan'do stood behind the speaker in a rough semicircle. Jake continued down without a word. He had the lingering feeling that he had been violated by the inspection and his mood was sour. He took a deep breath, smelling the cool, crisp air of Mirohm. *Time for business*, he thought and pushed the police interdiction from his mind.

The squat, humanoid Klan'do tapped a query into his datapad as Jake stopped a half meter away from the alien. He looked down at the alien who stood nearly two feet shorter than Jake. The mossy smell of the Klan'do assaulted his nostrils. "Twenty-seven minutes late," the Klan'do read from his pad.

"Police checkpoint." Jake tried to sound nonchalant as he shrugged. "Unavoidable."

The Klan'do offered a snort. He motioned for his minions to begin unloading the cargo before waving Jake to follow him. The Klan'do's short legs caused it to waddle as it walked back toward his spaceport office. Jake followed, trying not to laugh at the funny walk. The sight of the merchant raised Jake's spirits and by the time they arrived at the office, his sour mood had changed considerably, but still not to his usual sunny disposition.

The duo entered the Klan'do's office, a subset of offices that lined the spaceport like a strip mall. The merchant sat behind a large dura-crete desk built out of the floor. The entire office appeared to be constructed of dura-crete except for one overstuffed faux-leather chair. The soft cushion chair creaked slightly as the Klan'do rocked backed. The office walls stood bare, a solitary window, with a view of the landing pad, streamed in bright sunlight. Jake stood calmly as the merchant took his time going over the manifest. He had delivered to the Klan'do before and knew that business came before manners, or anything else.

Jake retrieved a small data pad from his belt and activated the internal and external cameras aboard the *Fortuna*. The external cameras showed more of the Klan'do's minions had arrived; a dozen employees of several races now bounded up and down the freighter's ramp, unloading the cargo. Anti-grav dollies rolled on and off his ship in a very systematic and efficient routine. Jake made sure the computer shut them out from the rest of the ship. He touched a tab on his pad, ensuring the cameras recorded everything, before putting it away.

"Everything is in order," the Klan'do said with what passed as a smile for the merchant. "Your account has been credited, minus the late fee."

"The checkpoint caused the delay." Jake protested. "Not my fault."

"The contract is quite specific, Captain Cutter," the Klan'do replied, his smile widening. "You give up ten percent for every hour you're late."

Jake opened his mouth to protest again, thought better of it, closed his mouth, and simply nodded. The Klan'do's smile filled his entire pudgy face. Jake knew nothing made the alien happier than saving a few credits, except maybe haggling over the lost credits.

"Are you available for another job?" The merchant smiled innocently at the Captain.

"Depends on which direction it's heading," the pilot muttered.

Jake had not seen his wife in two months and he needed a vacation. His mind drifted to the net-call he made after waking up from his nap. Seeing Pamela's brown eyes and tanned cheeks on the screen had brought a sense of warmth and normalcy to his life. She had seen his mood shift on the screen and her expression changed to concern in an instant.

"What's wrong?" she asked.

"Nothing, now," Jake said sincerely. Just her presence, even if just on a screen, lifted his spirits. "I passed a police checkpoint a few hours ago. Got boarded." He shrugged, trying to forget the entire event. "Delayed me a bit, but I'm almost back on schedule."

"You're alright?" she asked.

"Yeah, I'm fine." he said, the tension still draining. "They went over the ship pretty well, but didn't find anything."

"Did you expect them to?"

"No, of course not," he replied, his eyes widening at her tone. Maybe it was the long day, but her almost accusatory tone firmly entrenched his sour mood. He took a deep breath. "I just wanted to let you know that I'm coming home. Should be there in a couple of days. Have you thought about my proposal?"

"Jake," she said, her voice low. "I've told you before. I don't like to fly. What would I do on a ship all day long?"

"You'd be here...with me." He could tell she was

deep in thought.

"Jake," she said, shaking her head to dismiss the conversation, "we'll discuss it when you get home."

"Everything okay there?"

"Yes," she smiled. "I'll tell you all about it when you get here." A chime sounded in the background; something was cooking in the oven. She saw the inquisitive look on his face. "Baking cookies for an event tomorrow. Chocolate chip, your favorite."

Jake could almost smell the cookies. "An event?" He asked as his stomach rumbled, reminding him that he had not eaten in almost a day.

"Social gathering with some friends," she replied, vaguely. "I'll tell you about it when you get home."

He nodded. "Have fun, see you soon. Save a few cookies for me."

They signed off without another word.

"Which direction do you want to go?" the Klan'do asked, bringing Jake from his reverie.

Jake offered a half-hearted grin. "Home. The Heroz system. Got anything going that direction?"

The six fingered Klan'do typed in a query, saw the results and smiled. "Yes." He turned the data pad around for Jake to read. "Just sign at the bottom and the cargo is all yours."

"The cargo has been loaded, per your specifications," said the Klan'do into his holo-com. "He is scheduled to depart any minute." The holo-com showed a dark shadowy figure, out of focus and unrecognizable. The merchant moved his eyes from the holo to his data pad showing a large deposit of credits. His eyes widened, a smile crept across his thin lips. This was not the first time he had done business with the Government, but this had definitely been the most profitable.

"You've done us a great service," the disembodied voice said.

The roar of engines interrupted the conversation. The Klan'do turned to stare out of the window, watching the *Fortuna* lift from the pad. The figure on the screen paused, cocking an ear to listen. The engine roar subsided.

"Was that Captain Cutter?"

"Yes," the Klan'do said, forcing his eyes from the window, to his data pad, and finally back to the screen. The alien smiled, nodding absentmindedly. "He should be in the Heroz system in three days."

Dust and smoke billowed across the dura-crete spaceport pad as the *Fortuna* lifted. Jake Cutter throttled up, adding thrust and smoothing out the bumpy ascent. He piloted the ship in a northerly direction away from the mercantile area of Mirohm. He flew low, following the edge of a sprawling city. Once clear of the congested space-lanes, Jake pulled on the flight yoke, nudging the throttle a bit more. The streamlined, cigar-fuselage design of the freighter headed straight up and left the moon.

Jake felt the heat of the atmosphere dissipate as the black emptiness of space consumed his ship. The ship continued away from the moon, heading for the navigation beacon at the edge of the system. *Twenty minutes to the nav-beacon and three days to home*, he smiled and pushed the throttle to max.

The nav-beacon requested a destination query and Jake turned, happily typing in *HEROZ*. The computer confirmed the course and relayed the ETA. Jake smiled cheerfully as he sat back in the pilot's chair and let the computer handle the minor course change. He let out a long, relaxing exhale. It would be good to get home for a week or so.

Maybe I can convince her to come with me, he thought as the ship banked slightly. The indicator revealed fifteen minutes to the nav-bouy. He leaned forward and flipped two switches, activating the star drive for faster-than-light travel. The computer accepted the input and a hum filled the ship as the engines prepared for jump.

Jake rotated his seat, propping his feet into the navigation chair. He nestled deeper into his pilot's chair and cocked his head, watching the stars beyond his canopy. The stress of the day diminished with each breath. The gentle hum of the engines pulled him toward the beckoning arms of sleep. Dreams filled his mind's eye. He recalled graduation day from the civilian flight school, celebrating with a few drinks with his fellow pilots. The image of the bar filled his mind: the smoke, the off-key band in the corner, the constant clink of glasses. The whiff of subtle perfume.

He saw her at the other end of the bar and felt his palms begin to sweat. She was beautiful, with long brown hair down to her waist, a tight-fitting blue skirt and matching top; her make-up applied perfectly. It took him almost an hour of teasing glances to work up the courage to simply talk to her, another half-hour before he bought her a drink.

The image shifted to a lakeside cabin and Jake smiled in his sleep. The multi-colored leaves fell with the autumn wind, crunching underfoot at they walked along the bank. He strolled hand in hand with Pam, her hair much shorter than when they met at the bar. He fiddled with the ring box in his pocket, hoping she would say yes. He dropped to a knee, the wet ground soaking his khaki pants. He pulled out the box, flipped the top open and asked her the question on his mind.

The scene morphed, the lake replaced with an expanse of ocean. They walked along the beach, celebrating their fifth anniversary together. The steady rumble of the waves masked their giggles and gently whispered affections. The sun set behind them, casting long shadows toward the ringed moons rising on the horizon. Jake felt the waves rush around his ankles and he stopped, letting the sand engulf his feet as the tide retreated.

"Pam," he pulled her close. "These last five years have been the best of my life." She snuggled against him, burying her head in his chest as he spoke. "I think it's time that I bought a bigger ship. One big enough for both of us…"

Jake startled awake as the communication panel chirped and a harsh voice filled the cockpit. "Freighter *Fortuna*, shut down your engines and prepare to be boarded."

Jake rubbed his eyes and checked the sensor panel. His heart raced as his spirits sank. Two police pickets rapidly approached his freighter on an intercept course.

"Again?" Jake shook his head as he rotated the chair forward. He pulled back on the throttle as a volley of warning shots exploded out of his cockpit window. He waited until the rocking ship stabilized before standing and moving to the engineering panel. Another round of warning shots jarred the ship and he again found himself reaching for the closest panel to steady himself.

"This is ridiculous!" Anger replaced his disbelief as he powered down the ship. He took an extra moment to ensure he left the master circuit on this time.

One of the TSA vessels roared past the cockpit canopy, the engine exhaust rocking the *Fortuna* in its wake. Jake stood transfixed, watching the ship bank, turn, and stop nose to nose with his freighter. Its forward spotlights slid across the ship, coming to rest on the cockpit, blinding Jake. He shielded his eyes, letting them adjust. His heart pounded as he realized that the ship's weapon ports were open. *They mean business.* A warning indicator flashed that the ship had target lock on the freighter.

This isn't right, he thought. He stumbled backwards, finding the communications seat with his legs and sat down heavily. He rotated the seat, facing the panel, and activated the camera playback from his cargo hold. Nothing looked out of place as he watched the Klan'do's minions haul in three large crates and strap them down in the hold. Jake glanced out of the cockpit and saw the nose of the second scout as the ship hovered above. A flash of panic chilled him, coursed through his body as the magnet grapples of the TSA Picket latched onto the freighter. He brought his eyes back to the replay.

The last Klan'do in the hold was strapping down a small silver box behind the other crates of cargo. Jake had missed it on his initial inspection. He silently cursed himself for not looking behind the other crates. The vibration of men entering his ship brought him back to his current situation. He turned off the playback, and felt a cold sweat creep down his spine. *Maybe they'll miss it like I did,* he thought.

The cockpit door opened and two armored officers entered, weapons up and ready. Jake slowly stood, raising his hands. The three men stood in silence for several minutes before their Commander arrived. Jake heard someone approach. The same Sergeant from the first encounter enter the cockpit, carrying the small, twelve-inch by twelve-inch silver box from the freighter's hold. The TSA Officer sat the box on the communication console before slowly removing his gloves and helmet. He wore an all-knowing smile as he slapped his gloves in his left hand again.

"Captain Cutter," the Sergeant said. "We meet again."

Jake lowered his arms, then crossed them. His eyes glanced at the silver box, the Sergeant's fingers slowly drumming on the metal. A chill shot down his spine and he lost all hope, like a kick to the gut. Still, he tried to play it off. "What can I do for you?"

"You can tell me about your cargo," the Sergeant replied. He patted the silver box on the navigation console. "Starting with this box."

"I'll have to check the manifest," Jake replied truthfully. He felt the sweat forming on his brow. "I didn't check any of the contents before I launched."

The Sergeant smiled. "No need. We both know what is in this box, don't we?"

"Actually, uh, no," Jake protested. "I...I have no idea what is in there."

The Sergeant offered an assuring nod at the pilot that mimicked *Sure..sure.* He drew his pistol in an explosion of motion that startled Jake. Jake stumbled backwards as the TSA Officer blasted the lock with one shot. Smoke and the stench of ozone filled the confined cockpit. Jake, shocked at the speed of the draw, faintly heard the atmospheric scrubbers kick on to remove the acrid odor. The officer re-holstered his weapon as fast he drew it, knocked the melted slag of the lock away with a glove, and popped the lid open.

The Sergeant inspected the case, shaking his head. Jake strained to see around the lid and only caught sight of a couple pieces of paper. Jake watched the officer shuffling through papers and other objects, but nothing recognizable. The Sergeant stopped his shuffling, and raised his head. He stared at Jake, the twinkle of glee in the officer's eyes made his heart sink.

"Captain Jake Cutter," the Sergeant smiled. "You are under arrest for theft of confidential government material, the transport of contraband, and smuggling."

Chapter Two

Fading sunlight streamed through high windows, casting long shadows across the courtroom. Bound and shackled, Jake Cutter shuffled before the Blu'clic system Magistrate. The metal restraints bit into his wrists and ankles. He strained for even the smallest movement, thanks to the electro-magnet that connected the cuffs to a belt around his waist. The presence of two armored police officers on either side of him assured everyone present that the prisoner would not be going anywhere.

A dozen other prisoners, bound like Jake, lined the back wall, each escorted by a guard as they waited their turn before the magistrate. An equal number of black armored TSA Officers, short barreled rifles cradled in their arms, stood silently along the adjacent walls of the room. A few other beings occupied the courtroom: the Chandrillian Magistrate and his two aides, several bureaucratic lawyers, and a holographic jury of Jake's peers. The jurors—Human, Hazmora, Klan'do, and Blu'clic—aligned themselves on Jake's left, their flickering images standing silently. Two desks, one for the Prosecutor and the other for Jake's court appointed attorney, sat on either side and behind the accused.

Jake bent at the waist and lifted his left arm as high as he could, straining against the electro-magnet. He barely managed to brush his matted brown hair from his eyes before standing erect. He winced as his hand brushed the bruises on his face and again as he stood, shifting his cracked ribs. He checked his hand and saw no new blood. He gave silent thanks that the blood no longer flowed from the gash along his left temple.

The arresting TSA Officers had hauled him out of the *Fortuna*, roughly tossing him into the picket ship's brig. He slid across the floor into the feet of a scarred and tattooed Hazmora. The red-tinted humanoid alien was thin, even for its species, with a mane of spiked, jet black hair trailing down its back. The alien howled as Jake impacted its ankles, roared in anger, and pummeled Jake with its long arms. Jake curled into a ball. The beating lasted a few seconds, until a TSA guard stunned the alien with a single laser bolt to the chest. The alien, thankfully, remained unconscious for the trip to Blu'clic.

The Magistrate banged his antique gavel. Jake shuffled a few steps forward and stopped in a bright circle of light emanating from a hidden source in the ceiling. He squinted against the light as the murmur in the hall quieted.

"Jake Cutter," the magistrate began. He was a slovenly, overweight Chandrillan with large, rabbit-like ears, snout nose, and four large, round eyes. Jake had never seen a Chandrillan before and could not help but imagine a white, fluffy tail in the seat. He thought that he might have laughed under other circumstances.

The Magistrate continued. "You are charged with theft and smuggling. How do you plead?"

Jake opened his mouth to speak when he felt a hand on his shoulder. He turned to see a man in an expensive suit step up beside him. The man reeked of cheap cologne and wore a smarmy expression of superiority. Jake took an instant dislike to him as the man flashed a toothy smile.

"Your Honor," he began. Jake realized he was an attorney. "My client is a simple man, with no criminal record. He is an honest, hardworking, family man. Mr. Cutter only resorted to this type of behavior to ensure that his family was well provided for."

"Wait. What?" Jake stammered, astounded. "No!" He tried to hold up a hand in protest, but the electromagnet resisted and his hand failed to lift. "Damn it!" he screamed in frustration.

The gavel banged. "Mr. Cutter, you will refrain from using such language in my courtroom," the Magistrate admonished.

Jake took a deep breath and nodded. "Sorry, Your Honor." He motioned toward the lawyer with his head. "I don't know who this man is, but he does not speak for me."

"Mr. Cutter, that is your attorney," the Magistrate acknowledged. "He is here to assist you in your defense."

Jake turned his head to look at the attorney. He squinted against the bright light of the circle. "How can he speak for me when he hasn't even *talked* to me?"

The attorney held out his arms, palms up. "Your honor, my client is clearly distraught..."

"Damn right I'm distraught!" Jake yelled. "I'm being set up and you're helping them."

The gavel banged again. "Mr. Cutter, this is your second warning."

Jake took another breath. "Sorry, Your Honor, but this man does not speak for me. I have not done anything wrong."

"You are entering a plea of not guilty then?" asked the Magistrate.

Jake blinked in confusion, thought for a moment, and nodded. "Yes, sir."

The lawyer shrugged his shoulders. "Whatever." He turned to head toward the empty desk and paused next to Jake. "Just so that you know, I already had a deal worked out for you; six months and loss of your merchant's license for two years." He smiled and shook his head. He patted Jake on the back. "Good luck."

"I don't want your damn deal," Jake whispered in reply. "I'm innocent."

The lawyer simply smiled, patted the prisoner on the back again, and exited the courtroom, whistling as he left.

The spectacle over, the Magistrate turned his

attention back to Jake. "You wish to have other counsel brought in?"

Jake did a slow look around the courtroom and realized that there would be no justice for him today. The TSA police stood stoic behind their armor. The jurors sat bored and disinterested, several held data pads in their hands, steadily typing away. The prosecutor leaned back in his chair with his hands behind his head, his face a mask of smug satisfaction.

Jake sighed. He had been bullied into firing the lawyer. He had been bullied from the moment the police boarded his ship. The only course open to him was to follow it through and see what would happen next.

"No, sir," Jake said slowly. "I will represent myself."

"Very well, let's get started."

The sun had long since set and overhead lights illuminated the courtroom. It was well past dinner and Jake's stomach rumbled loudly. How long had it been since he had a meal? A day? All he knew was that for the last two hours, the evidence had been presented: docking permissions, manifests, video of the scout's pursuit of the *Fortuna*, and a silver box that had yet to be opened; the contents labeled *classified*. The only item not submitted into evidence was the video from his ship showing the Klan'do merchant planting the silver box. Jake had attempted to refute a couple of items, but his knowledge of the law was limited and the prosecutor stymied him at every turn. A foreboding filled Jake as the holographic jury returned from their deliberations, their images coalescing in the jurors' box one after another.

"Has the jury reached verdict?" The Magistrate sounded bored.

"Yes, your honor," said a smallish woman as she stood. Jake stood as well because he thought it was the proper thing to do. He received an icy stare from the Magistrate.

"Proceed," said the Magistrate politely.

"Jake Cutter, Captain of the freighter *Fortuna*, you are found guilty of all charges."

Jake felt gut-punched and let out the breath he did not know he had been holding. His shoulders slumped, his head drooped. He felt as though his whole life had ended.

"Thank you," the Magistrate smiled. "Dismissed." The holographic jury vanished and the judge turned his attention to Jake.

"Mr. Cutter," he asked. "Do you have anything else to say before I pass sentence?"

"I'm innocent," he said hopelessly.

"Not according to your peers," the Magistrate stated matter-of-factly. He shook his head. "You are hereby sentenced to ten-years hard labor at a penal colony outside of the Tri-System. Your ship will be impounded and your accounts frozen."

"Ten years?" Jake yelled, anger and disbelief attacking him all at once. "The lawyer you had in here said six months!"

"The lawyer you fired, Mr. Cutter?" Jake paused for a moment before nodding. The Chandrillian continued. "Maybe you should have listened to him.

"Sergeant, remove Mr. Cutter from my courtroom. "Court adjourned!"

Jake Cutter struggled with the electro-magnetic restraints as the police officers roughly escorted him from the courtroom. He turned his head to see the Chandrillian Magistrate, the prosecutor and the defense attorney – who had entered from a side door – laughing. They waved at someone and Jake caught a glimpse of what he thought was a Klan'do before being shoved down the corridor.

"Move it," one of the officers commanded. Jake fell to his knees. He tried to stand, but his legs buckled. His mind raged, unable to focus on a single thought or action. The officers grabbed him by the shoulders and dragged him toward the detention area. The drab duracrete corridor tore through his pants and cut into his knees. The pain brought him focus and he managed to get his legs under him. Depression and despair sapped his strength.

The trio left the bleak sub-corridors of the building and stepped into the common area of the courthouse. Jake shuffled along on autopilot, head down, staring at the marbled tile on the floor.

"Jake!"

A woman's voice echoed down the judicial building. The escort stopped and Jake turned his head to see a woman walking toward him. The brunette wore a tight fitting black outfit, and a thin layer of makeup. Her shoulder length hair fell from her head like a cascade, the right side tucked neatly behind her ear. Jake felt a resurgence of hope at the sight of his wife, and thought that Pamela had never looked more beautiful. She stopped a few feet away, staring at him with her brown eyes.

"Is it true?"

"I'm innocent, Pamela," Jake pleaded, reaching for her with shackled hands. The electro-magnets kept his hands close, and she recoiled slightly at the sight of the cuffs. "I swear. I would never knowingly carry contraband."

She stood quietly before him, unmoving, her eyes moving up and down as she surveyed Jake. He knew how he looked, bruised and bloody, wearing ragged clothes. He gulped, filling his voice with all the strength he could muster. "Stay strong," he said. "I'll get out of this. I'm innocent."

"I know," she replied. More silence.

"One question. I have to know." Jake began, breaking the quiet. "Were you ready to travel with me?"

She stepped forward and took his head in her hands. She slowly, sadly, shook her head *no*. She saw the hurt in his face and offered an explanation. "That ship is no place to start a family."

"A family?"

"Jake," she said, tears welling in her eyes. "I'm pregnant."

The armored guards pulled him away from his wife. He felt her hands slip from his face as the TSA officers dragged him backwards down the corridor. "No! Wait!" He protested and struggled against their hold, resisting as best he could with the electromagnetic shackles that bound him. The Officers simply tightened their grip on the prisoner, hauling him toward the shuttle dock. They rounded a corner and he lost sight of Pamela, still standing in the corridor.

"Jake!" she called, her cry cut off by a blast door as it slid closed.

The escort dropped him unceremoniously at the foot of a shuttle ramp. Jake looked up, into the cold eyes of the Sergeant that had arrested him. The man, gloves still slapping his left palm, stared down at Jake, smiling.

"Congratulations, Mr. Cutter; or should I say Prisoner Cutter?" He towered over the prisoner, grinning ear-to-ear. He pocketed the gloves, replacing them with a wooden baton from his belt. He stood, smacking his left palm gently with the two-foot long cudgel. He nodded and the guards hoisted Jake to his feet. "Too bad you won't live to meet that child."

The movement was swift and Jake barely saw the wooden baton swing before it hit him in the stomach. He doubled over as the other guards moved into a tight circle around him.

He never felt the beating the officers gave him. He

thought of Pamela and his unborn child as his mind dove in on itself. The world around him disappeared. He did not even acknowledge when the officers bodily threw him into the prison transport. The door slid shut, leaving him alone in a three-meter by three-meter hold.

He lay on the deck, G-forces pressing his body as the ship launched. The ship went weightless on the edge of the planet and Jake rose from the deck a half-meter before someone activated the artificial gravity. Jake grunted as he impacted the floor.

His entire universe spun out of control. Pain racked his body. Jake forgot about Pamela, the child, and all the good things in his life. He closed his eyes and wished that death would take him.

Chapter Three

The beatings continued sporadically for the first few hours of the flight. Jake curled into a fetal position every time the door opened. A guard would enter, slap Jake in the face or punch him in the ribs, and then leave, laughing. Finally, the Sergeant and two others entered. The man knelt on one knee beside Jake, contempt in his eyes.

Jake stared up at him through hazy eyes, smelling the man's foul breath. He shuddered.

"That's enough," he said, rising. He headed back for the door, paused, and turned back to Jake. "For now."

One of the other officer's tossed a round container into the room before closing the door. The container of liquid rolled, coming to a stop against Jake's left knee. He grunted with effort as he struggled to sit up. He fumbled for and found the container, removing the lid with difficulty. The cool water burned as it snaked its way down his throat. Jake dragged himself to the bulkhead and propped his head against the wall under a small porthole. He winced as he craned his neck to stare out of the window. He watched the stars as he faded in and out of consciousness. The ship exited the Tri-System boundary, heading for deep space.

The citizens of the TSA had determined early on that they had no need to be reminded of the criminal element in their midst, so all convicted felons were sent out-system. The citizens lived their blissful lives, while the prisoners were often forgotten. A prison sentence, no matter how short, almost always meant life. The citizens of the TSA simply did not care. Jake reminded himself that, until very recently, he was one of them.

He watched the stars, his mind drifting from the trial, to Pamela and to the child he would likely never see, to the beating, to thoughts of what awaited him in prison. He had heard the stories: bad food, prison gangs, forgotten prisoners left there well past their sentence. With each subject that flitted through his mind, his depression grew, and he knew that he would never leave the prison alive.

The shuttle banked and Jake received his first look at his new home. A gas giant planet with a dizzying array of rings grew larger as the ship approached. The shuttle continued its gentle turn, moving passed the planet. Jake saw vast oceans of purple, interspersed with black and yellow storms. Jake had seen enough planets to know that a toxic atmosphere awaited him. The ship leveled from its long turn and slowed. The ringed-planet began to shrink and Jake, realizing the gas giant was not his destination, grimaced as he craned his neck in the other direction to look out of the window.

He had a brief glimpse of a brown moon before the blast shield shut without warning, cutting off his view. The shuttle entered the moon's atmosphere and Jake scrambled to find something to hold onto, gripping the edge of the porthole as best he could. Pain coursed through his body with every jolt from the turbulent decent. A massive bounce jarred him and he lost his grip, sliding across the floor as the ship continued toward the planet. Finally, the flight smoothed out and Jake lay still, gasping for breath. The shuttle landed a few minutes later and Jake rolled onto his back, surprised he was still alive.

The guards arrived soon after landing. These men wore different uniforms, dark green with name tags over their left breast pockets. The emblem of the TSA Prison Authority rested on their right sleeves. Neither was armed, but that offered little hope to Jake in his current condition. They hoisted him to his feet, and Jake stood on trembling legs. The pair escorted him out of his cell and off the shuttle. Jake shuffled along as best he could despite the electro-magnetic resistance of the cuffs. A maze of rock corridors left him disoriented and lost, convincing him he could not find the docking bay if he tried.

Eventually, he arrived at a small desk with a young, bored looking officer sitting behind it in a well-worn chair. He wore the same uniform as Jake's escorts, with Ensign bars affixed to his collar. The officer gave a cursory glance at the display on the computer panel sitting on the desk and, without a word motioned for the guards to take the prisoner away.

Jake shuffled along between the guards, arriving at the next station, identical to the first down to the bored officer, a minute or two later. The Officer rose from a chair and stepped around the dented and dusty metal table. He nodded to the escorts, "Dismissed," and the two men disappeared back up the corridor the way they came.

The Officer produced a small device from his belt, pointed it at the prisoner's shackles, and Jake's cuffs fell away, clattering to the stone floor. Jake rubbed his wrists until the man produced a thermo-knife. Jake froze as the TSA officer proceeded to cut off his tattered and bloody suit. Jake tensed as the heat of the thermo-knife came close to his skin. Small heat welts crisscrossed his body as his clothes fell away, and Jake moved his hands to cover his private parts, his sore wrists forgotten. A flush of red brought color to his cheeks.

The officer retreated back to his desk as a toothless old man appeared from a side corridor. Dressed in haggard clothes and long stringy hair, he offered Jake a pair of miner's coveralls, a shirt, and a pair of worn out boots. Jake nodded his thanks and began to put on the clothes. The shirt and pants were too small and the shoes too big.

"Don't worry, you'll lose enough weight to fit those in no time," the old man smiled.

The old man collected Jake's ratted and bloody clothes, depositing them in a chute hidden behind the officer's desk. The officer continued looking at his computer screen, ignoring the two prisoners. The old man offered a cheerful grin to Jake.

"The name's Zreb. I guess I'm what you'd call the welcome wagon." He scratched his scraggly beard. "Welcome to Cla'nix." He pointed to the rock corridors around them and gave the newcomer a brief overview of the prison. "There are no rules here. The prison is nothing more than a series of caverns under the surface of the dead moon," the old man said. He led Jake to a small ledge that overlooked a large cavern. "This is the center of Cla'nix prison. The only guard post is up here in the administration area. Once you're down there," he pointed to the large cavern, "you are on your own.

"The entire prison is a kill zone for psychopaths and the criminally insane. Oh," the old man snickered, "there ain't no infirmary, so my advice..." He paused until Jake nodded his head. "Don't get sick. "

Jake took in as much as he could, but his left eye was swollen shut from the shuttle beating and his head throbbed, making it hard to concentrate. *No infirmary? I need a doctor now!* He shook his head to clear it and tried to get the details of the prison. He stood on a ledge overlooking the large cavern. A sheer rock face five meters tall prevented any prisoner from ascending to the ledge. Jake shifted his gaze to the cavern itself.

Light tubes lined along the ceiling and walls illuminated the cavern and Jake could see a multitude of alien faces looking up at him. Blue-skinned

Blu'clics; green-tinted Klan'do; reddish-brown Hazmora; huge, hairy Crendoshians; and dozens of other species all stared up the ledge at him. Several rubbed their hands together and Jake swore that one drooled. He averted his eyes and continued his survey of the cavern.

Rock walls and a dirt floor greeted his blurry vision. A half dozen tunnels led off the cavern. The old man pointed to one of them. "Those lead further into the moon. There are a few dormitories, but you," he looked Jake up and down, "probably won't get to use one." The old man snickered. "Any questions?"

Jake shook his head absently. He needed to lie down and sleep. He needed a...

The old man shoved Jake off the ledge. "Enjoy your stay."

Jake screamed as he fell five meters from the ledge, landing hard on the rock floor of the cavern. A plume of dust rose in the air. Jake tried to stand, but his legs buckled and he fell back to the rocky floor. Pain racked his body, fire consumed his ribs, and he fought for a breath. He rolled in agony on the dirt floor, fighting the tears welling in his eyes.

Rough, furry hands grabbed him, hoisting him off the floor. Jake struggled against the grip, looked down and recognized the paws as Crendoshian through swollen eyes. He stared face to face with the largest alien he had ever seen. The beast snarled, displaying sharp fangs. Jake felt hot breath on the back of his neck and struggled to turn, fear replacing the pain as he panicked. He craned his neck enough to see the an alien the likes of which he had never seen before. He recoiled from the beast, struggling to break free, but the Crendoshian grip was inescapable. The hairy beast, with only the slightest grunt of effort, spun Jake around to face the unknown alien, his feet a foot off the floor.

The creature stood on two long legs and resembled a mythological Succubus: reddish skin; deep, dark eyes; long horns curling outwards from its head; and a tail that twitched with agitation. Jake almost gagged as the scent of sulfur touched his nostrils. The demon alien took a step back and looked down. Jake involuntarily followed the alien's gaze. The beast shook one of its three-toed feet, dirt and dust fell from the alien's appendage.

The alien moved nose-to-nose with Jake. "I am the Lemox Demoness," she hissed. "And you, are, now, mine." Her tail whipped around, striking Jake across the face. The Crendoshian dropped him to the rocky floor, as the Demoness struck him again.

Jake never learned how to fight and had no idea how to defend himself. He simply curled into a fetal ball and wished for death to come quickly. His display seemed to enrage the Demoness and she beat him harder. Jake felt kick after kick on his back and heard his screams of pain above the roar of the crowd cheering on the alien. The impacts stopped and he opened an eye in time to see her turn her back to him and take a step away. She paused, turned her head to look at her victim, and lashed out one last time with her left foot. Jake's head snapped back but he somehow remained conscious. The alien walked away, two Crendoshians in tow, and the crowd groaned, displeased the show was over. He lay there several minutes before he crawled into a nearby corner and passed out.

Jake awoke stiff and sore; barely able to move. He attempted to survey his surroundings, only to find one eye functional and the other swollen completely shut. His body felt numb and on fire simultaneously; Jake closed his eyes to fight a flood of pain induced nausea. The wave subsided and he opened his eye again. He suffered a moment of confusion, then panic before he remembered where he was and what happened. He attempted to pull his legs under him and found his boots were gone. He looked down and discovered his coveralls and shirt missing as well. He tried to stand and failed. Using the rock wall for support, he tried again. On the third attempt, Jake forced himself to stand on wobbly legs. Chills coursed across his skin in the cool cavern and he felt exposed, vulnerable; literally naked to the world.

He stood alone in a small alcove off a corridor. He could hear the murmur of voices close by, but saw no one. Still holding on to the wall, Jake took a tentative step and then a second. He made it to the entrance to the alcove before a large Crendoshian stepped in front of him. The beast stood seven-foot-tall, a Gorilla-like behemoth, all fur, teeth, and muscle. The alien's red eyes burned with rage as it yelled at Jake in its guttural language. The screams attracted a crowd which quickly formed a semi-circle around the two. Shouts for the alien to kill the human filled the air. The alien screamed another verbal barrage. Jake stood, bent over from his previous beatings, and said nothing.

"Your nakedness offends her," came a humor filled voice from the crowd. "If you do not dress immediately, she is going to kill you."

Jake turned to find the speaker, an older Blu'clic man with a hint of blue tint to his skin and gray, thin fuzz on his bald head. The man leaned calmly on a crude walking cane. He was thin, but muscular, and held an air of complete indifference about the whole affair. The Blu'clic's companion drew Jake's attention. She stood tall, strikingly beautiful even in her dirty and tattered prison clothes. She looked very much out of place in the underworld of Cla'nix Prison.

She stood as tall as Jake, slender, with long brunette hair. Her skin was pale from not having seen the sun in months, her smile mischievous. She held onto the older man, her arm intertwined in his. The connection was neither protective nor possessive. Jake blinked, trying to figure out the situation between the two but the screaming of the Crendoshian would not allow him to think. He shook his head to clear it and re-focused on his current predicament.

He stared at the alien for a moment before spreading his arms wide, exposing his entire body to the world. "Well, as you can see I have nothing else to wear," Jake said wearily. "So, if you're going to kill me, just go ahead and—"

Jake awoke a few hours later, propped against a rock wall, his entire body throbbing in pain. The last thing he remembered was a large, hairy paw coming at his face. He flinched as the memory materialized and tried to scramble backwards. He bumped his head on the rock wall behind him and cried out, nearly in tears. "Ow!" He rubbed his head to deaden the pain, creating a wave of agony as his ribs shifted. He took several breaths, fighting more nausea, before finally opening his eyes.

The Blu'clic man and the human woman stood over him, smiling. "Hurts, does it not?" the man said. He offered a hand to Jake, his smile unwavering. Jake gave a skeptical look at the hand through his one functioning eye. The Blu'clic waved the hand, insisting that Jake accept it.

"Is that Crendoshian still around?" Jake asked, taking the hand and allowing himself to be pulled into a standing position. The Blu'clic was stronger than he looked, easing Jake upright while being attentive to his injuries.

"She's currently entertaining another new arrival," the woman said with a smile. "So, you've caught a reprieve." The woman's tone was upbeat, almost cheerful.

"Lucky me," Jake said, his voice barely above a whisper. "How long was I out this time?"

"Almost four hours," the man smiled. He tapped his stick on the floor and nodded to the woman, who produced a small satchel. She opened the bag and pulled out trousers, shirt, and shoes, offering the bounty to Jake. "These are probably a little large for you," the old man said with a nod at the clothes. "But, perhaps they will keep you from getting beat again for a few hours."

Jake moved slowly, painfully sliding the shirt over his head. He paused, breathing heavily from the pain and exertion. Once the pain subsided, he went for the pants. He placed his hand on the wall and realized that he had been moved. The trio stood in a small alcove on the opposite side of the cavern from the entrance. Jake spotted the trail his feet left in the dirt floor where he had been dragged across the cavern. Alien prisoners milled around, pointing at Jake and his new friends, but none approached.

Jake lifted his left leg high enough to get it into the pants. He lost his balance and the Blu'clic steadied him before he could fall. He stood unsteadily on two bare feet. "Who are you?" Jake inquired looking at his benefactor.

"You may call me Grag," the old man replied. "Or inmate 39480384 if you prefer. And this darling creature," he motioned to the woman at his side, "is Angel."

"Jake...Jake Cutter," he responded. "Thank you for this." He sat, with some effort, and began pulling on the shoes. Every movement caused an ache somewhere on his body. "But I have to ask why. Why would you help me?"

Grag smiled, shrugged, and ran a hand along his gray goatee. "Angel has a soft spot for the underdog. And, I was asked."

"By whom?" Jake asked, returning to his feet with the Blu'clics aid.

Grag smiled, putting his arm around the wounded man's shoulders. The trio started a slow trek away from the main cavern. "We have a benefactor, Mr. Cutter," Grag began, keeping his voice low. "Someone who does favors for Angel and I from time to time. In return, we do what is asked."

"And this...this benefactor asked you to help me?" Jake pondered. "Why?"

"That is a question you must ask our benefactor, Mr. Cutter," Grag responded casually.

Jake smirked at the non-answer. "Does he ask you to help others often?"

Grag offered a nod in Angel's direction. "Only once before."

"But why you?" Jake asked.

"A reasonable question," Grag replied as Jake slumped against the wall to catch his breath. The Blu'clic leaned on his cane and continued. "I am classically trained, Mr. Cutter. Trained in the martial arts of my ancestors. Before sentenced to an eternity confined by rock walls, I was a master instructor and military tactician for the TSA." He smiled. "I am convinced our benefactor researched my past to enlist me as an ally, if needed.

"So far," he concluded, "he has required my

services twice."

"But why?" Jake implored. "Why save me?"

"Again, that is a question you will have to ask our benefactor, Mr. Cutter. If you ever meet him." Grag turned toward the sound of a crowd coming toward them. "You may wish to stand up," he murmured. "Stand up, stand tall, and show no pain. Perhaps you will make it out of this alive." Grag winked. "Perhaps."

Grag and Angel moved away arm-in-arm as a crowd, led by what Jake thought was the same Crendoshian that beat him earlier, approached from a nearby tunnel. The Crendoshian roared as she saw Jake, took several steps toward him, and then stopped. She uttered a long series of grunts in Jake's direction.

"She asked where you got those clothes," someone yelled from the crowd.

Jake stood tall and defiant, although he felt like running. He did not understand it, but he inherently trusted the old Blu'clic. Jake made a fuss of straightening his clothes, all the while staring at the hairy beast in front of him. He said nothing, simply smiling through the pain.

Frustrated, the Crendoshian roared, turned, and shoved her way through the crowd. Most moved out of her way, those not fast enough were casually tossed out of her path. Jake stood silently as the crowd exited the tunnel back toward the central hub of the prison. The last to leave was the Lemox Demoness. She stared at Jake for a moment, before offering a nod in his direction. She flashed an evil smile before she, too, disappeared down the tunnel.

Jake breathed a sigh of relief as Grag and Angel reappeared. "You did well," Grag smiled. "May I suggest that you accompany Angel and I?" He cupped her chin lovingly with a scarred hand. "We have been asked to offer you food, shelter, and protection."

"But why?" Jake implored.

Grag shrugged, but leaned in toward the beaten man. "The request only asked that we look after you."

"What?" Jake asked.

Angel pulled a small handwritten note from her pocket. She glanced up, ensuring she had Jake's full attention before reading the note. "Take care of him. He is an innocent man."

"So, join us," Grag interjected as Angel put the note back into her pocket. He pointed down a nearby tunnel. "And welcome to Cla'nix Prison."

Grag and Angel moved Jake down a series of tunnels away from the main cavern. Jake, supported by his escorts, tried to memorize the path, but every step sent a wave of pain through his ribs, chest, and back. Jake closed his eyes and fought the nausea. The trio traversed a long rock corridor before stopping and backtracking halfway back up the tunnel. They turned and faced the wall and Jake started to ask what was going on when Grag and Angel pulled him through the rock.

The three prisoners stepped into a large oval cavern lit with light strips and a pair of lanterns. Rocks had been placed to the side to mimic a table and two chairs. They escorted Jake over to a set of three bedrolls, gingerly laying him down on the nearest one. Jake cautiously rolled over onto his back before relaxing onto the thin pad.

"I shall tend to Mr. Cutter," Grag nodded to his female companion. "Would you be a dear and go and see what our benefactor can provide by way of medical supplies, or at least some water?"

Angel nodded, patting Jake's hand before walking away. His vision blurred and he lost focus before she disappeared through the solid rock wall. It was the last thing he remembered before darkness enveloped him.

He awoke to the smell of smoke. He blinked his eyes open, trying to get his blurry vision to focus. It took him a moment to remember where he was, and then panicked as he remembered the smoke. He sat up too quickly, shifting his ribs. He rolled over and vomited from the pain, each heave sending a new wave of pain coursing through his body. Hands found him, gently supporting him until he finished, and then laying him gently back down.

Jake slowly opened his eyes and stared into the dark eyes of Angel. She smiled reassuringly. "Good morning."

Jake relaxed, feeling the pain return to a tolerable level. He nodded, mumbling, "Morning. Where am I?"

"Our home," Grag answered, appearing over

Angel's shoulder. "You have been asleep for a couple of days. Hungry?"

The rumble of Jake's stomach answered, but he blanched at the thought of eating. He turned his head and saw a small fire pit, smoke gently wafting upward to a small exhaust hole in the rock ceiling of the alcove. The rock walls were unadorned, as he imagined they would be, but there were several items scattered about the room that caught his interest. The blankets he felt beneath him and the food being top of the list.

Angel moved toward the fire to prepare a small plate of food. Grag gingerly helped Jake to a seated position. Cutter crossed his legs and leaned against the rock wall. He pointed to the scattering of light sources and patted the blankets. "Where did you get all of this?"

Angel arrived with two disposable plates that had seen better days, passing one to each man. She left, returning a moment later with a plate of her own. The three sat in a semi-circle and Grag began his explanation.

"Our benefactor, Mr. Cutter," he said in between bites of some type of meat. "And we stole the rest. We discovered a cache in a hidden tunnel a few months ago. There were a few blankets, clothes, a canteen, and a note addressed to Angel."

"The note said, 'I may need your assistance soon,'" the woman chimed in. "'I hope this will make your stay more comfortable.'" She shrugged.

Grag smiled. "Last week we received another note. It said, 'Take care of the new arrival.' Once you arrived, beaten and bloody, we knew that you were the one referenced in the letter. Our new charge, as it were."

Jake picked at his food and drank from a cup provided by Angel. The water was cool, soothing his throat. "And you don't know who this benefactor is?"

Grag nodded. "I have an idea," he offered a knowing smile. "But that is not important. What is important is that he wants you healthy and ready to assist him in *his* endeavors."

"How do you know this?"

"Why else would he ask us to assist you? There are many games being played here, Mr. Cutter. You and I are merely pawns." The Blu'clic extended his hand, motioning Jake to do the same. Jake did as asked, and Grag dropped two pills into his outstretched hand. "For now, take these and rest. We will discuss our plans later."

Jake, without thought, followed the instructions. Something about the alien engendered trust. A flood of warmth filled Jake and the world grew hazy. Grag and Angel laid him on the blankets and Jake Cutter felt the world dissolve around him.

Three weeks. Three weeks he remained hidden. Three weeks Angel provided him food and tended his wounds while Grag moved about the population trying to discover the fascination with Mr. Cutter. Everyone seemed to be asking about the weak human, but no one would say why.

"We need to explore the fascination with you, Mr. Cutter," Grag said, appearing through the wall, returning from yet another fact-finding trip. He limped slightly, drawing a concerned look from Angel. He waved her off. "It is nothing. Someone does not enjoy my inquisitive nature." He shrugged. "I explained my determination to obtain answers to my questions." Jake wondered exactly what the old man had explained, and to whom.

Grag turned his attention back to Jake, ignoring the scornful look from Angel. "If you are ready, I think that we may wish to up the ante a bit." Jake looked confused and Grag smiled wryly. "If you want answers, then you need to be seen. Someone will make a play for you." Jake's eyes widened with the weight of what the Blu'clic suggested. Grag patted him on the shoulder. "Do not worry. Angel and I will be there to support you."

"Easy for you to say," Jake gulped. "I'll be the one getting beat to death."

"You are not dead yet," Grag shrugged.

"You know what I mean," Jake responded. He stood. The bruises were gone, his ribs mending, but he moved slowly, stiff from lying around for three weeks. His eyes glanced at a broken pane of glass leaning against the far wall of the alcove. His reflection revealed he had already lost weight in his short stay, his face and eyes gaunt.

"Well, if it's any consolation," Angel chimed in, "if we fail, then we all get beat to death."

"That is no comfort at all," Jake replied. A shiver

coursed through his body. "I...I don't know if I can...attack someone."

Grag put his hands on Jake's shoulders, staring him in the eyes as he spoke. His words were slow, precise, his voice low and comforting. "You live in a different world now, Mr. Cutter. You no longer have the option of running from a fight." He paused, letting the words sink in before he continued.

"In many ways, life is now much simpler for you," Grag continued in the smooth, soothing voice. "It is either kill, or be killed. It is up to you. Ask yourself, Mr. Cutter. Do you wish to live your life in fear, or do you desire to take charge of your life and your destiny?

"You can continue to be the gentlemen that you are, and you will die a slow, painful death at the hands of your enemies. If you choose that path, I should do you a favor and kill you myself. Here. Now. You would avoid the agony of a prolonged beating." Grag took a step back, his voice took a tone of harsh determination.

"Or, Mr. Cutter, you can fight. You can choose to live. If you choose life, then you must forget your upbringing. You must forget everything you have ever been taught about right and wrong. You must be cold...ruthless...merciless." Grag offered a knowing smile and his tone changed back to smooth, soothing. "If you want to survive."

Angel moved to Grag's side adding. "You cannot hesitate," she said. "I had my own choice to make, once upon a time. The choice I made...The choice you must make. Once you make it, it cannot be undone."

Jake rubbed his eyes, and ran a hand through his hair, before nodding slowly. He rubbed the three-week stubble on his face. The thought of finding out why an entire prison population was out to kill him outweighed the prospect of actually getting killed. And who was the benefactor that knew he was coming and wanted him to survive? He paused, struck by the sudden change in his attitude toward life and death. He realized that he had already made his choice.

"What do you have in mind?"

"Mr. Cutter, all you have to do is take a walk," Grag smiled, putting his arm around Jake's shoulders and steering him deeper into the cave. "But first, I think we need to teach you a few things about prison life."

Two tall Crendoshians, one under each arm, suspended Jake off the ground, feet dangling. Jake saw the Lemox Demoness raise her talon to strike and tried to roll his head with the punch, but the two Crendoshians holding him kept him stationary. His face took the full brunt of the attack. Somewhere, in the back of his mind, Jake was thankful that her claws were retracted. His head snapped to the right, spittle and blood raining on the Crendoshian holding him. The alien roared in outrage and yanked Jake's arm out of its socket. Jake cried out in pain.

The four of them stood in the center of the central hub of the prison. Dozens of prisoners formed a circle around them. Jake sensed a presence and turned his attention to the administrative ledge above the cavern. The Sergeant stood there, with three other guards. The TSA officials smiled in anticipation of a bloodbath, save for one guard. He stood off to the side, fidgeting, his fingers touching the pistol at his belt.

Does he want to help...or simply end my suffering? Could he be the benefactor?

Jake lost that train of thought as the pain in his shoulder brought him back to his current predicament. Jake's right arm hung useless, and the alien had no way to hold him upright. The Crendoshian changed position and grabbed onto Jake by the waist, propping him back upright.

Where is Grag? Jake's mind screamed, as the Demoness hit him again. He grimaced, refusing to yell out again and stared defiantly at the Demoness.

"That the best you got?" Jake spat between gasps for breath. "I thought you wanted to hurt me."

The Demoness moved in close, the stench of sulfur assaulted his nostrils over the smell of his own blood. A savage smile full of teeth creased her face and Jake thought her breath was worse than the sulfur. "I am going to kill you, human. Hurting you is just for fun."

"What did he...promise you?" Jake asked, gasping for breath through the fire in his chest. He continued baiting the alien as Grag instructed. "A pardon? A...a reduced sentence? You know he...he is lying...don't you?"

The Demoness stepped back, smiling. She raised her right hand. One at a time, her inch-long claws extended from her long fingers. "A pardon and a fortune. The Secretary's offer was quite generous." She licked her claws, the black onyx glistening in the artificial light. "And quite specific that you had to die."

The Secretary? Jake thought, but did not dwell on it. He had to get more information and keep the Demoness from gutting him like a sea bass. He fought his fear, focusing on the moment and smiled, playing a bluff. "The Secretary? You got...the agreement in writing...didn't you?"

The Demoness stopped licking her claws and stared at him. Jake shook his head and pursed his lips before he continued. "If it's...the same man...he has a history...of...breaking promises. How do you think...I...ended up in here?"

"You lie," the Demoness replied, but Jake heard uncertainty in her voice.

The Crendoshian, still dripping with Jake's blood, growled and howled at the Demoness. She turned her attention to the large alien.

"I will kill him when I discover what he knows about the Secretary!" she screamed in frustration.

The Crendoshian holding Jake's waist let go and howled at the Demoness. The other gorilla-like alien released Jake's left arm and he fell in a heap on the dirt floor of the cave.

"Now!" Grag's voice echoed through the cavern.

Grag and Angel appeared from the edge of the crowd, standing behind the blood splattered Crendoshian. The alien turned in time to take a sharpened pike through the chest. Angel twisted the arrowhead pike with a grunt of effort. The

Crendoshian grabbed the wooden spike sticking from its chest as it howled in pain. Angel withdrew the pike and the alien fell to the ground, almost face to face with Jake. Jake stared bewildered, as life faded from the Crendoshian's eyes.

Grag moved to stand before the Demoness, the walking stick supporting his limp. He glanced at Jake lying on the ground at the Succubus' feet. "I said, now!"

Jake's heart pounded, threatening to explode from his chest. He summoned all the strength he had and lashed out with a quick kick. His boot, reinforced with metal from a mining axe, connected with the weakest point of the remaining Crendoshian—its knee. The sliver of metal tore through the fur, muscle and tendons, shattering the knee.

The alien howled, falling to the floor. The Crendoshian rolled on his back, grabbing and cradling its damaged knee. Jake struck again, mustering all the strength he had and fighting the pain ravaging his body. The metal tipped boot connected, slicing through the alien's throat like tissue paper. Jake turned away in horror as blood gushed, focusing his attention on Grag and the Demoness. He noted that the crowd stayed back, although screams for blood and vengeance filled the cavern.

Grag moved with a speed that Jake had not thought possible for a Blu'clic that old. He dodged a swipe from the Demoness, back stepped to avoid her lunge and poked the Lemox in the chest with the tip of his stick. The alien howled in frustration and, blinded by rage, attacked the old man.

Grag appeared calm to Jake as the Blu'clic swatted away the Succubus' slashes and kicks with ease. Grag continuously moved to his left. He ducked another attack and the Demoness' claw sparked against the rock wall of the cavern. Jake stared in wonder as Grag allowed himself to be backed into a corner.

The crowd surrounded the two, closing in as the Demoness advanced on the Blu'clic. Angel brandished the bloody pike in the air, warning the crowd to stay back. The prisoners stepped back, but continued to watch Grag and the Succubus. Jake saw the fire of determination in Angel's eyes as he limped to stand next to her. He stood hunched over, his right arm limp, and noticed that no one wanted to confront her and the pike. He turned his back to the crowd to watch Grag.

The walking cane poked the Demoness in the chest again. She swatted, but Grag deftly moved it from her reach and poked her again. The man smiled and Jake swore that Grag was enjoying himself. The Demoness threw herself at Grag, hoping to crush him against the wall. Grag ducked, sliding out of the way as the alien hit the wall at full speed. Her claws dug deep into the soft igneous rock and her head rebounded off the wall. The Demoness' head snapped back, her eyes rolled back into her head, and she collapsed unconscious. Her claws, still imbedded in the wall, kept her body from sliding to the floor of the cavern.

Grag stood, brushing the dirt from his clothes. He moved to stand beside Angel and Jake. Barely breathing hard, he handed the cane to Jake and raised his hands. "The show is over. Leave us. The Demoness will not be in a good mood when she awakes." He looked over the crowd. "And I assure you, none of you will want to be here when she does."

The crowd parted, many with looks of concern and some in awe at the three humanoids who had defeated two Crendoshians and the Lemox Demoness. Jake watched them leave, but knew they wouldn't go far. Many would hide in the shadows to see what happened next. He looked down to stare at the Crendoshian at his feet.

Angel handed the pike to Grag and wrapped her arm around Jake. She touched his cheek as a tear streaked through the dirt and blood on his face. "I've...I've never killed anyone before."

Grag moved to stand beside him, taking the cane from his hand. Grag leaned the pike and the cane against the wall next to the unconscious Demoness. "Remember, Mr. Cutter, that they were going to kill you."

Jake turned his head to Grag, shocked at the callous tone. "That will make it easier?"

"No," Grag shook his head. "That makes it right."

Angel tapped Jake on the left shoulder and he turned to see her smiling. "What?" His brow furrowed in thought, confused at her grin. He felt Grag's hands grab him from behind. Powerful arms wrapped around his chest, holding him stationary.

"Now," the Blu'clic said.

Angel snatched Jake's dislocated arm.

"No...no!" Jake protested, trying to resist the woman. The arm snapped back into its socket and Jake's painful scream filled the cavern, scattering the last of the prisoners as it echoed through the prison.

Jake fought off the tears, as he rubbed his throbbing shoulder. He looked up at the ledge and saw the Sergeant shake his head in disgust before storming off. Two of his minions followed, leaving the third guard standing alone. The man looked over his shoulder nervously at the retreating Sergeant before making eye contact with Jake. He nodded curtly before he turned, following the others.

Jake breathed through the pain. "I think I may know who our benefactor is."

Grag and Angel followed his gaze, but saw nothing on the empty ledge. Grag shrugged. "We can discuss that later. For now, let us awaken the beast and determine who this mysterious Secretary of yours is, and why he wants you dead."

Chapter Four

Angel rolled forward, came to her feet, and lashed out with a one-two punch. Her fists connected, sending Jake staggering backwards. A light haze of dust filled the cave as she followed with a round house kick to the head, which he managed to block, although sloppily. Angel stepped back, brushed the hair from her face and allowed the dust to settle.

"You are getting better, Mr. Cutter," Grag said, appearing from the shadows at the edge of the cave. He moved to stand beside Angel.

The woman smiled, barely out of breath while Jake gasped, hands on his knes. He rubbed his arm from the impact of the blocked kick. He dropped to a knee, exhausted; his lips dry and parched. Sweat streamed down his face, his bushy beard dripping perspiration onto the dusty floor.

"I blocked one," Jake managed a small smile. "She still hit me twice."

"That is improvement," Grag smiled. "It is the first thing that you have blocked in two months."

The trio stood in a small cul-de-sac, several tunnels removed from the main cavern. The roughly circular alcove opened into a ten-meter sphere, perfect for teaching Jake hand-to-hand combat techniques. The occasional passerby would appear to investigate the noise, disappearing quickly at a glance from Grag.

Jake stood and retrieved a small canteen from a rock ledge. He drank heavily, draining the contents before tossing it off to the side. He stood tall, back straight, moving with a grace he had not had since his youth. Angel had mentioned more than once that muscle had begun replacing his flab. He flexed, confident, as he made his way back to the center of a circle drawn on the dirt floor. Dust shook from his clothes with each step. He smiled, nodding toward Angel. "It won't be the last one I block."

Angel looked to Grag and rendered a knowing smile. Grag returned the smile, shrugged, and nodded. The woman began to slowly circle Jake. He turned, keeping her ahead of him. She was three-meters away when she attacked, a leaping front kick aimed at the man's head. Jake saw the woman lift in the air, her foot growing larger in his vision. Time slowed as he tried to lift an arm to block the kick. A sense of déjà vu flitted through his mind and he remembered the last few months in a blur.

Grag and Angel became the only friends Jake had on the prison moon, other than the mysterious benefactor. Jake was not naïve enough to think they simply wanted him to survive, he knew they had their own reasons for helping him. That did not matter to him, he only knew he needed their help to survive.

The Lemox Demoness, once conscious, had not given up any information easily. Grag and Angel escorted the alien Succubus to a secluded area and persuaded the alien to talk in ways that Jake had never thought possible. The Demoness screamed, writhing in agony for days. Her cries attracted wave after wave of prisoners loyal to the Demoness. The trio, Angel and Grag mostly, repelled each attack. Jake watched the interrogation, his own feelings about taking a life forgotten. He realized there were things much worse than death.

The Demoness did not know who the Secretary was, only that he contacted her through one of the guards. She was told that Jake was an enemy of the state, and his death would grant her a pardon and enough wealth to buy her own moon. The guard who had delivered the message had been found with his throat cut several days later.

"You should kill her," Angel protested, watching the Succubus limp away. The alien looked over her shoulder, staring daggers at the trio. "Leaving her alive could come back to haunt us."

"Better to let her live," Grag smiled, before adding, "for now. Word will spread of what we have done. The mercy we show today may buy us time to train Mr. Cutter."

"It may also get us killed," she offered.

Grag ignored the quip and put his arm around Jake, as the Demoness disappeared around a corner that led to the main hub of the prison. Jake watched the bloody and beaten Demoness leave, as Grag continued. "Obviously, there is more going on than we know.

"The Demoness is contacted by the mysterious Secretary, and then the guard that delivers the message dies days later," he summarized. He tapped Jake on the chest, shaking his head. "You are an enemy of the state? Who says things like that?"

"I'm no one's enemy." Jake shook his head. A headache blossomed from the information and the implications. "I'm a...was a merchant. A simple merchant."

"Not anymore," Angel chimed in. "You are now a convict, with a rather large price on your head. If you want to live, you will need training and you will need to change your way of looking at the world."

Jake had only heard the first part of the statement. "Yes, I want to live."

"Excellent," Grag smiled. "The first thing you will need to learn, Mr. Cutter, is how to survive.

"Angel," Grag nodded, "teach Mr. Cutter how not to get hit."

Two months and Jake was only beginning to learn that lesson. He watched as Angel's foot grew larger in his vision. He moved to his right, raising his left arm up to block. Angel anticipated his move to the right, took the block, planted her feet, and used the momentum to lash out with a spin kick. Her right foot hit Jake between the shoulder blades, sending him face first into the dirt.

Grag took his place sitting on a small ledge

overlooking the makeshift arena. He laughed quietly as Jake picked himself off the floor.

She pushed him back to the floor with her foot. "What did you do wrong?"

Jake rolled over, staring up at the woman. "I blocked the kick, but I..."

Angel shook her head. "You moved to the right. You *always* move to the right."

"But I'm right handed and it feels natural..."

"You must learn to do unnatural things," she interrupted, holding up her hand. "I knew what you were going to do before you did. You are predictable."

Jake took a deep breath, trying to control his emotions. Rage trickled to the surface as he picked himself up off the floor. *I'm trying, dammit.* He had never been in a fight before all of this started. He knew he had a lot to learn, but he thought he was making pretty-good progress. He shook his head. *No, I am making progress.* Jake let the rage boil and attacked Angel. His vision narrowed, focusing only on the target before him.

Muscle memory moved his hands and feet. Jake did not think, he *flowed.* Punches and kicks lashed out, catching Angel by surprise. The woman backpedaled, blocking the fury of the attack. Jake executed a back-spin kick, catching Angel in the stomach. The woman landed hard on the floor and stayed there sucking in air.

Jake stopped, his tunnel vision expanding to take in the whole room again. He heard a rhythmic booming sound that slowly coalesced into Grag's clapping hands. Jake took a moment to catch his breath, then walked over and offered a hand to Angel. The woman took it, allowing Jake to pull her to her feet.

"Where did that come from?" she asked.

"I...I don't know," Jake stammered. "Are you okay?"

"I'm fine," she smiled.

Grag stopped his slow clap and made his way down from his perch. He landed lightly and glanced at Angel, receiving a nod that she was fine before he turned his attention to Jake. He looked the man up and down. "What did you feel when you attacked, Mr. Cutter?"

"I..." Jake gulped. "It wasn't me." He shook his head. "My body moved on its own. I wanted to attack, and it just happened." He shrugged, confused by his own actions. Grag nodded, rubbing his chin. "And your surroundings, were you aware of the world around you?"

Jake slowly shook his head. "No," he said softly. "I saw her. Nothing else."

Grag smiled. "Progress." He clapped Jake on the back. "We have progress. Still a long way to go, but we have progress."

Jake started to respond, when shouts of a crowd interrupted. The sounds grew louder and shadows played on distant walls. Grag, Angel, and Jake formed a small semi-circle, waiting quietly.

A crowd, led by three guards and the Demoness, rounded a distant curve in the stone cavern, stopping at the edge of the cul-de-sac. Several dozen inmates followed. The mob parted and Jake watched a Crendoshian drop the leg of a man it dragged through the prison. The leg belonged to a man who wore the tattered uniform of the TSA Police, his face bruised and bloody.

"Mr. Cutter—." Jake raised an eyebrow, realizing the speaker was the Sergeant that had arrested him. "I must say that I am surprised you are still alive. I figured you for a short life span here on Cla'nix."

Jake said nothing.

"I see you've made friends," the Sergeant continued, nodding toward Jake's companions. He also pointed to the guard lying in the corridor. He kicked the guard in the ribs, eliciting a groan. Jake saw no weapons and wondered why the other inmates let the Sergeant go unmolested. "It's good that you have friends in here, because you have none outside of these walls."

The Sergeant pulled an envelope from his pocket. The crowd turned unusually quiet as the man took his time unfolding it. The crinkling paper gave a faint echo in the now quiet stone corridor. He raised the tone of his voice, creating an off-key, female falsetto.

" 'Jake,' " he read. " 'I haven't heard from you since I last saw you in the courthouse.' " The Sergeant paused, looking over the paper to make sure his audience was listening. Jake's eyes widened, his heart pounding. *Pamela!* He took a tentative step forward, but Grag touched his arm, keeping him from taking another step.

Emotions and memories hit Jake like a wave on a

beach. He had been so focused on survival that he had forgotten about Pamela and the baby. The baby! A smile touched his lips. *I'm going to be a father soon.*

" 'I don't know how to tell you all that has happened since you left,' " the Sergeant continued, a hint of sadistic glee in his voice. " 'Your ship was confiscated and sold to pay your legal fees. Without your income, I lost the house. Our friends have stopped calling.' " He flipped the page and kept reading. " 'Jake, I lost the baby; a miscarriage. The Doctor said it was stress from worrying about you.'

Jake's smile vanished and his knees buckled. He fell to the floor. Grag and Angel stepped forward to grab him and hold him upright.

" 'I don't know what to do,' " the Sergeant read, his voice rose to a higher pitch, mocking. " 'I've lost everything and it's all your fault.' " Jake distantly heard the Sergeant. His mind sought refuge somewhere far away. It wasn't far enough. Jake's subconscious recognized the tone of the letter had changed. Shock set in, Jake's emotions overloading his system. All he could do was kneel on the floor and listen.

" 'I've filed for divorce. As a convict, I don't need your consent. It's done. Goodbye, Jake.' "

The Sergeant finished his narration and Jake saw the glee in his eyes. The TSA official tossed the paper to the cavern floor and, as a final insult, crushed the paper under his boot. He turned, motioned for the other guards to follow, and lead the way through the crowd that had gathered to watch. He paused beside the guard as the prisoners kicked dirt on the beaten man. The guard pulled himself to his knees, making eye contact with Angel. The Sergeant kicked him in the chest, sending the guard back to the floor.

"No more, Dawson," the Sergeant said. "No more assistance to the prisoners." The prisoners filed past the guard, pointing and laughing at Jake as he collapsed all the way to the floor. Others—a few of them—walked away with their heads hung low.

Angel dropped to her knees, holding Jake's head in her hands. "Jake? Jake!"

Grag watched as the last of the prisoners left, grabbing the guard—Dawson—as they passed, dragging him down the corridor. Dawson clutched his chest from the Sergeant's kick, as they dragged him away. Grag waited until they were gone before he finally turned to Angel. "Get him up," he whispered. "This is the second round in the campaign against Mr. Cutter. Now that they have weakened him mentally, they will be back."

The two gathered Jake in their arms, escorting him toward their hidden cave. Jake shuffled along, numb from shock. "We must expedite his training." Grag mused and Angel nodded her agreement.

They reached the cave entrance and the trio slipped past the holographic wall that hid their home. The holo-generator, a gift from their benefactor, Dawson. They laid the withdrawn Jake on his makeshift bed before Grag stepped back into the corridor, scattering their tracks. He returned a couple of minutes later.

Angel lit a torch in the close confines of the cave and saw, for the first time since she had met him, fear in Grag's eyes.

"What is it?" she asked. "What worries you so much?"

Grag slid past Angel, heading deeper into the cave. "Prisoners have access to information that they should not be privy to. Guards are colluding with prisoners to undermine and destroy Mr. Cutter. Someone is desperate for his demise. That letter had one purpose: demoralization.

"And it worked," Grag pointed to Jake who had rolled into a fetal ball in the corner of their hidden cave.

"They will soon attack, en masse," he speculated. He stared into the woman's eyes. "Round three is going to be bloody."

Chapter Five

"Time to rise, Mr. Cutter."

Jake opened his eyes to slits, allowing the light in. He raised his head, focusing on the speaker. His two companions stood over his makeshift bed, arms crossed, sad expressions peering down at him. Jake rolled over onto his right side, staring at their boots on the rocky floor. He closed his eyes. "No."

"It's been almost a week, Jake," Angel said. "You need to get up and get moving."

"No," Jake repeated, rolling over to his other side, turning his back to them.

Jake heard one of them kneel beside him. He turned his head, cracked an eye open, and saw Grag staring at him. "I understand your pain, Mr. Cutter," the Blu'clic began. "But it is time to stand up and face your destiny. The universe awaits."

"The universe can go to hell." Jake spat, closing his eye.

"Jake," Grag said, his voice soft. "At this point, today, you have two choices before you. Stand and face the demons that haunt you; face your destiny.

"Or, you can stay here, wallowing in your self-pity, and die. The Demoness and her minions will eventually find this cave. When they do, we will all perish."

"I can leave here, give myself up," Jake offered, opening his eyes again. He propped himself on his left elbow, the stone floor biting into his skin. "That will at least keep you and Angel safe."

Grag laughed lightly. "That is doubtful, Mr. Cutter. Angel and I are now marked, just as you are. We became targets the moment we helped you. If you were to surrender, our strength would decrease by one-third. Our demise would surely follow yours."

"Jake," Angel asked, "Do you want to die?"

"What?"

"Do you want to die?" she repeated. "You've been lying here, sulking, ever since the Sergeant read the letter. It appears you've given up, so I ask again, do you want to die?"

He collapsed back onto the stone floor. The letter. Pamela. A baby lost. The divorce. Thoughts and emotions overwhelmed him rolled over to hide his face. *Everything I had in my life is gone. My wife. My job. My friends. Nothing left...nothing.*

"Yes," he muttered.

He felt hands grab his left leg and drag him off the bedroll. He opened his eyes, shrieking in protest and scrambling for a purchase on the slick floor. Angel hauled him across the room, dropped his foot, cocked her right leg, and kicked him in the stomach. Jake rolled into a ball as the woman began his beating. She punched and kicked his abdomen and chest. He rolled, protecting his stomach and she began working on his back.

Jake unfolded, lashing out blindly to repel the woman. She easily parried his flailing arms and kicked him in the ribs. Jake felt a bone fracture and breath left his lungs. Time slowed and his mind screamed, *Fight back!*

Supporting his ribs with his right arm, Jake kicked. She took the impact on the left hip. Jake used the momentum to roll away and stood, his eyes never wavering from the woman. Adrenaline surged, ready to parry the next attack as his right arm supported his broken rib, left arm up and ready to block.

A rhythmic boom, boom, boom, filled the cave. Jake quickly glanced at Grag. He stood next to Jake's bed, clapping. Jake turned his attention back to Angel. The woman stood, relaxed, arms crossed over her chest. The clapping stopped.

"I thought you wanted to die," Angel mocked.

"Not being beat to death," Jake shouted. The adrenaline rush subsided. The pain in his ribs flared, the room began to spin, and his legs buckled. He dropped to his knees, his left arm keeping him upright. His right arm never wavered from holding his ribs.

Grag nodded to Angel as he approached Jake. The woman disappeared into the recesses of the cave as the Blu'clic knelt before Jake, his voice soothing. "Yet if you surrender to the Lemox Demoness, that will be your fate. Do not, for a moment, think you will receive mercy from her, or the guards."

Angel returned with medical supplies. She gingerly removed his shirt, careful of his ribs, and began applying bandages to Jake. Grag continued. "If you go to them, Mr. Cutter, your death will be long and painful."

"So I ask again," Angel asked, cinching the bandage tight around Jake's chest. He tensed as the ribs contracted. "Do you want to die?"

"I did," he replied through clinched teeth. "I do?" he asked himself. The flood of emotions returned, confusing and conflicting. Grag and Angel helped Jake to his feet, escorted him to his bed, and laid him gently on the blankets.

"What other option do I have?" he asked, squirming until he found a comfortable position.

"You can continue your lessons. Learn to fight," Grag replied. "You have the instincts, or you would have let Angel beat you to death just now. You can learn to fight, to survive. And then, you can face your destiny."

"And what is my destiny?" Jake asked, the sarcasm a little more prevalent than he wanted.

"To discover the truth," Grag responded, stepping forward. "To discover why you were sent here. To discover the identity of The Secretary. To survive, Mr. Cutter, to survive."

"Your move, Mr. Cutter."

Jake rubbed his chin and scraggly beard thoughtfully, sitting cross legged on the floor staring at a makeshift chess board. He stared down at his ragged clothes, momentarily distracted by Grag's near pristine prison uniform. *How does he look so clean and kempt?* he wondered.

Their hidden cave had not changed in the two months of his self-imposed sequester. The rock walls sat bare, the dirt floor filled the air with dust whenever any of them moved, the smoke from the small cook fire still found its way out of the small ventilation hole in the ceiling, and food still appeared from their benefactor. Beaten and bruised, Dawson apparently still provided for the trio.

Jake moved his rook across the board. He held his forefinger on the piece carved out of rock into something resembling the classic chess piece. His eyes glanced to Grag, but the old Blu'clic kept his face passive, revealing nothing. Jake removed his finger, sitting back. "Check."

Grag leaned forward, shaking his head slightly. He moved his queen, capturing the rook. "Check-mate."

Jake's smile faded as he leaned forward, eyes scanning the board. Abruptly, he sat back, "Damn it." He knocked his king over in defeat. "Tell me again what I'm supposed to be learning, other than how to lose? Pretty sure I already know how to do that."

Grag flashed a disarming grin as he began setting up the rock pieces for another game. "Chess is a game of strategy, of anticipation. It will assist you in developing a strategic mind."

"Strategic...?"

Grag held up his hand to stave off the interruption. "If you wish to survive, to find the person responsible for your troubles, then you must learn to anticipate your opponents' next move."

"But I'm here in..."

"You must also learn to plan your attack based on their probable course of action," Grag continued, undeterred. "Anticipate their moves, while plotting your own strategy. Of course, you must also be flexible in the event they do the unexpected."

Jake leaned forward, deep in thought. He nodded slowly. "I understand," he said, an idea forming in his mind. "Another game?"

Grag smiled. "Of course."

Fourteen moves and Jake's king was once again on its side in defeat.

"Damn it!"

"Do you know what you did wrong?" Grag asked setting up the board for another game, once again.

"Of course not!" Jake spat in frustration.

"You fixated on one word that I said," Grag explained. "You heard," he air-quoted, "'unexpected' and attempted an unorthodox attack from the start. You did as I expected. You must learn to incorporate the unexpected in *conjunction* with what is anticipated. Lull your opponent into thinking they have you figured out, and *then* pounce. Understand?"

Jake nodded absently, before shaking his head. He was getting a headache listening to Grag.

"We have time," Grag smiled. "Plenty of time to

learn the lesson." He lifted his arms in the air, encompassing the room. "We are not going anywhere."

"I believe we have come to an impasse," Grag said, nodding.

The Blu'clic sat cross legged across from Jake, the chess board separating them. The board sat mostly empty with only a few pieces remaining in play. A pile of rock pieces sat on either side of the board. Jake sat hunched over, studying the board while he absently stroked his grey streaked beard. His eyes roamed the board, following the possible moves he had at his disposal. He leaned back, stretching his spine before crossing his arms. "Stalemate."

Grag nodded. "You have improved, Mr. Cutter. Congratulations."

Jake offered his thanks, as he leaned forward to study the board again. He was so close to winning.

"Grag."

Both men looked up to see Angel materialize through the holographic wall. She leaned against the rock wall, clutching her right arm. Blood streamed down her face from a cut on her forehead and her nose. A puffy bruise threatened to close her left eye. Jake and Grag jumped to their feet, moving across the room to assist the woman.

"Jake," Grag ordered, "check the corridor. Clean the prints."

Jake nodded and left the two in the alcove. He moved up and down the corridor, pausing to listen, but heard nothing in the way of pursuit. He left a trail of prints down a side passage before retracing his steps to the holographic wall. Using an axe handle wrapped in tattered cloth, he swept back and forth, disturbing all of the prints except for the ones he had just produced. With a final look up and down the cave, he stepped backwards through the wall back into their haven.

He turned to see that Grag had placed Angel on the pile of blankets that Jake used during his recovery. Angel winced in pain as Grag touched her ribs. The alien handed the woman a small tube. "Bite down." Angel did as instructed, and Grag, without preamble, returned her right arm to its socket. The woman yelped before letting the small tube drop from her lips.

"What happened?" Jake asked, grabbing a small bandage from their dwindling medical supplies and kneeling next to Angel. He began wiping the blood from her face.

"The Demoness," Angel began. "She hasn't forgotten about you, Jake."

Grag offered her a cup of water and she took a sip, then another. She nodded her thanks before continuing.

"She and her merry band of malcontents cornered me on the way to the supply drop." She rubbed her shoulder, massaging the muscle. "She gave me a message for you. The bounty on your head has gone up. If you surrender, they will kill you quickly. If they have to search for you, well, it will not be quick. Or painless." She winced as her ribs shifted.

"And that goes for Grag and I as well," she continued after the pain subsided. "There is a price on our heads as well, for helping you."

Grag sat back, nodding. He lowered his head, but Jake saw the same thoughtful look on his face like when they played chess. Grag played move-countermove in his mind. "Any word on the guard, Dawson?" he asked without looking up.

"She didn't say anything about him," Angel responded. "Luckily, they found me before I made it to the supply cache. I would imagine word would get back to the Sergeant if I had been caught with an armful of supplies."

Grag looked up, staring at Jake. "What do you suggest we do?"

Jake looked around the small cave. Fear knotted his stomach as he thought of losing his only friends. He looked at Angel, the pain on her blood-streaked face and slumped in resignation. "I'll surrender to them. To save the two of you."

"A noble sentiment, Mr. Cutter," Grag shook his head. "But also the easy way out." He sighed deeply. "And I thought you were over your death wish. We discussed this before, only a few weeks ago."

"But things have changed," Jake protested.

"Have they?" Grag demanded. "There is still a bounty on your head, and ours. There is still a mystery to solve. Tell me what has changed."

"They are hurting Angel," Jake replied. "I can't be

responsible for that."

"Mr. Cutter," Grag shook his head. "Angel and I were targets before you arrived. We will be targets after you surrender to them. Do you know why we assisted you on your arrival?"

Jake nodded, "You said our benefactor recruited you."

Grag continued. "Correct. We were enlisted by the Guard, Dawson. He knows something about your past, something that we have not yet determined. There are forces at work here that we do not yet understand."

"So, I'm nothing but a pawn in someone else's game," Jake sighed. He began tending Angel's wounds again. "Pawns are there to be sacrificed."

Jake startled awake, staring up into the humorless eyes of Grag. The old man grabbed his arm and hoisted him to his feet. Jake rubbed his eyes, still half asleep. "You are not a pawn, Mr. Cutter," he whispered in the dim cave. Jake looked across the room to see Angel sleeping soundly. Grag grabbed Jake's chin and turned his head forward, staring into his eyes. "You are the prize in this little game."

Jake had spent the night tending to the wounds of Angel. He felt responsible for her beating. *I don't care what Grag says. If they had not helped me, they would not be in this situation.* His self-pity lasted deep into the night, long after Angel had drifted to sleep. Grag, his calm demeanor lost, stormed off after Jake's admission, leaving the man in silence. Jake had succumbed to sleep early in the morning, only to be awakened by a still furious Grag.

"If you wish to give up, then walk out that door right now and never return," Grag ordered. "Take the easy way out. Let whoever is behind all of this win." Grag stepped forward almost nose to nose with Jake. "But ask yourself this. Do you really think they will allow Angel and I to live?"

Jake recoiled from the Blu'clic's words. He took a step back, but Grag matched his movement. "What do you want me to do?" Jake asked.

"Fight, Mr. Cutter," Grag said. The alien's words were thick with venom and anger. "Fight! Fight for yourself."

Jake bumped into the cave wall and Grag moved within inches of him. "Fight for the truth. Fight for your wife, Mr. Cutter, your family. Do not give up on them."

Jake sat down heavily, the cave wall scratching his back as he collapsed onto the dirt floor. Thoughts of his ex-wife, his lost child filled his mind. The happy memories he tried to cling to faded. Faces blurred, replaced with a backlit door and the silhouette of a woman. She turned, blocking the light source, and Jake could see Pamela holding a small baby. She lingered for a moment before turning her back to him and stepping through the door, leaving him forever.

A tear streamed down his face, followed by another and another until he openly wept, sobs racking his body. "I have...no family. Nothing...nothing to fight for."

"You are wrong, Mr. Cutter," Grag said, lifting the man to his feet. Grag pointed to the woman across the cave. "You have her. Fight for Angel, for all she has been through, and continues to endure."

Jake shook his head dismissing his words. She was not his responsibility. Angel was not his burden. The tears slowed as his own thoughts returned to haunt him. "She would not be in this situation without me," he mumbled. His shoulders slumped, gulping for air after his weeping. "It's my fault."

"No, Mr. Cutter," Grag said. "This can all be traced to your mysterious Secretary." He stepped back, offering a hand to pull Jake from the wall. Jake wiped the tears from his face, streaking his face with dirt, accepted the hand, and the two men walked to the center of the cave. Jake stoked the small fire, feeling the heat of the fire alleviate the small chill in the air. Grag retrieved two canteens and the two sat in front of the fire.

"Remember when you told me that it was a government box that led to your arrest?" Grag asked. Jake nodded. "That is another tie to this Secretary. Do you want this man, the TSA, to send another innocent soul to prison?"

Jake sat quietly before shaking his head.

"You can give up," Grag began, his voice soft, his features glowing in the firelight. The calm demeanor grew with the warmth of the fire. "Or you can fight. We've had this talk before. Every time there is the slightest setback, you want to quit. That may have worked for you as a freighter Captain, when you had other options. But you are a prisoner now, and your options are limited. It is time for you to decide, Mr. Cutter. Life or Death. Surrender or truth. It is very simple, Mr. Cutter."

"Is it?" Jake retorted. "I'm never getting off this rock. So does it really matter?"

Grag sighed. "If you wish to live, you will find a way."

Jake looked over to see Angel staring at him. The pain in the woman's eyes overwhelmed him. No, not pain. Sadness. He saw the pity in her eyes. He looked to Grag and let the man's calm attitude enshroud him. He would never again disappoint someone who cared for him.

He looked back to Grag. A fierce determination burned inside him. "What do I need to do?"

Sweat poured from his body as Jake ran in place. He dropped onto the dirt floor and performed twenty push-ups before bounding to his feet to continue his cardio. He counted to fifty and dropped onto his back to do flutter kicks. The task complete, he returned to his feet. Twenty minutes, three times a day he conducted this ritual. Jake's days were filled with training. Calisthenics interlaced with a series of chess games and hand-to-hand combat. He dropped for another series of pushups.

Angel had healed over the past weeks. Jake's

attitude had improved as she regained her health, as if the two were connected. And Jake thought they might be. The two were becoming close, but Jake still did not understand the complex relationship she had with Grag. Were they lovers, or was it more like a father protecting his daughter? Jake had not worked up the courage to ask.

He bounded to his feet to run in place, his feet kicking up the dirt and filling the small cave with dust. He was alone in the cave. Angel had left an hour earlier to make a supply run. It had been two weeks since her last attempt and supplies were low. The usual twenty-minute excursion stretched to forty and Grag left to look for her, leaving Jake to continue his training alone.

He dropped to his back again for more abdominal work; crunches this time.

He returned to his feet as Angel emerged through the holographic wall. She supported Grag under one arm. "Jake."

"What happened?" Jake inquired as he maneuvered around the table and chairs and other obstacles in the room to assist. Grag wheezed, a bloody spittle flying from his lips with each breath. The two gingerly laid the Blu'clic on the pile of blankets.

Grag grabbed Jake's shoulder. "Think before you act." Grag fell back, unconscious.

"What happened?" Jake repeated.

"I was stopped by the Sergeant," Angel began. She found a rag from the bedroll, wet it from a canteen on the makeshift table, and began wiping the spittle from

Grag's lips. "Detained for questioning. He wants to know where you are."

"Did he hurt you?"

"No," she said. "It was all a distraction to draw you and Grag out." She ran her hands along the Blu'clic's ribs. She nodded, satisfied nothing broken. "When Grag showed up, six prisoners jumped him. He killed four before the other two managed to subdue him." She rubbed her arms. "The Sergeant held me so that I couldn't help." She looked up at Jake. "They stopped short of killing him so that we could deliver another message to you."

"What?" Jake felt the pit in his stomach grow exponentially.

"Surrender or this continues."

"No," Jake said, resolve and determination filling his voice. "This ends. Did you get the supplies?"

Angel shook her head. "No." She paused, a hint of worry in her eyes. "Jake, they had one more message for you."

"What?" Jake asked through gritted teeth.

Sadness filled her voice. "Happy Anniversary. You've been here a year."

Chapter Six

A low voice, calling for help, pulled Jake from restless slumber. He lay quietly in the dark of the cave, wondering if he heard something, or dreamt the cry. He slowed his breathing, willing his pounding heart to slow. He turned his head and saw Angel lying on the blankets across the room, softly snoring. The hairs on his neck perked up as he realized that Grag was not in the cave.

Jake rose from the waist and cocked his head, listening. He came to his feet still unsure if he heard or dreamed the mournful call. He trotted silently through the dark, his rough, calloused feet padding softly across the floor. Muscle memory moved him through the rock-strewn cave, sidestepping obstacles en route to the holographic wall. He paused, listening for a sound, anything to help him determine if what woke him was real or a dream.

Nothing.

Jake eased his head through the hologram into the brighter lit cave beyond. He blinked, letting his eyes adjust, before scanning the corridor. Alone, Jake stepped through the wall into the tunnel. "Grag?" he hissed.

Hearing nothing, he expanded his search, moving swiftly down the rock corridor, his bare feet quiet on the rough stone floor. Hard calluses had developed on his feet over the past year and the rough stone no longer hurt his feet. He paused at an intersection with another tunnel, the rock walls joining into one. He listened for any sign of life and heard only silence. Fear gripped him, and adrenaline surged as he continued to the next intersection. He paused again and then he heard it, a distant whimper. Jake inched his way toward the sound, his back hugging the wall.

A glance around the corner revealed a figure on the floor, his back to Jake. Two Crendoshians stood over the body, blood covered their hands. One giant alien kicked the figure on the floor and smiled as the figure grunted in pain. The victim rolled with the kick, now facing Jake.

Grag!

Grag stopped the roll, curling into a small ball to protect his front. He lay on the stone floor of the cave, battered and bloody, his breathing ragged. One of the Crendoshian's placed a foot on Grag's neck and let loose a howl of victory. The other Crendoshian stood silently, alternately watching both ends of the corridor. Its giant paws clinched and unclenched, anxious. It paused, sniffing the air and Jake pulled back. He waited a half dozen heartbeats before he risked another glance.

Grag lay still on his left side, the Crendoshian foot still on his neck. Both gorilla-like Crendoshians nodded their pleasure at their victory and bellowed their triumphant cries, the sound echoing through the corridor. Jake looked passed the two, to the corridor beyond, and spied the toes of a foot edging out of a junction a few meters away.

Trap, he thought as Grag let another moan escape.

Jake felt his rage boil, but fought to keep it in check. They had taken the strongest man Jake had ever known and turned him into...Jake, a year ago. He closed his eyes and stroked his neck long beard, developing his plan of attack. In his mind's eye, he played move and countermove, the same game that Grag used to teach him strategy. Another ragged cough echoed through the corridor and Jake sneaked another peak.

The scene remained unchanged, except the Crendoshian had removed his foot from the Blu'clic's neck and Grag's gaze met Jake's. The Blu'clic shook his head slightly, and raised four fingers on his right hand. Jake nodded and retreated around the corner. He forced himself to breathe, calming his racing heart. Four enemies: two visible, two not. A calm fell over him as the plan formed in his mind. A small, menacing grin split his face. Jake looked around the tunnel and found what he wanted. He picked up a medium sized rock, stood straight, exhaled, and bolted around the corner.

The rock sailed through the air, hitting the nearest alien—the one who had kicked Grag—square in the face. Jake was a half a heartbeat behind the rock. The alien howled as the rock crushed its nose, sending a blood curling wail echoing through the prison. Jake bypassed the screaming Crendoshian and attacked his partner.

Jake grabbed the alien by the scuff of its neck and, using his body as a fulcrum, hurled the Crendoshian around the corner into the two lying in wait. Without waiting to see the carnage down the corridor, Jake attacked the alien with the bloody face. The reddish-yellow blood mixed with the fur on the large alien's face, creating a ghastly image that would have terrified Jake a few months earlier. The blood and rage in the alien's eyes only spurred Jake's adrenaline. Jake jumped, using a nearby boulder to catapult himself up and over, landing on the Crendoshian's back. Wrapping his legs around the alien, Jake joined his fists, and brought them down on top of its head.

The Crendoshian let out a deafening roar and reached behind it, trying to grab Jake. He shook his hands, trying to alleviate the pain of hitting the hard bone head of the Crendoshian. He knew he only had seconds before the others joined the fray. Jake rotated his body and pummeled the alien on the side of the neck. The attack stunned the Crendoshian long enough for Jake to grab the alien's head on either side, scream in frustration, and wrench violently. The alien screamed in pain, staggered off balance with the twist, and Jake hit the Crendoshian again, driving the alien toward the wall. Jake slid off the alien's back as its head impacted with a sickening thud.

Jake whirled to face the rest of the attackers as the other three aliens rounded the corner. One held a shank made of metal, dripping blood. The largest of the Crendoshian's held a small boulder in both hands. The third, Jake thought it was the one he had propelled down the rock corridor, sported a bloody gash down the left side of its torso. Jake saw the blood seeping from the alien and classified it as the lessor of the threats.

The rock toting alien raised the boulder over its head and, with a roar, hurled the stone at Jake. Jake dove to his right, rolling with the momentum as the boulder hit the wall. It dropped, finally coming to rest on the head-crushed Crendoshian lying on the floor. Jake came to his feet with a rock of his own, paused long enough to set his feet and threw the rock with all of his strength.

The largest alien appeared ready to dodge the counterattack that never came. Jake's rock flew straight into the overgrown nose of the shank wielder. The alien tried to block the flying stone with his knife hand, inadvertently cutting himself in the arm. The rock connected, the force of the blow knocking the alien off his feet. The Crendoshian fell backwards, its head impacting the wall. The alien slumped to the floor, unconscious.

As soon as Jake launched the rock, he moved toward the alien that had thrown the stone. The Crendoshian turned its head, involuntarily watching Jake's rock sail through the air. The alien winced, distracted by his partner's misfortune. It turned at the sound of Jake's footfalls, just in time to take Jake's flying leap in the face. The Crendoshian stumbled backwards into the third, wounded alien. Both screamed in pain as they fell into a heap on the floor.

Jake landed lightly on his feet and waited to see if anyone stood. None of the aliens did, one was unconscious and the other two stayed on the stone floor in pain, nursing their injuries. He nodded, listening for other attackers. He heard footfalls coming from two directions and prepared himself for another attack.

The Demoness appeared, a small band of her henchmen in tow. Jake saw the Succubus' eyes widened as she spied him, and she smiled menacingly. She lashed out with her tail, catching one of her henchmen across the chest and propelling him across the tunnel. He hit the wall hard, the Hazmora's head snapped back. Unconscious or dead—Jake wasn't sure—the alien slumped to the ground.

Jake turned his gaze down the other tunnel leading to the intersection as Dawson and three other guards arrived. Dawson's face showed the remnants of a beating, the dark purple and green bruises fading. His companions carried TSA issued rifles, pointed at the floor. The Demoness took a step forward. Her smile faded as the guards surrounding Dawson raised their weapons.

"Not now," one of the men said. "The Sergeant is off-world and he wants to be here at the end."

"I have him *now!*" she raged.

"No," the guard repeated, drawing a bead on the

alien.

The Succubus growled. She glanced at Jake before turning her attention to the guard. "You will pay for this, human." Without waiting for a response, she turned and retreated up the corridor, her entourage in tow.

Jake turned to see the three rifle armed guards disappear up the corridor. One paused, whispering something to Dawson before following the other two up the tunnel. Dawson placed his back to the wall and nodded to Jake as he moved to his mentor's side.

Grag's breath came in shallow gasps. His eyes fluttered as Jake knelt beside him. Jake examined Grag's wounds. The Blu'clic winced, but remained silent.

"Hang in there, Grag," Jake said. The alien smiled weakly, but stayed silent.

Jake stole a glance up the corridor, and then raised his head. "Angel!" His call echoed down the tunnels. Months of fighting and strategy had not covered first aid. "Angel, come quick!"

The corridor grew quiet except for Grag's ragged, raspy breathing and Dawson's foot nervously tapping the stone floor. Jake felt his heart pound in his chest, heard the rapid pulse in his ears. Footsteps approached, breaking the silence and announcing the woman's arrival. Her eyes widened at the scene and she rushed to Grag's side.

Jake moved back as Angel, tears in her eyes, dropped to the floor beside her mentor. "Grag? Grag!"

The Blu'clic opened his eyes. Grag showed no more

pain, only a sad smile as she held his hand. Jake moved back to Grag's side, assisting Angel as she gently rolled Grag onto his back. The alien raised his trembling hand and touched the woman's face, stroking her cheek as her tears flowed.

Footfalls announced the arrival of another group. Jake squeezed Grag's hand one last time then stood and moved to the center of the tunnel. He felt adrenaline flood his system again and he resolved himself to take as many of the attackers as he could to the afterlife.

"Grag," Angel spoke softly, her face close to the alien. Her hand supported his head. "Don't leave me. I need you."

The man smiled. "My fate was decided long ago. You are the only bright light in my universe." His voice faded, but his words were clear. "Take care of Jake. If we were right, this is only the beginning for him. He will need your strength."

"And I need yours," she implored.

He coughed, then smiled weakly. "You have it." He nodded slightly. "You always have and you always will." He pulled her closer and whispered something into her ear that Jake could not hear.

"Now, go. Leave me," Grag said, relaxing his neck and letting his head droop. She let his head down slowly, keeping her hand under his head. "I do not wish for you to die with me."

Angel heard footsteps and turned her head to see the Demoness and six of her alien minions come into view. Three Crendoshians, a Blu'clic with blue skin darker than Grag's, and two Hazmora fanned out in the corridor, facing Jake. They smiled at the sight of Grag and the pool of blood that surrounded him. Their smiles vanished as their attention turned to Jake.

He glanced at Dawson, standing in the opposite tunnel, his hand touching the stun baton attached to his belt. Jake noticed that his holster sat empty and realized that he had been disarmed. *By whom?* he mused.

"Jake?" Angel asked, interrupting his thoughts.

"Take care of Grag," Jake said. A calm, cold resolution filled him. Grag died trying to keep him safe. No more. He finally understood what he had to do to survive. He made eye contact with each of the other prisoners. "I've got this."

"Six on one," hissed the Demoness. "You really think you can handle those odds?"

Dawson stepped forward, clearing his throat. The Demoness raised what passed as an eyebrow. "Six to two," she said dismissively.

Jake's smile was cold, calculating. "Try me."

Jake watched as the Demoness studied the situation. Her eyes focused on the four Crendoshians lying in the corridor.

Jake imagined what went through her mind as she calculated the odds. He nodded as her eyes found his. "Yeah, you're going to need more," he confirmed her unspoken thoughts. "A lot more."

"Soon," she barked. She focused on Dawson. "You should choose your allies more carefully, dead man." The Lemox Demoness turned on her heels and left the tunnel, her minions following in step behind her. Jake remained where he stood, willing his heart to slow. His right hand dropped the shank that he had picked up from the Crendoshian slumped against the wall.

Jake faced Dawson. "Thank you."

Dawson nodded. "There are supplies waiting. Get them quickly. I don't know how much longer I can assist. My days may be numbered." Without waiting for a response, the guard turned and disappeared up the tunnel.

Jake knelt next to Angel. Tears streamed down her face, leaving trails in the dust and dirt that covered her. She threw herself into Jake's arms, openly sobbing on his shoulder. He patted the woman on the back, providing what comfort he could. His gaze moved to Grag and he watched the Blu'clic nod before taking his final breath. A long, ragged exhale was the last sound that Grag ever made.

Angel continued to cry, her mournful weeping echoing in the corridor. Jake inhaled, fighting his own tears. *Time to mourn later*. Jake lifted Angel with him as he stood. She shook with frustration, and loss. Her knees buckled and Jake cradled her in his arms. He hoisted her off the ground and she put her arms around his neck, burying her face in his chest. "He's gone," she cried.

"I know," Jake said, straining with carrying his charge as he made his way toward their hidden cave. "And I promise you, they will all pay."

Chapter Seven

Jake gently wiped Grag's blood from Angel's hands. She sat on the stone and dirt floor of their cave, staring blankly at nothing. Her body rocked with sobs, oblivious to the world. Jake fought to keep his own feelings in check, right now was not the time to break down. The woman would be no help if the Demoness attacked and Jake needed all of his wits and senses.

Jake finished with her left hand and moved to her right. She showed no response, only tears. The dirt from the cave mixed with Grag's blood creating a tough, cake batter goo on her hands. Jake took his time, slowly and methodically removing the reddish-brown mixture. It gave him time to think...to plan.

He removed most of the grime from her hands before gently lifting the woman and placing her on her bedroll. She curled into a ball, knees into her chest with her arms around her knees. The tears were streaming less now and Jake chalked that up to exhaustion. A few minutes later, Angel had sobbed herself into an uneasy sleep.

With Angel temporarily pacified, Jake set to the task of cleaning himself. The luxury of running water filled his thoughts as he reused the filthy rag from Angel's cleaning. Jake spot checked his clothes and was grateful he didn't have a mirror. What he saw by looking down made him realize that he really did not want to see the extent of his year in the Cla'nix prison.

Grag's blood mixed with splotches of green and silver-flaked Crendoshian blood stained his clothes. Jake ran his hand down his pants, watching a plume of dust expand with each pat. He found a long tear down the right leg. He let out a little laugh. "Knife was closer than I thought." The sound of his voice echoed in the small chamber and he stole a quick glance at Angel. She remained in her fitful sleep.

Jake finished his inspection and cleaning of his clothes and moved to his face and head. He tried to untangle his long and unkempt beard. He ran a hand through his matted hair. He pulled it away and found crusted dirt interlaced with Crendoshian blood. He sighed and tried to remember the last time he had been fortunate enough to get one of the showers. *Four months?* he pondered. *Five?* He remembered the icy water as it cascaded down from the guard level catwalk. He shivered. *The irony was, it wasn't even a shower*, he thought. *It was the guard's attempt to break up a brawl in the common area.*

He smiled as a thought suddenly entered his mind and he stopped picking at his clothes. He stood perfectly still in the cave, his only movement the rise and fall of his chest with each breath. And his eyes.

They darted left and right as the thought morphed into a plan. His right hand started tracing invisible lines in the air as the scenario played out. His smile grew.

He turned to look at Angel, still sleeping on her mat. Jake knew he would need her help, but she needed time to mourn. He nodded his head. He would use that time to finalize the plan. Jake lay down on his own mat, the smile still plastered on his face. *I'll have to pick a fight. Before I'm through*, he thought, *everyone will get an icy shower.*

Over the next several weeks, Jake learned how much trouble he had been to Angel and Grag. Angel stayed catatonic and Jake, who had been dependent on his benefactors for months, was suddenly thrust into the lead for their survival. Shelter could be checked off the list, Grag had seen to that. Now, after two weeks and their stores were depleted, food was priority. Dawson had told him to pick up the supplies, but Jake had no idea where the drop point was located.

"Angel," he shook her gently. "Angel, where do you get the food?" He was embarrassed to think that for a year someone else had waited on him, bringing him food and water twice a day. He shook his head. "Angel."

"Down the corridor," she mumbled, still half asleep. "Turn left, then...left...right. The guard...Dawson, has been leaving food for us." Her voice trailed off as she drifted back to sleep.

Jake shook her again, but she lay still and would not awaken. Her mind and body had almost shut down after Grag's death. Jake knew that she was getting better, but she needed more than Jake could give her. She needed Grag. *No*, he thought, *she needs some good news for a change.* Jake sighed.

He had no choice but to venture out. He tucked two makeshift blades in the rope belt he wore around his torn pants, grabbed the small canteens sitting nearby and left the cave.

Jake travelled quietly through the crisscrossing caverns, his footfalls nearly silent on the rough stone. He had no concept of time, but knew by the lack of activity, it was early morning in Cla'nix Prison. The omnipresent light fixtures lit the way as he turned the first left, then a second. A dead end, and from the lack of tracks on the floor, no one had entered this cove in months. He backtracked, taking a right, then left. Another dead-end, but there were prints in the dirt. Someone had been there in the last few days. Jake searched, but no food. He continued the search for another quarter hour, finding nothing. The rock walls began to all look the same and he stopped. He knew he had to, at the least, find his way back to familiar ground. He took a knee in the middle of the tunnel and listened.

Silence surrounded him, except for the faint sounds of running water. Not the drip of water through rocks, but the sound of a powerful stream of water. Jake knelt in pensive silence for a moment, rubbing his bearded chin. *The guard's stash? A waterfall? A trap?* He picked a rounded stone the size of his head off the ground and placed it in the middle of the tunnel. He took a few steps, turned to survey his path marking, and then continued down the unfamiliar corridor toward the sound.

Jake's callused feet trotted lightly. He paused at an intersection, listening intently. A sleepy Hazmora stumbled past, oblivious to Jake's presence. Jake paused, watching the alien trudge along the dirt corridor, disappearing around a distant bend. He turned his attention back to listening and heard the water, louder but still distant. He placed another rock in the path and took the left fork.

The natural cave began a lazy descent. Jake felt a slight, warm breeze replace the usually cool temperature of the cave as Jake made his way downward. The rough stone corridor gradually evened out until Jake was walking down a smooth, seamless tunnel. He stopped, crouching on the smooth surface. He examined the tunnel, running his hand along the almost glass texture. "Machine bored," he muttered.

Humidity flooded the tunnel and sweat poured down his face, matting his hair to his head. He wiped his face with his tattered shirt sleeve, his hair in his eyes. He removed one of the blades from his rope belt, cut a small length off his shirt to tie his hair back and out of his eyes. He stood and continued his journey down the smooth tunnel.

Flittering light from up ahead caused Jake to halt and study his surroundings. The smooth cave walls doglegged to the right, but he could not see beyond the turn. The water roared, drowning out all the other sounds in the universe. He had no idea if anyone pursued him and knew he would not hear them over the roar if they were. He continued his trek. The smooth walls bore none of the prison light sources. All the light emanated from what had to be a waterfall up ahead. Jake squinted and raised his hands to shield his eyes. He looked up and down the corridor, ensuring he still traveled alone. Confident he was undetected, he continued down the slick tunnel.

The humidity in the tunnel increased and the sticky sweat worsened. Jake wished he had brought a canteen of water before remembering that he was, in fact, out *looking* for food and water. He shook his head to clear the thoughts when he saw the end of the tunnel. Jake squinted against the bright light, almost blind after a year below ground. His back hugged the wall as he inched along, making his way cautiously the last few meters.

A waterfall covered the exit of the machine burrowed corridor, cascading water creating a curtain with intermittent rainbows. Jake found the rock surface slippery as he tentatively made his way down the last few steps. He stepped into a small pool at the end of the tunnel, the water cool on his bare feet. A chill shot up his back and he smiled. It was the most pleasant sensation he had felt in months. He eased forward, standing directly behind the waterfall, and let the spray soak him.

After pausing a moment in the improvised shower, he edged closer to the cave opening. The waterfall covered most of the cave entrance, all but a small section on the left where bright sunlight streamed in, untouched by the cascading water. He peered passed the falls into the bright sunlight from a clear, bright, powder blue sky. His brow narrowed. "This was supposed to be a dead world," he said aloud, his voice lost in the roar of the waterfall. He shook his head. "More lies."

He knelt, cupped his hands, and tasted the water. It was cool, clean and fresh; the best he had ever tasted. He filled the two bottles he had brought, drained one, and refilled it. Jake sat his back to wall and let his body relax. The vantage offered a view beyond the edge of the waterfall and he took in the details of the mountain enveloped valley.

A forest sat in the distance, beyond a small lake fed by the waterfall. The lake led to a lazy river that stretched out of sight through the wood. The trees were not large, only ten meters or so tall, but provided an elegant beauty that he found he had missed. The kilometers-wide forest jutted against large mountains that encircled the entire valley. The mountains formed a creavice at the opposite end of the valley and Jake thought the river flowed in that direction. Jake thought the jagged rocks would make a formidable climb and pondered if the river could lead to an escape. Something in the distance momentarily reflected the sunlight and Jake shifted to get a better view. The unmistakable shape of two hammerhead shaped Trillinden Mark IV freighters brought a smile to Jake's face. The river escape forgotten, Jake narrowed his eyes to focus on his new escape route.

The freighters were favorites of smugglers across the tri-system for their speed, maneuverability, and durability. Their modular design made customization easy. Rarely were two Trillinden freighters the same after they left the assembly line. The ships sat seventy-five meters long and forty wide. A long flat snout, which housed the sensor and navigation packages, protruded from the front. It widened out after a few meters and then blossomed into the main compartment of the ship.

The main section of the freighter housed the cargo area, reached by a long sliding door on either side of the ship. The large cargo doors allowed for easy loading and unloading, and offered a quick exit if modified as a troop ship. Jake had looked to buy one a few years back, but found them very expensive. They also seemed to attract more than a fair share of surveillance from the Tri-System Authority. Ironic, since the ship he had purchased, a low-end tug converted to haul freight, had apparently attracted them as well.

The hammerhead cockpit extended from the top of the main cabin, running above and parallel with the snout. The hammerhead melted into the body of the ship, forming the small swept-back wings necessary for atmospheric flight. The swept back design of the glass canopy housed the small maneuvering thrusters and the four seats of the cockpit. The glass design provided an uninterrupted forward and peripheral view. The last three meters of the snout, running beneath the canopy, protected the cockpit from the massive thrust of takeoff.

The four engine nacelles ran along the hull, gracefully emerging from the superstructure as they extended from the rear of the ship. The two dorsal engines sat ten meters apart, while the ventral engines had a wider base of twenty-five meters. This off-set of the engines accounted for the freighters legendary maneuverability.

Jake smiled as he wondered if these were designed as troop ships to deliver prison guards or as smuggler ships full of black market cargo. He thought back to a year earlier. *I don't think this was the ship that brought me here,* he shook his head. *Doesn't matter. One of these ships is my way off this rock.* He nodded as another piece of his plan fell into place. Satisfied that he had seen enough of the valley, he shifted and prepared to make his way back up the corridor when he saw the orchard.

On the far edge of the lake, brown trees with red leaves and green-orange fruit stretched from the water to the mountains, at least three hundred meters. Green-orange: Darlencko fruit. The most nutritious, delicious, and precious fruit in the entire Tri-System. It was also the most narcotic and addictive.

Jake's eyes widened. *Contraband. Explains the freighters.* He thought back to a TSA briefing for new freighter captains. One piece of the fruit could sustain a man for a day. That was the good news. The bad news; Darlencko fruit was so delicious very few people had the willpower to only eat one. Only two alien races,

Traxillian and O'glenz, were known to be immune to the addictive effects of the fruit. Two pieces in a TSA Standard twenty-seven-hour day and a humanoid would become hopelessly addicted. Men, and several species of aliens, had been known to sell all of their possessions, result to thievery – or worse – just for another piece of fruit. Three pieces in a TSA Day and the fruit turned poisonous; its precious nutrients transmuted into a lethal toxin. The effect was near instantaneous, the death excruciating.

Jake stood and ran down the slope toward the waterfall before his thoughts caught up with him. The fruit provided the final piece to his plan. A few pieces of the fruit was all he needed to give him the strength to escape and to exact his revenge for Grag. The formulating plan foremost in his mind, he missed a rocky trail leading down the ridge. Jake focused on a more direct approach and made his way down the rocky slope in front of the waterfall. He jumped the last handful of meters, splashing into the cool water.

The water engulfed him. He kicked hard, emerging neck deep in the lake. He swam two strokes before he froze in place, stopping all movement. He had moved from his hiding place, down a rocky slope, and jumped into a body of water without thinking, without verifying he was alone in the valley, without checking to make sure there wasn't a deadly creature lurking beneath the surface of the pool.

Stop, Jake, dammit! he admonished. *Use your head.* He quickly swam to shallow water, staying low. With only his eyes and the top of his head protruding from the water, he took a long look around. Nothing stirred. He appeared to be alone. Keeping his eyes on the valley, he duck-walked low in the water toward the orchard.

He stopped a few meters into his journey as something nibbled at his toes. Keeping his panic in check, he stopped, looked down into the clear water, and smiled as he shooed away a school of small minnows. Jake breathed a sigh of relief and, keeping to the shallow water, made his way to the orchard side of the pool.

Well, you said you needed a bath, he thought as he emerged from the lake at the closest point to the orchard he could find. He crawled onto the dirt bank, lying on his stomach in knee-high tall grass. He turned and looked over his shoulder at the clear lake. A film of pollutants—blood, dirt, and grime—slowly dissipated in the water. The water washed away the filth, but not the worries. His washed body could present a problem once he returned to the prison. Putting the thought from his mind, he ran, sloshing and waterlogged, toward the grove of trees. He stopped, propping himself behind a treetrunk to catch his breath. His breathing and heartrate nearing normal, he turned and surveyed the valley from this new vantage point.

The waterfall dropped over a hundred meters into the lake. Even knowing where to look, he could barely spot the well-hidden entry behind the waterfall. The distance reduced the roar of the waterfall to a distant rumble. He heard birds and looked skyward, but saw nothing. Chill bumps crossed his arms as a breeze filled the valley, cooling his wet skin. He smiled as he looked at the waterfall again. Anyone that stumbled upon the orchard would never know the entrance to the most despised prison in the Tri-System was only a few hundred meters away.

Jake spent a few minutes in the orchard, wandering through the trees, studying the fruit. He raised his arms and looked skyward, enjoying the cool breeze and sunlight. Long shadows began to recede as the sun arched across the sky and he wondered how long he had been gone. He looked at the shadows and guessed almost two hours. The prison would be coming to life soon, and that greatly diminished his chances of returning undetected. He needed to move.

Jake pulled two pieces of the fruit from the nearest tree. The fruit was coarse, almost bristly to the touch, and heavy. The green/orange orb sat neatly in the palm of his hand. He hefted a piece and wondered what kind of weapon it would make. *Another time,* he thought as he placed the fruit in his one remaining pocket. He stared at the tree and ran his hand along it fondly. "I'll be back."

Jake left the orchard, heading back toward the waterfall, and to Angel.

He found the trail leading up the ridge and stone steps to the cave entrance behind the waterfall. He tested each step as he kept an ear open for anyone else. The roar of the waterfall masked everything in the valley. He paused at the opening of the cave long enough to top off both canteens in the small pool behind the waterfall. Satisfied, Jake made his way through the smooth tunnel. He travelled quickly, the tunnel morphing to natural rock and he continued to ascend the stone corridor. The tunnel opened to a larger cavern and he paused. He took out the fruit, placed it on the stone floor then dropped to the ground and rolled around in the dirt to cover his swim in the lake. He knew he still looked clean, but hoped it would pass a cursory inspection. He stood, took the fruit and continued to follow his rock trail. Within minutes, he found his way back to the familiar tunnels and caverns of the central complex.

Sticking with the shadows, Jake made his way through the prison. He paused twice, allowing small groups of prisoners to pass. He kept an eye out for the Demoness or guards, but saw neither. He desperately wanted to find Dawson, but that was secondary. He had to get back to Angel. His feet padded soundlessly on the stone floor as he found the tunnel to their hidden cave. He erased his prints using the cloth covered pickaxe handle and disappeared behind the holographic wall.

Jake knelt beside Angel, still curled up on her bed. He touched the canteen to her chapped lips, pouring a bit of the cool water. The woman licked her lips, opening her eyes for the first time in days. She drank a few more sips before attempting to rise from her bed. Jake patiently assisted her as she drank.

Jake left the canteen with her, produced one of the blades from his belt, and cut a piece of Darlencko fruit. Angel took the offered morsel, eyeing it cautiously. She sniffed the orange slice, before nibbling a corner. She smiled and she ate the rest of the slice in one bite.

"That's delicious," she said, holding out her hand for more.

Jake cut another slice which disappeared into her mouth in one gulp.

Jake smiled. "Slow down." Each bite produced a flush of color to Angel's cheeks, life returning to her eyes. He offered her the final piece of the small fruit. "There are enough nutrients in that to last the day." He nodded knowingly. "Probably, more than either of us has had in the last six months."

Jake told her of his trip down the cave, the valley, and the orchard. She nodded as she ate.

"You said there is an orchard of these?" she asked. She took a drink of water from her canteen and turned to face Jake, her face bright. "Fresh water, too?"

Jake nodded, taking his first bite of the fruit. Warmth filled his body like a shot of whiskey. He ate the remainder of the slice and forced himself to slow down, taking his time to cut one piece after another. He watched her as she watched him take the last bite and knew that he had found more than just food and water. He had found some of the hope that she so desperately needed. "And something else," he began, hoping that rest of the news would put her firmly back in the land of the living.

"What?" she asked, licking her fingers, savoring the Darlencko fruit juice. She took another drink of water then turned the rest of her canteen over her head. The cold water splashed, washing grime, blood, and dirt from her hair. Her tangled hair soaked up the moisture.

"I found a way off this rock," he continued. Her eyes opened wide and she stared at him, begging for more information as he took a drink of water. "They have two ships near the orchard. Trillinden freighters."

Her eyes brightened. "Trillinden? Here?" She raised an eyebrow. "What are they smuggling?"

Jake smiled, pointing to her face. "You just ate the evidence."

She smiled. "Thank you, Jake."

"You took care of me for the last year," he took her hand and squeezed gently, "the least I can do is take care of you for two weeks."

"You've done more than that," she returned the squeeze. "You've given me hope again. Hope of seeing Grag's killers punished. Hope of getting out of this hell." Tears welled, but she stifled them. Jake saw her strength and determination returning. *Another day, maybe two, and she'll be ready.*

She wiped her eyes and smiled. "So, what's the plan?"

Jake's eyes showed mischief as he smiled. "First, I'm going to show you the way to the valley. We need to regain our strength, and I think the sunshine will do us both good."

"Sunshine?"

"This isn't a dead world," he said, smiling.

Her face brightened. "And then?"

"And then, after we return...retribution."

Chapter Eight

Mark Dawson felt the walls close in around him as he hedged his way through the dank tunnels of Cla'nix. The passageway narrowed and he turned sideways, sacrificing speed for only an instant, to squeeze between the converging walls. The rough stone scraped his chest, back, and his knees, but he continued unabated. He could hear his pursuers gaining over the pounding of his chest. Time was running out.

Dawson had grown accustomed to the berating—the mental torture at the hand of the Sergeant. He had even healed from the numerous beatings he had endured for helping the prisoners, but the game had gone too far. The Sergeant had allowed prisoners into the garrison area.

Dawson awoke to two Hazmora dragging him from his bed, their long arms wrapping him tightly as they escorted him from his small room. The two prisoners held Dawson tightly, presenting him to the Sergeant in the main admin area of the prison by suspending him off the floor. The Sergeant stepped forward, shaking his head as if sad, before executing a rapid one-two punch to Dawson's mid-section. Dawson gasped for air as the Sergeant stepped back.

"Where are Cutter and his companions?" the Sergeant sneered. "I know you've continued to help them, even after our chat."

Dawson saw the backhand coming, but could do nothing to avoid the blow. His jaw stung, his ears rung. He tasted blood.

"Where are they?" The Sergeant repeated.

"I don't know," Dawson replied, gaining his breath after the initial punch. He lowered his head, sucking in another breath. The Hazmora hoisted him higher and Dawson used the momentum. He pulled his legs up to his chest before lashing out with all the strength he could muster. His feet caught the Sergeant in the chest, propelling the Senior Guard backwards into a wooden table. The table collapsed under the man's weight, splintering and scattering pieces across the room.

Dawson turned to his right, spitting blood into the Hazmora's eyes. The alien screamed in rage, releasing Dawson as it staggered backwards, wiping its face. His right side free, Dawson punched the other Hazmora, feeling its nose crunch under his fist. The alien released him, grabbing its wounded snout and howling in pain. Dawson turned to face the first Hazmora, ducking under its swing. He grabbed a handful of the creature's mane, stepped backwards, and propelled the alien across the room into its counterpart. The two reddish-brown aliens collapsed to the ground and lay in a heap, unmoving.

Shouts and footfalls echoed through the stone walls and Dawson ran back to his sleeping quarters. The alcove contained a small desk with a lamp, his unmade bed, and a chair that held his work clothes. Foregoing his work clothes for the pair of shorts and shirt he wore, he slipped on his shoes and then fell to his knees, feeling around under his bed. His hand latched onto a small satchel and he yanked it from its hiding place inside his mattress. He stood, attaching the small pouch via a clip to his waistband. He pulled on the small container, satisfied that it was fastened securely to his shorts. Footfalls echoed closer and Dawson left his alcove.

He moved quickly down the rock aisle, slipping into another sleeping alcove. He blended into the shadows, watching as the search party—two guards, and a Crendoshian—ran past, straight into Dawson's sleeping quarters. He waited until he heard the desk flipped over and saw the bed thrown out into the corridor before he left his hiding place and ran toward the administrative area.

I need to get to the shuttle bay, he thought. He returned to the admin area, breathing a sigh of relief that it was empty except for the unconscious Sergeant and the two Hazmora. He turned right, heading down the long tunnel to the launch bay. The distant door—a hundred meters done the corridor—opened, revealing the Lemox Demoness and her entourage of prisoners. He slid to a stop at the sight of the Succubus. The alien smiled and waved her minions forward. Dawson turned, fleeing back up the corridor as the alien horde's roar echoed through the prison, charging in pursuit.

Dawson found his way to a narrow set of tunnels. He squeezed his way through the first narrow notch, relieved that the corridor widened somewhat. He guessed that only a few of the Succubus' minions would be able to pursue. *I'll take any advantage I can get*. He heard the horde reach the narrow gap, followed by the crash of rock. Dust filled the passage and Dawson stopped, hands on his knees as he gasp for air, and turned to check on his pursuit.

A Crendoshian stood at the mouth of the passage he had just traversed, its massive form blocking the light. Dawson watched as the alien pounded the cave walls, creating a small landslide of rock, but did not widen the entrance. The Crendoshian howled in frustration and nursed its bloody fists before stepping aside. With the alien out of the way, the smaller prisoners filled the corridor. Dawson shook his head, turned, and ran.

He felt the walls close in around him as he hedged his way through the dank tunnels. The passageway narrowed and he turned sideways, sacrificing speed for only an instant, to squeeze between the converging walls. The rough stone scraped his chest, his knees, but he continued unabated.

Another turn, another narrow passage; a small door, about waist high, carved out of the cave wall. He wedged his way through the opening, stood, and ran a dozen meters before he stopped, shaking his head. He placed his hands on his knees, gasping for air. *I can't keep running. No place to hide.* The sounds of pursuit grew closer and a calm resolve filled him. He picked up a stone twice the size of his fist, hefting the rock to get the feel for its flight capability. The aliens drew closer and he cocked his arm back.

The first alien that came through the narrow passage was a two-foot tall, blue Traxillian. The diminutive alien dove through the opening, rolled into the corridor, and jumped to its feet ready to run in pursuit. The Traxillian took two steps before spotting Dawson. Its eyes widened in horror as it caught sight of the rock. It took a step back, raising its arms to block the inevitable throw as it lowered its head.

The next prisoner, a Hazmora stripped to the waist, stepped through, bumping its head on the low opening. Howling in pain, it grabbed its head, rubbing the point of impact, and staggered into the retreating Traxillian. Both aliens fell in a pile as the third pursuer, a smaller-than-average Crendoshian, stuck its head out of the breach in the rock wall.

Dawson, with a grunt, hurled the rock at the Crendoshian's head. The alien, now halfway through the aperture, raised its massive arm, deflecting the rock. The stone flew straight up, impacting on the cavern roof and dislodging several small rocks. The alien released a howl of rage and pain as the ceiling fell, stopping the alien's movement through the opening, and burying it in the avalanche of rock.

Dawson turned his head as dust filled the corridor.

He turned back and saw the opening sealed. He sighed in relief and continued down the tunnel at a more relaxed and cautious pace. The corridor continued to narrow and widen at random intervals. He found evidence of prisoner habitation and knelt to examine the remains of a bedroll. He turned the pile of blankets over and turned away quickly as the skeleton of an unidentifiable alien stared up at him. He rolled the bedroll back the way he found it and continued in silence.

The sound of running water greeted him and the TSA Officer paused, listening. His parched mouth led the way and he inched forward, stopping short of the opening to a large cavern. Dawson stuck to the shadows, listening for activity. Confident he was alone, he began to move, but froze as shadows played on the rock wall ahead. He retreated quickly into shadow as a figure appeared out of a tunnel to his left. The figure stopped, surveying his surroundings before dropping two orange/green ovals and a couple of canteens. The man lay down on the floor, rolling in the dirt.

Dawson's eyes widened when he recognized Jake Cutter. *What is he doing? Where did Jake get Darlencko fruit?*

The answer seemed obvious as Cutter completed his dirt bath and began to recover his items. Dawson watched him go and turned his attention to the tunnel. Confident he was still alone, the guard left the shadows of the narrow passage and moved quietly to the mouth of the tunnel from which Jake had emerged. The sound of rushing water grew, as did Dawson's sudden thirst. Cautiously, he made his way down the tunnel.

The rough to smooth stone transition surprised him. He stopped, running his hand along the seamless texture of the tunnel wall. He nodded his head as a piece of the puzzle slid into place. He touched the small pouch attached to his shorts, reassured by its presence, and continued toward the sound of a waterfall. He arrived at the mouth of the cave and the valley appeared before him.

Dawson spotted the freighters instantly and exhaled a long sigh of relief. A weight lifted from his shoulders and he knew that his time as a prison guard would soon end. He nodded as his eyes roamed the valley and he saw the orchard. The final piece of the puzzle fell into place. He saw the stone steps leading down to the valley and bounded the stairs two at a time. He needed to collect evidence.

Dawson reached the valley floor and tugged a small metal cylinder from the pouch attached to his shorts. He activated the device and began to record a slow panorama of the valley. He tried to dictate what he saw, his words lost under the roar of the waterfall a dozen meters to his right. Dawson walked away from the waterfall, parallel to the small lake, looking around for a good vantage point for his transmission. He found a small recess in the rocks halfway to the orchard and moved in that direction. He settled there and began his dictation again.

"This is Mark Dawson, Lieutenant Junior Grade,

on special assignment for the Parliamentary Committees of Commerce and Internal Affairs. I have been undercover on Cla'nix as a Prison Guard for almost eighteen months." He took a breath. "And I have finally found the secret of the prison.

"As evidenced in this holo, Cla'nix houses not only a prison, but a viable atmosphere." He panned the recorder across the valley as he identified areas of interest. "There is an orchard of Darlencko fruit...a sustainable water source," he paused as he refocused the holo-recorder on the distant ships, "and two freighters capable of hauling contraband anywhere within the TSA."

A hint of movement near the waterfall distracted him and he sank deeper in the shadows. He turned his head and watched as the Sergeant, the Demoness, and a handful of guards emerged from behind the waterfall. They descended the stairs single file, taking each step one at a time. The guards pushed anti-grav carts while the Sergeant barked orders and pointed to the distant Trillenden freighters. The guards nodded and proceeded past Dawson into the orchard. The Sergeant and the Demoness followed them to the edge of the orchard and stopped less than five meters from Dawson's hiding place.

Dawson, still in shadow, steadied the recorder on the rock in front of him. He ensured the device still recorded as he strained to listen.

"Have you found Cutter?" asked the Demoness. She shimmied her tail, sending a plume of water in every direction.

"No," the Sergeant replied, a bruise forming on the side of his face. He took a piece of Darlencko fruit, produced a knife from his pocket and sliced the orb. He tasted the meat of the fruit, crinkled his nose and spat. "Another week," he said, addressing one of his men as he pointed at the fruit. "Look on the east side of the orchard for the ripest."

He turned his attention to the Demoness. "And I've been informed that Dawson has eluded your team." He touched his face. "We need to find him, and quickly. There is something about him—"

"We need an advantage," interrupted the Demoness. "I thought the death of that Blu'clic would lead us to them. Cutter is more resilient than we were led to believe."

"The Secretary gave us all the information he had," the Sergeant countered. A yell from the orchard drew the man's attention. He turned, saw the full crates of fruit, and nodded, pointing to the freighters. His minions followed a footpath from the orchard toward the forest, crossed a wooden bridge over the lazy river, and eventually disappearing into the trees. The Sergeant shook his head.

"Where was I? Oh, the Secretary gave us all the information he had. His information was correct, at the time. I've seen the change in Cutter." The Sergeant shook his head again. "He is not the same man that I arrested last year."

"Nonetheless," the Succubus hissed. "He and the girl must be found."

"And Dawson."

The Demoness nodded. "And Dawson."

The roar of engines interrupted their discussion and they turned to watch one of the freighters lift from the far side of the valley. The ship rose, edging its way toward the Sergeant and Succubus. The quad-engine freighter hovered for a moment before turning ninety-degrees and rocketing out of the valley. Within seconds, it was a distant dark spec in the early afternoon sky.

Three of the underlings arrived a few minutes later, without their anti-grav sleds. The Sergeant ordered them back toward the waterfall before turning toward the Demoness.

"I may have a lead," the Sergeant said as the two started walking back toward the cave. "Two of my holo-emitters are missing. It may be possible to track them using a..."

Dawson followed the two on the video, their words lost to the distance and the waterfall. He sighed, feeling the stress of the moment fade. He lowered the recorder and wiped the sweat from his brow. He stared at the lake for a moment, thinking how good it would feel to go for a swim. He shook those thoughts from his head as the last words came back to him.

It may be possible to track them...

Dawson peeked around the rocks and saw that he was once again alone in the valley. He exhaled sharply, before pulling a small expandable satellite dish from the end of the cylinder. He set up the small antenna, pointing it toward the northern horizon. He flipped a switch on the side, changing the device from record to transmit, and raised the device to his face. "I request immediate dispatch of an interdiction team to commandeer the prison and arrest the Sergeant-in-Charge."

Chapter Nine

Angel heard the waterfall at the second turn, the roar of the water sending chills down her arms. She gripped Jake's hand tighter as he led her down the rocky corridor. Butterflies filled her stomach; she felt like a teenager sneaking out for the first time. The corridor smoothed out and the noise of the waterfall increased. She felt the temperature and humidity rise, but all of that was secondary. After seeing how clean Jake was, she only wanted to take a swim in the lake.

All day she had wanted to get started on the journey, but she knew that they had to wait until after midnight, prison time. The risk of running into someone in the corridor, or down the smooth tunnel, would be greatly diminished in the early morning. So far, the plan worked. Neither she nor Jake had seen a soul since leaving their hidden cave.

They silently padded down the passage. Empty canteens hung around their necks. Angel's smile grew as the cave grew lighter. They rounded a final curve and bright light assaulted her eyes, forcing her to squint. "Why is it so bright? I thought it was the middle of the night."

"They must have the prison set on a different clock." Jake responded. "The only thing I can think of is the guards are running both operations. They have to man the prison, so they work there during the planet's night. Then, half sleep and the other half work out here during the prison's night. Exhausting, but effective," he concluded.

Angel nodded, but said nothing. They had reached the waterfall and the sight, smells, and sound of the valley overwhelmed her. She never knew that all of this had been so close to the prison on what she had been told was a desolate moon. "Wow," was all she said.

"What?" Jake yelled.

"Wow!" she exclaimed.

Jake nodded. "Stay here, take it all in," his voice raised above the roar of the falls. "I'm going to scout around and make sure there is no one else about." She nodded and Jake disappeared around the edge of the waterfall.

Angel sat down near the small pool behind the waterfall. She removed her haggard leather sandals and dipped her toes in the water. The cool water tickled her toes and, with a smile, she thrust her feet into the water up to the ankles. Chills raced up her legs and across her arms as the sensation engulfed her. Muck, dirt, and blood washed from her feet, leaving the pool a murky brown. She leaned back on her hands, closed her eyes and threw her head back. The anticipation of submerging her entire body in the water left her breathless. She took in a deep breath and let it out slowly.

"Angel?"

She opened her eyes to see Jake standing at the edge of the waterfall, water soaking his shirt and pants. He motioned for her to come to him and she did. She stood beside him, the splash of the waterfall drenching her.

Jake leaned in close. "We are alone. Go, enjoy your swim. Try to stay low in the water. If you see anyone or hear anything, hide."

Angel gave him a strange look, unsure of his intentions. "Where are you going?"

"I'm going to be in the orchard across the pool," Jake replied, pointing. "It's time to pick some fruit to set the trap." He looked around the edge of the waterfall at the far end of the valley. "One of the transports is gone," he nodded. "When you've finished with your swim, I'd like to head over there and scout the other."

Angel tightened her grip on his hand, "Are you sure that's wise?"

Jake patted her hand and nodded. "I'm sure it'll be fine. Now go," he pointed at the small lake a few meters below them, "the water is great."

Angel made her way down the stone steps. Halfway down, she found a ledge a few meters above the lake and stood there, watching the water cascade down. Jake moved past her, making his way down the steps to solid ground, and the orchard. She breathed in the clean air, held it, pinched her nose, and jumped from the ledge. She fell three-meters and entered the lake feet first, the cool water embracing her as she sank beneath the surface. Months of dirt, grime, sweat and tension drained away as momentum pushed her down. She kicked, stopping her downward motion. She spread her arms as she slowly exhaled, floating beneath the surface of the water. Her body relaxed and began floating up. She kicked, broke through the surface, and took a gulp of air before opening her eyes.

She treaded water while she surveyed the closest thing to paradise she had known in years. The waterfall sat to her left in a mist of vapor, creating ripples and eddies in the lake. Squinting her eyes against the sun, a cloudless sky welcomed her. She turned and got her first good look at the forest, barely making out the top of the freighter beyond.

Angel surveyed her pasty skin, sadly shaking her head that she had not seen the sun for what seemed like an eternity. She and Jake had discussed the effects of UV and they knew to limit their time out in the sun. The last thing they wanted was to go back into the prison clean and sunburned.

She smiled at the thought of once again having bronze skin. She let that thought hang as she ducked her head under the cool water. She ran her fingers through her hair to remove debris, dirt and grime. She surfaced and saw an expanding cloud of dirt; like the waterfall pool, only much larger. Satisfied, she swam toward the orchard. If anything happened, she wanted to be close to Jake.

She stayed in the shallow water, fighting off the

occasional school of small lake creatures. She splashed and dunked herself, cleansing her body and soul. Angel couldn't remember the last time she had enjoyed herself without Grag. The thought of Grag stopped her in mid-stroke, made her gasp for breath, and she sucked in a mouthful of water. She choked and stood up in the shallow water, bending over with a hacking cough.

She flinched as a splash next to her announced the arrival of Jake, his arms wrapping around her almost instantly. "Are you okay?"

"Fine," she coughed. She shrugged out of his protective grip, but he did not let go. His grip comforted her and enraged her simultaneously. She patted his arm and he released her. "I just swallowed some water, that's all." She stared up into his brown eyes and saw his innocence gone. The eyes staring back at her were intelligent, cold, and knowing. She turned away.

"I think it may be time to check out the freighter," she said, changing the subject. "I think I've had all the swimming I care to do today."

Jake offered his hand and she took it. He helped her out of the pool and led her toward the orchard. They took shelter among the trees, their vantage point giving them a good view of the waterfall and the lake. Clouds moved across the sky, casting shadows, as birds floated on a slight breeze high above.

"Eat another?" Angel asked, pointing to the Darlencko fruit on the branches above their head. Her stomach growled with anticipation.

He shook his head. "Not yet. I don't think we are outside the twenty-seven-hour window." He pointed toward the mountain side of the grove. "There is a trail over there that leads in the direction of the freighters. Are you sure you're okay?"

Angel nodded, wringing out her hair. "Yes, I'm fine." A hint of annoyance in her voice. She let it go, smiled, and nodded toward the trail. "Let's go check out this ship of yours."

A packed dirt path from the orchard lead to a meters-long wooden bridge overlooking a river. The two paused on the bridge, watching the water flow from the waterfall side to a distant break in the mountains. Jake calculated it would be at least a two-day trek to reach the crevice. They continued their journey, the path gradually changing to a leaf covered trail through the forest. Jake held Angel's hand as they travelled through the trees. He breathed deep, enjoying the quiet and the shade of the wood. After the cramped confines of the prison caves, the open air of the valley left him feeling free.

Jake released her hand in the heart of the wood. He led the way, occasionally stepping over a downed log or around a bramble bush. He picked his way carefully along the trail, not knowing if the smugglers had left traps or not. He doubted it, but took no chances. Angel followed along behind, quiet and contemplative.

Jake kept a watchful eye on the woman. He did not

know for sure what caused the incident in the pool, but he had an idea. It would be some time before she could truly put Grag out of her mind. That led to his own thoughts of loss: Pamela and now a baby never meant to be. *It took months for me to come to terms with it. Its only been a couple of weeks for her.* Being out of the prison, alone with him, might be the best therapy for her. *Then again,* he thought, *it might make her miss Grag more.*

They stepped from the cool, shady wood onto a sun scorched plateau. The sun shone high overhead and the two started to sweat. More puffy clouds had moved in, but provided little respite from the sun. The temperature rose sharply in the direct sunlight and Jake stopped for a moment, drinking from one of the canteens hanging from his neck. The liquid cooled his body as it quenched his thirst. He wiped the sweat from his brow, hoping they had enough time for one more swim before they headed back inside.

A dirt path crossed the plateau, leading to a hard-packed dirt pad. The outlines of the missing freighters landing gear left deep impressions in the blasted earth. Jake felt the transition from dirt to scorched earth under his bare feet as he trotted across the landing field. He paused, crouching as he reached the open hatch to the freighter. He held out his arm, motioning Angel to a spot behind him. Jake listened for several minutes before waving Angel forward and the two moved up the ramp.

The metal floor felt cool on his feet as he quietly ascended the ramp into the ship. The searing sun abruptly disappeared as he entered the shadow of the interior. The temperature of the freighter, after sitting in the mid-day sun, made Jake wish he was still outside where there was at least a slight, cooling breeze. He paused at the top of the ramp, letting his eyes adjust to the dim interior.

A thick layer of dust and dirt covered everything in the ship. Deck panels lay strewn about, circuit boards sat halfway out of their slots or were missing entirely. Exposed wires hung from the ceiling and crisscrossed from control panel to control panel. Debris of all kinds—bottles, food wrappers, clothing—littered the freighter. Jake shook his head as he surveyed the freighter. "Damn."

He turned to Angel, silhouetted as she stood at the top of the ramp. "They must be using this one for spare parts to keep the other flying."

She nodded as Jake stood and moved inside. He carefully made his way through the debris on the deck over to one of the control panels. Jake picked up a discarded circuit board and inspected it in one of the random sunbeams that lit the interior.

Dark scorch marks covered the board, as if someone tried to repair it but only made it worse. *Looks like my first attempt,* he thought as he sat it back down.

Jake moved in a counterclockwise route around the compartment. He paused outside the first room leading off the main and saw Angel squat at the top of the ramp, watching him as he explored. He smiled and continued, sticking his head into each room and calling them off absently as he mapped the ship. "Galley. Crew quarters. Cargo bay." He spied a small walkway leading up to a separate deck. He snapped his fingers. "Cockpit."

He turned to Angel. "Be right back," he said before bounding up the steps to the control center of the ship.

The cockpit sat in shambles, much like the rest of the ship he had seen— maybe worse. More than half of the circuit panels, control gauges, and digital displays had been pulled. The navigation/communication console had been ripped from the bulkhead. The co-pilot's seat had been removed and now rested, upside down, in the pilot's seat; the co-pilot's control panel ransacked. Jake shook his head and returned to the main deck.

"It would take a lot of work to get this ship flying again," Jake looked at Angel. She now lay on the floor, peering into the darkness underneath one of the displaced deck panels. "But, on the bright side, they won't be able to follow us when we take the other one.

"What are you doing?"

Angel raised her head from the opening in the deck. "Did you know there was another deck under here?"

Jake moved to lie on the floor next to Angel, brushing away the debris to clear a spot for him. "No, but it makes sense. These are supposed to be some of the best smuggling ships in the Tri-System, because there are so many hidden compartments." He peered into the darkness underneath the deck. "Almost as much room here as in the standard cargo bay."

"The Darlencko fruit may be contraband, but it's not illegal everywhere. They wouldn't necessarily need these compartments for that," Angel said, thinking aloud. "I wonder if they are smuggling something else besides the fruit."

"Like what?"

"Slaves," she stated.

Jake pushed himself up from the floor. "Slaves? Where would they get..." His eyes widened. "Prisoners. Selling prisoners to the outer rim worlds." He shook his head. "No wonder so many convicts never return from Cla'nix." He cocked his head to one side, listening intently. Angel started to say something and Jake held up a finger: wait.

"Do you hear that?"

"Hear what," Angel responded, cocking her head, mimicking Jake. Distant, rolling thunder seemed to be getting louder. Her eyes widened, curious. "What...?"

Jake grabbed her hand and escorted her deeper into the freighter. He found a dark corner and squatted down behind another disassembled control panel. "Sit tight, we might be here a while." An inquisitive mask covered Angel's face. Jake gripped the woman's hand comfortingly before he rose and made his way to a small porthole in the main cabin. He craned his head skyward.

"It's the other freighter," he said over his shoulder. "The smugglers have returned."

Chapter Ten

Jake watched through the porthole as the freighter flared high, arresting the ships rapid descent with a sudden, bone jarring deceleration. He glanced away to look at Angel as the ship leveled off. She squatted, anxious. She saw Jake looking at her and she nodded. A pit developed in his stomach. They had come so far, neither wanted to be discovered, that would mean certain death. He pushed those thoughts aside and turned back to the porthole. The ship stabilized, the landing gear locked into place, and the freighter settled onto the packed dirt in a cloud of dust.

The billowing dust obscured the landing, but Jake had flown enough to know that the pilot was good. Jake turned away and hid his face as the interior of the scavenged freighter filled with a fine layer of the dust. The whine of the engines wound down and silence once again filled the valley. Jake returned his face to the small porthole and saw that the other freighter's landing gear sat in almost the exact spot of the imprints Jake had noticed on his way into the derelict freighter.

He heard the ship pop and hiss as it cooled after reentry, plumes of steam and exhaust escaped the freighter as it purged its systems. Eventually the ramp lowered and the occupants descended.

A man Jake did not recognize exited first, followed by two TSA enforcers that Jake did recognize from the prison. The lead man pointed up the ramp and said something that Jake could not make out. The others gave a hearty laugh and tugged on a thin line that led up the ramp. A dozen blind-folded prisoners, all wearing electro-magnetic cuffs, descended the ramp. The thin line bound their hands and feet into one long human and alien chain. Two Crendoshians followed the prisoners.

"Zrek," one of the rear guards called. "Prindell says the aft hydro-generator redlined twice on reentry. It needs to be replaced."

Zrek, the unknown man, stopped, and cursed. "Fine," he yelled in the general direction of the cooling freighter. Annoyance filled his voice. "You stay here and help him repair the ship. I'm sure there is a spare over there," he pointed toward the derelict. "Find it and get the ship back to full operation. These prisoners are on their way to the war in twelve hours. The ship should be ready to fly in four." Without waiting for a response, the man grabbed the line and led the bound prisoners toward the forest.

The man nodded. "Will do," he said, tossing a mock salute at Zrek's back before heading for the derelict, and Jake.

Jake moved from the porthole, crossing the small hold to kneel beside Angel. "We are about to have company," he whispered, his voice calm and even. "Two men, but only one is coming aboard."

Angel nodded, moving into a more suitable position to defend or attack. She slunk deep into a crevice between two panels near the door to the galley. Jake moved to stand in front of her, shielding her as much as possible. He slid deep into the shadow as he felt a vibration through his feet. Heavy footfalls announced the arrival of the guard.

"Fix my ship," the man muttered, mocking Zrek. "Do this...do that." The guard kicked a discarded computer core lying on the floor. The core arched across the cabin, shattering as it hit the far wall. "That SOB would be nothing without our support."

Shadows played on the walls as the man moved through the ship toward the main cargo hold. He paused in a sunbeam, staring out the porthole as the Crendoshians and Zrek escorted the prisoners into the forest. He ran a hand through his black, shoulder length hair before scratching his crooked nose. He turned away from the window and Jake could see brown eyes scanning the debris strewn cabin. The man shuffled noisily through the ship, pausing occasionally to pick up a random object and inspect it before tossing it over his shoulder. He moved to the next sunbeam and paused, again looking out a porthole, this time toward the distant waterfall. He took a cautious glance around, produced a flask, and took a long drag. Satisfied, he replaced the flask to a pouch on his belt.

Jake left his position by Angel, moving closer to the man's path.

The flask stowed, he searched for the elusive part he needed. He continued to move toward the rear of the cabin, toward Jake and Angel. The man's shadow crossed over Jake's hiding spot and Jake tensed, coiled like a spring to strike. The guard paused, suddenly spooked, and listened to something that attracted his attention. Without warning, the man spun, drew his pistol, and fired. He held the pistol steady as he moved toward a dark corner. He fired a second time, killing the small animal he had wounded with his first shot.

He holstered the weapon as a voice called from outside, "Dranald, you okay in there?"

Dranald scowled at the voice. "Yes, Prindell, I'm fine." Contempt filled his voice, "Just another Kratt-beast in the ship," he called. "You want it for dinner?"

"You know I don't eat those things," Prindell replied, his humanoid silhouette filled the top of the freighter's ramp. "Just find the damn part so I can fix the freighter."

Dranald smiled, bent over, grabbed the dead animal by the tail, and hurled it toward the ramp. "Here, have it anyway!" Prindell ducked the flying carcass, disappearing down the ramp. Dranald laughed. "I don't need it stinking up the ship."

Jake carefully picked up a meter-long pipe from the floor and moved from his hiding place, approaching Dranald from behind. The guard stared out of the ship, taking another draw from his flask. He carefully stowed the container back into his belt and turned to continue into the freighter. His eyes widened as he saw Jake. The pipe connected with Dranald's ribs, the crunch of bone echoed through the ship's hold. Dranald doubled over as Jake swung again, an upper-cut aiming for the man's lowered head.

The impact knocked the guard completely off his feet. The body appeared to levitate off the floor, hanging in the air for several seconds before crashing to the dusty, debris strewn floor. Jake turned toward the ramp, anticipating Prindell's return. He counted the seconds, but no one came.

Jake let out the breath he did not realize he held and unceremoniously dropped the pipe, it landed on Dranald's body before rolling onto the floor with a soft, metallic clang. He moved to the dead man's body, knelt, and began to search his pockets. The first thing he retrieved was the pistol from the man's holster. He rolled the gun over in his hand, examining the weapon before setting it on the deck beside him. Jake then moved to Dranald's pockets. That search revealed the flask, a prison access key, ten gold coins, and a small communicator. Jake tossed five of the coins, the flask and the access key to Angel before pocketing the other five coins. He then turned his attention to the communicator.

It was a standard short range device very common in security details. He had used similar devices before on large transports. "Two channel encryption," he muttered, "nothing fancy." He pocketed the comm unit and then continued his check of the man's clothing.

He undressed Dranald, held up his shirt, and shook his head. He unlaced the boots, removed them and held them to his feet. He offered them to Angel. "Too small for me," Jake whispered, turning toward the woman. "Should fit you if you want them."

Vibrations and loud footfalls on the ramp signaled the return of Prindell and cut off her remark. A Hazmora silhouette stood backlit in the doorway to the ramp. The guard blocked the light, dimming the interior of the ship. "Dranald?" Prindell asked. "Where the hell is my part?"

Jake grabbed the pistol from the deck beside him and pointed it at the perfectly backlit target at the top of the ramp. He had never fired a pistol before; had never even held one. His fingers turned bone white as he gripped the pistol tightly; held at a forty-five-degree angle that he knew was wrong, but could not correct. Time slowed as Jake sighted down the barrel at the alien.

Jake jerked the trigger, a dull green laser bolt impacted to the Hazmora's left. Prindell moved faster than Jake expected as the Hazmora headed for cover behind an overturned computer console. His hand went to the low-slung holster on his left leg as he moved to his right.

"No!" Jake yelled, firing again.

The Hazmora did not flinch as the bolt zipped past his head, a shower of sparks descended on him from the impact of the energy beam. Prindell, almost to the computer console, raised his weapon, bringing the pistol in line with Jake.

Jake fired a third time.

The third bolt hit Prindell in the left shoulder, spinning him as he fired. The errant bolt tore a hole in a panel near Jake, but did no damage to its intended target. Jake watched the Hazmora grimace, switch the weapon to his right hand, and raise it again. Jake, getting a feel for the pistol, adjusted his aim and fired another shot.

The fourth bolt hit the pilot in the center of his chest, throwing him backward. He impacted the bulkhead and slid down behind the computer console he sought as cover. Jake ran, shoeless, through the debris on the deck, and crouched at the top of the ramp to scan the landing zone, expecting a squad of guards to come running at the sound of the gunfire. Silence greeted him.

He exhaled, sitting heavily on the deck of the freighter and willed the hammer in his chest to slow. His heartrate under control, he moved to examine Prindell's body. He grabbed the Hazmora's pistol and tossed it to Angel before a quick search of the man's pockets yielded another ten gold coins, another communicator, and an aerial map of the valley. Angel came and knelt beside Jake as he studied the map in the late afternoon.

Jake checked the shadows outside the ship."We don't have much time. We need to replace the part they were talking about and get out of here. Today." He smiled, "Say goodbye to Cla'nix."

His smile faded as Angel shook her head. "What?"

"Not yet," she replied. She began stripping off the pilot's clothes. "There are still a couple of tasks to complete before we leave."

Jake started to object, but the determination in her eyes quieted his protest. He pulled off his old rags and started putting on the pilot's clothes; it was a close enough fit, if a bit awkward. He tried the shoes. They fit perfectly. "What's your plan?"

Worry filled her voice. "I'm working on it."

It took almost a half hour to find the replacement part that Dranald had been sent for. Angel watched as Jake removed the device from its slot in the engine room, cradling it carefully in his hands. He nodded and Angel led the way out of the derelict ship. The afternoon sat on the horizon, the light hitting the mountains and casting long shadows over the valley as they crossed the fifty-meters to the working freighter.

"Stand guard," Jake said. "This won't take but a minute or two."

She nodded and he disappeared to the rear of the ship.

Angel looked around, amazed at the contrast between the clean, operational freighter, and the one used for spare parts. This ship was spotless. A hint of flowers hung in the air. *Odd,* she thought, until she realized it was probably to mask the scent of unwashed slaves. She shuddered at the thought. An open deck plate toward the cargo hold seemed to confirm her theory and sent another shudder down her spine. She gripped the pistol in her hands tighter, comforted by the familiar feel of the weapon.

A trio of spacesuits hung in racks at the top of the ramp. Lights flickered sporadically on control panels, and a low hum reverberated through the soles of her boots. The vibration changed pitch and a series of lights on a distant panel changed from red to green. Jake re-emerged from the bowels of the ship a moment later.

"Done already?" she asked, turning her attention back out the door. The shadows grew longer, sunset was less than an hour away.

"Almost," he said, sliding past her and placing a foot on the short stairwell leading to the cockpit. "I want to make sure the ship is ready in case we need to leave in a hurry." He smiled teasingly. "You figure out how we are going to get into the prison and back out again in one piece?"

Angel followed the long finger of a shadow with her eyes. The shadow stretched from a ragged mountain ridge all the way to the orchard on the far end of the valley. Darlencko fruit glistened in the waning light. She turned back to face him, her eyes settling on a row of six satchels sitting in an open cabinet. She smiled as the final piece of her plan fell into place.

"Actually..."

The Jake Cutter Conspiracy

Chapter Eleven

The sounds of the waterfall diminished as Jake led the way up the smooth corridor. Angel, her hair still wet from a last dip in the lake, followed a few meters behind. Both wore their newly acquired clothes and carried newly acquired packs, each laden with Darlencko fruit. The duo carried their pistols out and ready. Angel had spent a half hour going over the proper stance and aiming techniques with Jake; she never said where she learned such skills and he never asked. He moved silently, his confidence high.

Darkness swallowed the valley behind them. The smooth corridor sat near pitch black save for the tiny lights that Jake and Angel carried, acquired from a storage locker on the ship. Jake could see the prison illumination strips up ahead and knew that they would soon be back in the general population. The engineered corridor changed into the rocky stone of the natural caves of the prison. Jake slowed, listening, and heard the rustling of prisoners ahead. He hugged the wall as shadows danced in the corridor ahead.

Another day in the prison had begun.

He stopped short of the main cavern, taking a knee as Angel came up beside him. Jake took a breath, trying to calm his racing heart. He stole a peek around his vantage toward the central hub of the prison and watched as a dozen or so prisoners milled about. Most of the prisoners stared toward the admin area, waiting on their morning meal. He followed their gaze upward and noted that the admin ledge sat empty.

Jake noticed that several prisoners held bowls to catch anything the guards may throw at them. Another small band of inmates entered the hub carrying held clubs and other makeshift weapons. They shoved their way through the crowd and Jake surmised they sought the weaker of the population. A small, blue Traxillian ran from two Hazmora. The little alien almost made it to a small cave before a Hazmoran club knocked it off its feet. Most of the prison population ignored the scene.

He pulled back, relieved that the aliens were disinterested in their environment. It made phase one easier. He stroked his beard, knowing that once they were seen with different clothes, packs, and weapons, that hell would descend on them. He took another breath, checked to make sure his weapon was fully charged and the safety was off.

"Are you ready?" he asked Angel, looking at her over his shoulder.

He saw Angel take a deep breath of her own and then nod. "Yes."

Jake removed the liberated pack from his shoulder

and pulled several pieces of the fruit from the bag. He took one final look at Angel, determination and anticipation filled her face. He holstered his pistol, crouched and walked toward the main cavern, staying close to the cave wall. He dropped into the shadow of a boulder and began rolling fruit up the last few meters of the stone corridor into the main cavern.

Jake's first bag empty, he discarded it and opened his second satchel. He rolled more of the fruit into the cavern, sending the green/orange orbs in every direction. His second bag empty, he dropped it and drew his pistol. Several pieces of fruit rolled through his peripheral vision and he turned to see Angel emptying her own bags of fruit.

Jake and Angel watched the predator and prey scenario continue to play out again, this time a Blu'clic attacked a Klan'do. The two grappled on the periphery of the cavern, away from where the orange/green fruit rolled into the cavern. The dozens of pieces of Darlencko fruit had completed their journey, stopping at random points throughout the central hub.

Angel looked anxious, but Jake calmed her. "Just wait. Once they take the bait, we move."

On cue, a green skinned Klan'do kicked a piece of the fruit. The humanoid alien looked down, saw the round orb and followed the rolling object it had kicked. The alien stopped when it did, staring down at the strange object. The alien looked around before bending over and picking up the fruit. He sniffed it before cracking it open and taking a tentative bite. A broad smile crept across his face as he took a larger bite. The Klan'do licked its chops before devouring the morsel. Juice and bits of fruit dripped from his chin.

The Klan'do looked around and, finding another piece of fruit, ran over to it, bowling over the struggling Blu'clic and the Klan'do in the process. He bent over and tore into the fruit, ignoring the shouts of anger from the two he had run over. The two stopped yelling when they saw him gorging himself on the fruit. Grunts, tweets, whistles, and a dozen other languages filled the cavern as prisoners descended on the Klan'do. The prisoners discovered other pieces of fruit and the melee Jake hoped for materialized before his eyes. More aliens filled the cavern and the fight grew.

The Sergeant and a squad of guards appeared at the ledge overlooking the cavern. Several of the guards laughed as the prisoners fought each other. Jake watched the Sergeant's features grow angrier as the TSA official realized what the prisoners were fighting over. He said something lost in the wind, but Jake thought he had a good idea of the obscenities the man released. The Sergeant turned and disappeared from the ledge.

Jake beamed, "Throw the rest."

In rapid succession, she emptied her satchel, tossing the remaining fruit into the middle of the fray. He watched the riot grow. Prisoners grappled for the fruit, several rolling around on the floor locked in combat. One pair rolled over a piece of fruit, leaving it crushed on the stone floor. Howls filled the cavern as others saw the damaged food and descended on the remains, fighting over the leftover bits. Jake searched for the original Klan'do and finally saw the green alien escape the main brawl. His eyes twinkled as he tore into his third piece of fruit.

"Let's move." Jake hugged the wall, staying in the shadows as he stepped into the main cavern. Angel followed close behind, her pistol in her hand behind her back. Jake's eyes scanned the melee, watching for threats. He felt Angel close behind and instinctively held out his arm to protect her. They were almost out of the cavern when an ear-splitting scream rose above the fray and stopped everything, including Jake and Angel.

The Klan'do prisoner that discovered the initial fruit dropped to his knees, holding his head in agony. His body rippled with seizures. His scream went silent as he ran out of air. His body forced another breath, and the scream echoed again. Blood and spittle flew from his mouth as the alien fell over on his side, his body convulsing. His second scream went silent and this time his body could not force another breath. The Klan'do died in silence, half of his third piece of Darlencko fruit still in his hand.

Silence reigned for several seconds before another prisoner dove for the discarded fruit, grabbed the half-eaten orb, and quickly finished it off. The melee resumed and the prison descended into chaos once again. Angel turned, saw Jake watching the fight, and pushed him forward, out of the central hub of the prison.

"Go," she hissed, and the two disappeared down the corridor leaving the free-for-all behind them.

"The Sergeant was furious," Angel said once they were alone again. They moved quickly down the tunnel, putting distance between themselves and the cavern. "But I did not see the Demoness." The two arrived at the holographic boulder hiding their alcove.

"I noticed," Jake replied. He stuck his head through the hologram and scanned their room. Nothing seemed out of the ordinary. He pulled his head back and looked at the woman. "The fruit won't keep them occupied for long," Jake surmised. "Now, go get whatever it is you need to get. Hurry!"

Angel handed her last satchel to Jake before disappearing through the hologram. He checked the bag, finding a half dozen more pieces of the fruit. "Enough for one more distraction." Jake took the sack and placed the strap diagonally over his chest before taking cover behind a large boulder. The sounds of the fight were still loud, punctuated by the occasional death scream.

He heard Angel exit the cave and turned to see the woman emerge from the hologram wall, a panicked look on her face, a long right claw around her throat. Angel continued to move into the corridor as the Lemox Demoness materialized from the holographic wall. Jake's eyes widened before he raised his pistol, taking a bead on the Succubus. His finger touched the trigger before the Demoness shook her head.

"No, no, no. Put the gun down, Jake Cutter," she hissed. The Demoness cocked an ear toward the distant melee, her expression unreadable.

"Angel?" Jake asked, his eyes unwavering from

their target.

"I'm fine," she struggled, her hands trying to pry the alien's arm from around her throat. The Demoness guided the woman into the middle of the corridor, forcing Angel onto her tiptoes. "Just shoot her."

Angel winced as the Demoness pricked her neck with her sharpened talon. "I would not do that, Jake Cutter." The Demoness' cautioned.

The Demoness moved to her right, further up the corridor toward the central hub. Angel shuffled along while Jake's pistol tracked the movement, never wavering. The Succubus toyed with Angel's neck, this time drawing a pinprick of blood. She bent down and licked the blood from Angel's neck. The Demoness drew her head back, licking her lips and smiled at Jake.

"Jake Cutter," the Demoness' eyes bored into him. "You are not the same man that arrived a year ago. You have," she paused, searching for the right word, "grown."

Jake closed his left eye, sighting down the barrel of the pistol. He had the shot. His finger tightened on the trigger. The Demoness began forcing Angel's head back and forth, in and out of his field of fire.

"Now, I understand the danger you pose to the Secretary," the Demoness continued, "and why he wants you dead."

Jake's finger stopped in mid squeeze. He opened his left eye as his finger released the trigger.

The Demoness' smile broadened.

"You mentioned him when I arrived," Jake stalled.

"So far all you have for your troubles are empty promises."

"Not empty promises," the Demoness purred. "A pardon, and riches beyond avarice."

Jake's mind raced, trying to find anyone named the Secretary in his past. He recalled every customer, every cargo handler, every shipyard manager, none of them had the resources or the power to lock him away...or kill him. His mind distracted, his eyes wavered from the Demoness for a moment.

Angel chose that moment to act, pushing backward against the alien's body and putting distance between her neck and the Demoness' talon. The Demoness tried to keep her grip on the woman, but Angel placed her feet on a small boulder on the side of the corridor and, using it for leverage, pushed back hard. The Demoness lost her momentum and her balance. She stumbled.

Jake snapped from his reverie, moved the pistol back to the target, and fired. Angel slipped from the Demoness' grip as the energy bolt flashed over her head, slicing through the alien's throat. The force of the impact threw the Demoness back two steps, but she did not go down. Jake fired again...and again...and again until the alien dropped to the ground. He stared at the Succubus lying at his feet as a wave of relief washed over him. He took a few steps and fired a final round between the glassy eyes of the Demoness.

"Are you alright?" he asked approaching Angel. He helped her from the rocky cave floor.

"Fine," she said tersely. He saw the anger and

embarrassment in her face. "She surprised me, grabbed me from behind." She shook her head before looking at Jake. "Thank you."

He dismissed her thanks with a wave of his hand. "I still owe you about a dozen times for saving my life the last year. But, let's save that for later. We still need to get out of here."

"Wait," Angel disappeared back into the cave.

Jake checked up the corridor, they were still alone. He listened and still heard the distant sounds of the riot he had created, although the sounds were muted now. He turned back toward the hidden cave as Angel emerged, fastening a shiny necklace around her neck. The pendent on the chain was a complex series of knots that formed a pattern that Jake had never seen before. He stared another moment before looking in Angels eyes.

"The only thing Grag ever gave me that I truly cherish," she said. "A gift that I couldn't leave."

Jake nodded, before checking the corridor again. "Ready?"

She listened for a moment. "Sounds like the fight is about over," she confirmed, her voice carried a cautious undertone. "I don't think we will get away clean."

Jake patted Angel's remaining satchel half-full of Darlencko fruit. "This should help distract them," he nodded up the corridor. "Let's go."

Prisoner bodies littered the floor of the central cavern of Cla'nix. Bits of green/orange fruit, blood, and body parts created a slippery, muddy wasteland. Those few prisoners still upright continued to fight over the last pieces of fruit, their exhausted swings almost comical.

Jake and Angel blended with the shadows of the walls, staying hidden as they approached the cavern. Three guards stood on the ledge, placing bets on who would be the last prisoner standing. The bets placed, one of the guards raised a rifle and shot two of the wounded prisoners who were attempting to get back into the fight. The guards laughed and exchanged their wagers. The sounds of the shots had no effect on those fighting on the cavern floor.

"Bastards," Angel whispered.

Jake nodded, handing the last satchel of fruit to the woman.

"Throw these when I tell you." His face a mask of cold malice.

"What are you going to do?" she asked, taking the fruit.

Jake did not respond. He stood, raised his pistol, and fired at the three guards on the ledge. Holding the weapon in a firm grip and controlling his breathing as Angel had taught him, he dropped all three of the guards in rapid succession. He shifted his aim to the melee, but the prisoners involved in the fight paid no attention to him.

"Let's go," he said, venom dripping from his words. He moved from cover toward the exit cave without further discussion. Angel followed on his heels, her back hugging the wall.

Shouts echoed through the cavern as another contingent of guards arrived on the prisoner level. The Sergeant who had arrested Jake led the way, pushing and shoving their way through the last dozen or so prisoners still fighting. One of the guards elbowed a prisoner, knocking the prize fruit from its claws. The alien screamed, grabbed the guard, and snapped his neck in one motion. The alien dropped the lifeless guard before retrieving his prize. The Sergeant shot the alien in the head and continued through the hub without pausing.

Jake and Angel dropped low at the sound of the shouting. They kept low, maneuvering around boulders and past bodies the last few meters to the mouth of the cave that led to the waterfall and the freedom beyond. Jake turned his pistol toward the melee as Angel slipped past him into the tunnel. The guards were halfway across the cavern, still pushing their way through the alien mass.

"Throw them," Jake said, nodding to the satchel. Angel stood from her crouch and hurled fruit into the cavern. Each piece of fruit bounced off a prisoner's head and everything seemed to stop.

The guards, seeing the pieces of orange/green fruit sail through the air, turned their attention toward the source of the objects. The prisoners, seeing the fruit bounce off each other, stopped to assess where the object of their desire originated. Everyone in the cavern turned to look at Jake and Angel squatting behind a boulder. An eerie silence filled the cavern as everyone contemplated their next move.

The Sergeant raised his weapon, pointing toward Jake. A thin smile crossed his lips.

A Crendoshian prisoner let out a blood-curling howl and bowled over the Sergeant and two others as she lunged at a piece of Darlencko fruit. The Sergeant's shot went into the ceiling. The howl frightened one of the guards who pulled the trigger of his rifle, sending a bolt into the wall a half meter from Jake. Jake snap-aimed a shot at the guard, missing him but hitting a second.

"Run!" he yelled and pulled the trigger as fast as he could in the general direction of the guards. The prison guards sought cover while the prisoners renewed their fight for fruit. Alien claws, fists, tails, and pinchers lashed out at anything within reach, prisoner or guard. Jake's bolts found targets indiscriminately.

Angel turned and ran down the tunnel toward the waterfall. Jake stole a glance, ensuring she was well down the tunnel, before sending a final volley into the cavern. A barrage of screams rewarded him. He stood and ran.

The two ran down the rocky tunnel, the downward slope adding momentum. The rocky ground gave way to the smooth-bored tunnel. They reached the waterfall and the dark valley in minutes. Angel stopped, putting her hands on her knees as she tried to catch her breath. The roar of the waterfall masked all other sound. Jake caught up to her a few seconds later, his breathing ragged. He looked over his shoulder and saw lights playing along the tunnel wall.

"Get going," he yelled to Angel between gasps. "I'll hold them off while you get a head start."

"No," she said, taking in a huge gulp of air. "We will fight them together."

Jake shook his head. "Go! I just need to delay them for a minute while you run to the orchard. I'll catch up." He smiled. "Promise."

Angel eyed him skeptically for a fraction of a second before standing on her toes and kissing him on the cheek. "I can't fly that ship, so don't take too long." With that, she disappeared down the stone steps and into the darkness beyond the waterfall.

Jake turned his attention back toward the tunnel, now brighter as the guards drew near. Jake fired a random shot up the corridor, rewarded by a scream. He ducked behind a boulder on the rock-strewn ledge behind the waterfall as a hail of laser bolts answered. The strobe of laser fire turned his attention to the waterfall and the superheated lasers passing through the water. The bolts vaporized the water into steam on contact.

Without looking, Jake fired another shot up the tunnel. No scream, but another hail of lasers answered. He risked a peek and saw the shadowy silhouettes of his pursuers, but no one advanced. He smiled and fired a handful of shots up the tunnel before taking two steps and diving through the waterfall. He passed through the water and felt the cool, almost icy fingers caress his body. He tensed, anticipating the full body shock at the end of the three meter drop to the lake. He closed his eyes as the water engulfed his body. The cold water hit him like a blow to the solar plexus and he gasped, letting out his breath. He somersaulted underwater and kicked for the surface.

He broke through, took a deep breath, and immediately started swimming for the orchard. He could hear the whine of the laser bolts as the guards continued to fire through the waterfall. The blue and green beams created an eerie strobe affect in the dark.

Jake crawled from the water on his hands and knees, gasping for air. Angel appeared at his side a moment later. He stood, turning to watch the sporadic firing through the waterfall. It stopped and Jake knew the Sergeant and his guards would be coming. The orchard was almost pitch black, lit only by the guards lights and a waning moon above.

Jake pointed to a spot near the waterfall. "They think we are still over there," Jake said, his breathing still ragged. He shivered as his body fought off the water's cold edge. "We need to move before they realize we aren't."

"I'm waiting on you," she said with a smile and, taking his hand, led him through the dark orchard toward the footpath.

Jake moved as quickly as he dared. He could not see, and tripped over roots and rocks every few steps. Angel had no trouble negotiating through the darkness. "How are you not tripping?"

"I can see the path," she replied. She stopped, placing his left hand on her shoulder. "I am from the

Zar'got system; Abrien, actually. Our planet goes through extremes of light and dark every solar cycle so we are finely attuned to see with little light. The stars provide ample illumination for me.

"So, just follow my lead, stay right behind me, and move as fast as you can." She turned her head toward the waterfall. "Looks like they are not going to give up easily." She pointed to her right. "They are through the waterfall."

Jake looked behind him and saw the light from their flashlights, crisscrossing the ground on the far side of the lake. He counted a dozen or so, stretching from the lake up the stone staircase to the waterfall. They were advancing quickly.

"Lead on," he said. "I'm going to need a couple of minutes to get the ship through pre-flight."

Angel resumed their trek through the dark, leading him into the forest. Jake clumsily tripped along behind her. He thought it somehow got darker as even the faint starlight had disappeared behind a living canopy. Their pursuers were gaining, noisily following the hard-packed trail. Jake turned his head, but could not see the lights of the guards. He tripped again, almost falling. He regained his footing and continued along the trail. "We have a two-minute lead, max," he whispered into the darkness.

"It's enough," Angel said, picking up the pace. "The edge of the forest is just up ahead. Then it's a quick dash to the freighter."

Angel was proven correct when, a few moments later, the landscape brightened as the forest canopy disappeared, revealing the starry sky and waning moon. The starlight created a colorless, bleak, but discernible landscape. Jake released Angel's shoulder and stared at the outline of the Trillinden freighter before him. The night brightened and Jake turned to see the planet of Yel'thi as it crested the mountains behind him. The freighter took a more defined shape in the planet's light. He heard the distant sound of the pursuit and knew time was running out. "Let's go!"

The two boarded the freighter at a run. Jake sprinted up the steps toward the cockpit, pausing to ensure Angel actuated the controls to raise the ramp and close the hatch. A mechanical hum, followed by a metal on metal scrape, confirmed the ramp nestled into its proper position. Jake continued into the cockpit.

Jake moved with purpose and precision; flipping switches, turning knobs, and adjusting power levels. A low hum filled the freighter and the interior lights grew brighter. He moved from the nav-com panel to the co-pilot's seat and back again. He glanced at Angel as she entered the cockpit.

"Sit here," he ordered pointing to the co-pilot's seat.

Angel moved past him to sit at the controls. Jake saw her eyes widen at the row after row of dials, toggle switches, and displays. He appeared at her shoulder, pointing toward a set of dials to her right. "When that center readout hits ninety-percent, flip that switch. Okay?"

She nodded, glanced out of the cockpit window and

froze. Jake followed her gaze and saw the Sergeant's angry face pressed to the glass. The man pounded on the glass. "Get out of my ship!"

Jake took the pilot's seat and calmly flipped a series of switches. The hum of the ship changed pitch as the engines came to life. A subtle tremble affirmed the completion of the pre-flight checks. Jake reached behind him and hit two more switches. The running lights and exterior ground lights flashed to life, illuminating the area around the freighter.

The Sergeant, now backlit by the running lights, pounded the glass with the butt of his pistol. "I'm going to kill you, Cutter!"

Jake looked through the canopy, past both Angel and the Sergeant, to see other guards outside the ship. A couple of them yelled for the Sergeant to move, brandishing their weapons at the ship. Several others disappeared underneath the freighter, apparently heading toward the ramp to try to break in.

"The gauge," he said, pointed to the indicator.

She nodded and flipped the toggle as instructed.

The re-entry shields activated, eliciting a pulse wave from the ship. The Sergeant and his entire squad of guards were catapulted from the ship. Jake saw the guards fly through the air, hit, and roll on the hard packed dirt. A tree abruptly stopped the Sergeant's tumble.

"The area is clear," Angel said, turning to face Jake.

Jake pulled the throttle back to hover. He felt the freighter rise from the landing pad, flipped a switch, and heard the landing gear retract. He watched Angel fumble with her safety harness as dust, rocks and debris filled the air outside. The shields flashed faintly as they absorbed multiple laser blasts from the prison guards. The small arms fire had no effect on the hovering freighter, although Jake and Angel both flinched involuntarily.

Jake lifted the freighter higher, piloting the ship in a lazy circle around the valley. The exterior lights illuminated the mountainside, giving him a new perspective on the landscape. He moved the ship toward the waterfall and saw the mountain lake that fed it, the orchard, and the valley below.

"It's beautiful from up here," Angel commented.

"Yes," Jake replied distantly. He stared at the lake, a thought forming in his mind. "That lake has to be what, forty kilometers wide?"

Angel nodded, staring at the waterfall in the spotlights of the ship. "At least."

Jake repositioned the freighter over the waterfall, reached back, and flipped two switches on the console behind him. Somewhere in the aft of the ship, servos groaned and a retractable laser cannon dropped from the belly of the Trillinden freighter.

A year of frustration, beatings, and loss culminated in one act. Resolve filled him. A chapter of his life appeared to close as he stabbed the firing button on the control pad before him.

Bright red lasers lit the night, racing from the freighter to the rocks around the waterfall. The rock exploded as the energy-intense bolts impacted. The lasers boiled the water on contact creating a super-hot steam bath that rocked the ship with thermals. Jake maneuvered the ship further away from the waterfall and fired again.

Ancient rock formations disintegrated under the barrage. The naturally controlled waterfall turned into an uncontrolled avalanche of water and rock. The lake, held in check for eons by the precarious rock structures of the mountain, poured into the valley. The orchard drowned in seconds as the lake flooded the valley.

Jake swung the ship around, hovering over the drowning forest. Angel pointed and he saw the guards running from the water, heading for higher ground. The water overtook the men; the tide sweeping them away in the blink of an eye.

"Jake," Angel called, pointing. Jake followed her finger and saw the derelict freighter, floating on the rushing water, bobbing in the current. Jake maneuvered the hammerhead cockpit lights to play on the sister Trillinden ship and saw a solitary figure holding on to the top of the craft where the sensor package once sat. The figure raised his pistol and popped off a trio of shots at the hovering freighter.

Do I kill him, or give him a chance to live, stranded in a flooded valley? he asked himself. *Is this the man I've become? Do I have the right to decide if he lives or dies?* Jake took another look at the man who had almost single handedly ruined his life and exhaled slowly, staring blankly at the controls.

Without another thought, Jake fired, vaporizing the water around the floating freighter. Superheated steam exploded from the rising lake, rocking the freighter violently. The ship rocked nearly vertical, the motion launching the Sergeant high into the air, his arms flailing in the ship's spotlights. He reached the apex of his flight and paused in midair, before plummeting back toward the rising, boiling water. The lake swallowed him whole, he disappeared instantly.

Angel turned to stare at Jake. He glanced at her briefly, turning away from the mixture of disbelief and relief in her eyes. "Grag is avenged," he heard her say and knew that a dark chapter in both of their lives was closed. He turned back to the controls, flipping switches, and set a course off world.

The Trillinden freighter left Cla'nix prison, never to return.

Chapter Twelve

Mark Dawson steadied himself against the stone wall as another tremor shook the cave. He ducked as dust, dirt, and small rocks pelted him from above. The ground beneath him steady once again, he continued through the tunnel toward the landing bay. He had to go the space-dock control room to release the shields before the assault team arrived.

Another tremor, accompanied by cries of panic. He turned, staring down the dark tunnel for a moment, wondering who was left to scream like that. He had witnessed the carnage in the main junction of the prison from his hiding spot. It was only after the Sergeant had chased Jake and Angel down towards the orchard tunnel that Dawson had emerged.

More screams, strangled off.

"What the hell...?" A new vibration traveled through the soles of his shoes. He turned, sprinting up the narrow stone corridor. He passed a junction and slid to a stop. Backtracking, he peered down this new tunnel. The stone was dark, foreboding, but he could see a gentle incline that disappeared into the darkness, and it pointed in the general direction of the space-dock. The vibrations grew, accompanied by a new sound—rushing water. Dawson entered the junction at a run.

The tunnel incline turned steep, but Dawson kept his legs pumping. His calves burned, his lungs ached for oxygen, but he could not stop. He managed a slight smile. He had a pretty good idea what had happened. *I just hope their escape doesn't kill me!*

He emerged from the tunnel a few hundred meters from the guard barracks and stood alone in the corridor, bending over with his hands on his knees to catch his breath. He cocked his head, listening. The air grew humid. The distant sound of rushing water filtered through the air, permeated by the occasional gurgling scream. Standing up straight, he forced his aching legs to move and headed toward his quarters.

He entered the barracks area and sighed in relief that he was alone. He reached toward a rock wall, his hand disappearing inside the structure. The wall disappeared, revealing an entire room including a holo-transmitter, two small duffle bags, emergency rations, a transmitter, and a wall of weapons. Dawson sorted through the rations, found a canteen, and gulped its contents dry. He tossed the canteen aside, grabbed another, and drained it. He exhaled sharply and began pulling off his tattered, dirty, and bloody shirt and shorts.

The small cylinder attached to his clothes buzzed for attention. Dawson slid on a clean pair of pants before moving to an alcove in the previously hidden room. He activated the transmitter attached to the cave wall. "Dawson," he snarled as the screen snapped to life.

He pulled on a shirt with some difficulty, as it clung to his sweaty torso. He felt filthy and could only imagine what he looked like after running the tunnels amid the constant rain of dust and debris. *Clean clothes helps,* he thought, *but I need a long shower.* He grabbed a gun belt from the wall and strapped it around his waist.

"Lieutenant," a young woman's face appeared on the screen. A battle helmet covered her head. The visor retracted, exposing her blue eyes. A small stem-mike extended from the left side of her face, hovering over her mouth. "I'm Ensign Panz, leading the strike team. What the hell did you do down there?"

"I haven't done anything," Dawson growled, gathering the few personal belongings he possessed. He stuffed them in a backpack as he continued. "We had a bit of a prisoner uprising. How bad is it?"

"See for yourself," the woman replied.

The screen changed, replacing her image with an aerial view of the valley, or what was left of it. The orchard and forest lay submerged under meters of water. A few tree tops from the forest rose out of the water, but there was no indication of the orchard at all. While he watched, the water level rose as the lake emptied into the lowlands and last of the tree tops disappeared. The view shifted and something caught his attention.

"Pan back to port," he said. The camera shifted and Dawson saw a Trillinden freighter dashed upon the rocks. The ship lay on its side, its fuselage twisted and scorched.

"Any sign of a second freighter?" he asked.

"We had a sensor echo a few minutes ago, but there is nothing on the scanners now," she said. The screen showed the water level continue to rise, drowning the freighter left behind.

The image flickered and the woman's face reappeared.

"I hate to interrupt," she began, but the look on her face said otherwise, "but we have a problem. Sensors indicate that the water has found a way into the prison. Water levels are increasing."

"Tell me something I don't know," Dawson muttered, strapping the pack to his back and picking a laser rifle from the mini-arsenal.

"It's destabilizing the cave system," she continued. "We estimate less than twenty minutes before the entire mountain caves in."

A smirk appeared on Dawson's face. "I did not know that." He stood up straight, feeling the weight of the pack and making a few minor adjustments to the straps. He jumped once, satisfied that everything was secured and picked up a rifle, comforted by its weight in his arms.

He nodded to the woman on the screen. "You may want to come get me," he smiled grimly. "Now."

Lieutenant Junior Grade Dawson stood rigidly at attention in his dark blue dress uniform. He desperately wanted to tug at his collar, but willed his right arm to stay at his side. His dress hat—a flat circle with a short bill—snuggled deep in the crook of his left arm and kept that hand occupied. He stared straight ahead, over the head of the Lieutenant Commander behind the desk, and out the window at a sparkling green sky.

"So," the Lieutenant Commander said, leaning back. Dawson lowered his eyes to look at his new Commanding Officer, a tall man with not quite regulation greying hair, dark eyes, and a small nose. His longer hair hid what Mark thought to be massive ears. A small scar sliced diagonally across the man's chin. The chair creaked with the strain, but kept the Officer upright. "You have been cleared and returned to duty after the disaster at Cla'nix." He lowered his gaze to his desk and sighed, "And assigned to me."

Dawson lowered his eyes and read the name on the desk. *Lieutenant Commander Dagon Aoffa.*

Aoffa looked up with accusing eyes and Dawson snapped his head up, staring out the window once again. "You lost what? Two-hundred prisoners? Plus, a contingent of guards?"

Dawson remained silent. He had already been briefed about his new boss and knew contradicting him was a road to nowhere. Besides, the events at Cla'nix had been thoroughly reviewed at the tribunal and he had been exonerated.

"Yes, sir," Dawson said. He could feel the sweat

beading on his forehead. "The Garrison Sergeant ran an illegal smuggling operation out of the prison, using guards and prisoners alike," Dawson continued. He felt like he was back at the tribunal, facing five old Admirals that held his career in their hands. "His body, what was left of it, was found in the flooded valley."

"I know all of that, Lieutenant," Aoffa scoffed. He stood, towering a full head over Dawson. "I read the report." He came around and sat on the edge of his desk, staring at the younger officer at eye level. "What I want to know is why it took escaping prisoners to unravel the operation, instead of the man sent in to conduct the investigation?"

"Some prisoners escaped?" Dawson asked, feigning ignorance and trying to change the subject.

Aoffa smirked. "You didn't know that..." He reached behind him on the desk and opened a small folder. He read the names and closed the binder before turning back to Dawson. "...Jake Cutter and a woman named Angel escaped?"

Mark looked him straight in the eyes. "No, sir."

"Hmmm," Aoffa said, standing and returning to his overstuffed chair. It creaked again as he sat back. "You know these prisoners?"

Dawson thought for a moment. "I know of them," he said slowly.

Aoffa picked up the folder and flung it at the young officer. Dawson caught it in his right hand. "Familiarize yourself with them. Your new assignment is to track down these fugitives and retrieve them."

"Sir?"

"You heard me," the Lieutenant Commander said. "Get out of here, and don't come back until you find them. Dismissed."

The Jake Cutter Conspiracy

Chapter Thirteen

Jake Cutter threw his head back and downed the shot of whiskey in one fluid motion. He felt the liquid fire slide down his throat, warming his entire body. He closed his eyes, savoring the sensation before slowly and deliberately setting the empty shot glass on the bar, right next to two others.

He ran a hand through his short, black but greying hair and let out a sigh. His bloodshot eyes studied his reflection in the mirror behind the bar. The mostly grey goatee added a bit of sophistication to his features. The dark jacket was new, picked up a few days back on some backwater world. He could not see the rest of his outfit in the mirror, but knew that the jacket matched his black pants tucked neatly into a pair of stylish boots. A holstered pistol rode low on his right thigh.

He raised his eyes, noticing the diorama over the mirror for the first time. A large breasted, feathered bird stood on skinny legs, one wing pointing directly at Jake. The bird in the painting winked and gave the half-drunk pilot a thumbs up. He read the scorched wooden plaque over the diorama. "*Busty Ostrich Bar*," he muttered, nodding his approval.

Aliens from a dozen worlds patronized the bar. An ancient music player, broken by a single shot to its midsection, sat at the end of the bar. The entry wound lay black with scorch marks, broken wires protruding out of the blast hole. Thick, acrid smoke hung in the air in one corner of the establishment. Jake watched as a blue skinned Blu'clic exhaled another puff of some horrible smelling smoke, adding to the dense layer. Glasses clinked as a dark-eyed Hazmoran barmaid picked up empties in the lounge.

He nodded to the bartender and pointed to his glass. The robotic bartender poured another before rolling away, wheels squeaking. Jake reached for the glass, sighed, but did not pick it up. He wanted to be left alone, but his current employer kept sending errand boys to harass him. Cue the alien sitting on the stool beside him, talking incessantly about nothing. Jake stared at the mirror and let his mind wander, briefly re-living the last six months.

After the prison breakout, Jake and Angel traced the Klan'do merchant that had set him up. They found his burial location on a distant, desolate moon and very little information on his demise. Jake and Angel stood in a howling wind, wearing respirators in the thin atmosphere. The barren, lifeless landscape provided an appropriate backdrop as they stared down at the alien's shallow grave.

"Loose ends tied up," Jake muttered, throwing a

data pad across the landscape.

They left the small moon and headed for the core systems to find Jake's ex-wife. A brief exchange of laser fire with a TSA picket changed their plans. He woke a few days later to find Angel gone, leaving Jake alone with only a note saying she would be back.

Alone. Which was exactly what he wanted, but the errand boy's incessant pestering would not let him be. A change in tone caught his attention and Jake turned to face the alien. "Would you care to repeat that," Jake asked, his speech slightly slurred.

He stared into the eyes of a two-foot tall, blue Traxillian. He paused for a moment, eyeing the creature, before his slurred speech gave way to raucous laughter. The blue alien stood on the bar stool, its normally blue eyes an angry red. Even on the barstool, the alien stood a half head shorter than Jake.

The voice was small and angry when it spoke. "I said, the boss wants to know why you haven't delivered the shipment yet." He leaned forward, forcing his bad breath into Jake's face. "You have been on the ground for six hours."

Jake stopped laughing and recoiled slightly at the alien's halitosis. He waved his hand in front of his face to dissipate the foul odor. "I'm still three hours ahead of schedule." He offered a half-drunk smile before pointing a finger at the alien. "I'll deliver on time." He wobbled slightly on the barstool.

"You will deliver now," the Traxillian said, pulling back his tunic to reveal a small laser pistol tucked into his waistband.

Jake sat silent and still, concentrating on the blurry alien beside him. He downed his shot of whiskey and motioned to the bartender for another shot.

"No more," the alien intervened.

Jake eyed the diminutive alien, shaking his head to focus the blurry image. He smiled and lunged for the alien's head. Jake felt the full effect of the alcohol. In his mind, he was moving at lightning speed; unstoppable and precise. In reality, the move was a slow, clumsy swipe that the Traxillian easily avoided. The alien jumped back out of reach, onto the next stool and into the waiting arms of a dark-haired woman.

Jake continued his lunge although the alien was well out of reach. His alcohol numbed mind recognized the woman as he missed the alien and continued off the stool. He turned his head as he fell, locking eyes with the woman as his momentum carried him off the stool and deposited him on the deck.

"Wha—?" he muttered, as he hit the wooden floor. A small plume of dust rose from the impact.

"Let me go," the Traxillian struggled. He was strong by his species standards, but no match for the woman. The alien turned enough to get a look at who held him and his eyes bulged as he recognized her, his eyes drawn to the pistol she wore in a cross-draw leather holster on her left side. The brown leather provided stark contrast to her dark one-piece suit and menacing eyes.

His struggles stopped immediately. "I...I thought you were gone."

Angel sighed, staring down at Jake. "I was."

Jake smiled as he fell into a peaceful sleep.

Pain.

A burning sensation followed by the sound of a loud pop. Another pop, more friction induced heat, this time on the other cheek. Jake slowly opened his eyes. Blinding light flooded in and he closed them tightly. His head pounded, fighting his cheek for supremacy in pain. He did not know which was worse, his head, the light, the echoing pop, or the searing pain on his cheek. Another pop, more pain, and Jake decided that the pain in his cheek was worse. He opened his eyes in time to see the little blue Traxillian pull back his tiny fist. Jake could not stop the alien and felt the sting of the alien's hand again.

"Damnit, stop!" Jake swiped at the alien, who deftly jumped out of the way. Jake grabbed his head and closed his eyes, fighting off the hangover headache that hit him far worse than the alien could have.

"He is awake," the alien said sarcastically. "Happy?"

Jake opened his eyes to see who the alien was talking to. He looked past the angry blue blob to see a woman sitting on a stool, her back to the wall. She held a pistol in her hand. Her eyes flashed with a combination of contempt and anger. Jake blinked the cobwebs from his brain. The woman came into focus and he recognized her immediately, or at least thought he did.

"Angel?"

"Hello, Jake," she smiled, her tone sarcastic. "I see you're doing well. What's it been, two months since we went our separate ways?"

Jake took a moment to look around, discovering the three of them were in a room stacked full of boxes of various alcohols. A door marked *EXIT* sat to his left, another door to his right. The clinking of glasses and murmur of voices filtered from the right-hand door. He stood and found a chair and sat as the room began spinning. He gulped down a bitter taste, his mouth dry from the whiskey.

"You mean since you abandoned me on D'rik." The room finally stopped spinning, the bitter bile subsiding in his throat. "Two TSA cops come busting in the door. I look up and you're gone." Jake shakily stood. He steadied himself on the wall, pointing an accusing finger at Angel.

"Two months. Two months on the run, working for Frendlo'pan. Two months of getting shot at by the TSA and getting harassed by blue boy here," he pointed at the alien. His head pounded, reminding him of the fire in his cheek. "And now you show up out of the...blue." He stumbled over the word, finding it somewhat humorous to use it twice in the same sentence.

"Sorry."

"Sorry?" Jake shook his head, rubbing his tender cheek. Anger filled his voice. "Why did you leave?"

"You didn't read the note?"

"Of course I read the note!" Jake replied. "It said

you needed to do something and you would be back soon. Soon is not two months later."

She looked down at the floor for a moment, watching her shoe move in a circle in the dust that coated everything. "I needed to..." She paused for a moment before finally raising her head and looking at Jake. Her voice cracked slightly when she continued. "I had to visit Grag's home-world."

Jake's anger vanished instantly. "Oh," was all he could say. "You...you could have told me." He closed his eyes against the headache.

"I needed to go alone," she said, sadness filling her voice. "I promised him, long before you arrived, that if anything happened to him, I would visit his home."

Jake nodded and silence filled the room.

"This is all very touching," the Traxillian said in his high-pitched voice, "but you have an appointment with my boss in twenty minutes. So, if you're done with this sentimental reunion, perhaps we can conclude the business we started two hours ago in the bar."

"You are late."

"Unavoidable, boss." The Traxillian threw a glance at Jake before lowering his eyes and staring at the plasti-crete surface of the landing pad.

The O'glenz trader, Frendlo'pan, removed himself from his hover-limo and approached Jake and Angel. The hover-limo lifted a half meter once relieved of the alien's bulk. The large, crab-like alien dismissed the Traxillian with a wave of a pincer. The blue alien backed away and moved over to stand with the other minions of Frendlo'pan's entourage, at the front of the vehicle.

The brown carapace of the O'glenz smuggler glistened in the hazy sunlight as he made his way across the landing area. Jake thought the alien's shiny exterior was a combination of the setting sun and a fresh coat of wax. Frendlo'pan stopped in front of Jake and studied him from head to toe, pincers clacking together. Jake stood, unflinching.

"You arrived on my planet before sunrise," the boss stated, pointing a pincer at the ship sitting nearby, "and yet you wait all day to deliver my merchandise. Why?"

"I guaranteed on time delivery, not early," Jake said, his head still pounding. "If you want early delivery, well, that'll cost you."

Frendlo'pan stood for a moment in silence. Jake watched the O'glenz eyestalks moved from Jake, to the Trillinden ship, to the woman, and finally, back to Jake. "And who is your charming companion?"

"She is my guardian Angel," Jake replied, knowing that she hated it when he called her that. He blinked a few times, fighting off the effects of the alcohol. He raised a hand to massage his bruised cheek. "And my partner."

The alien looked her up and down. "Obviously, the brains of your operation."

"Obviously," she replied with a curtsy, before

shooting a hostile look at Jake. She turned her attention back to the O'glenz. "But your deal was with Jake, not with me."

"So it was," the smuggler replied and shifted his attention back to Jake. "You have my cargo, yes?" Jake nodded quietly. "Then I shall take delivery."

"Payment first," Jake smiled. He extended his left hand while his right hand went to rest on the handle of the laser pistol strapped low on his right leg. He saw Angel cross her arms, her hand strategically near the butt of her cross-draw pistol. He relaxed, feeling a wave of relief that she was with him.

"You don't trust me?" Frendlo'pan asked, spreading his pinchers in mock shock.

"Of course," Jake replied, "but payment first. What is the O'glenz motto: Business before...everything?"

The O'glenz trader nodded and motioned one of his minions over. A light-green skinned alien—of a race that Jake did not recognize—moved from the hover-limo and joined the trio. Producing a data pad, the green alien typed in a series of commands. Satisfied with the readout, the alien spoke in a quick baritone. "All I need is your account number to complete the transaction, sir."

Jake's face produced an annoyed look that he first offered to the alien, and then to the O'glenz trader. "Cash only, Frendlo." Jake used the informal—and borderline disrespectful—shortened name of the alien as his right hand found a more reliable grip on his pistol.

Frendlo'pan bristled for a moment, before

motioning the accountant away. Another alien, a younger version of Frendlo'pan, took his place and opened a small satchel. Fifteen-thousand credits filled the satchel. "Satisfied?" asked the O'glenz.

"Almost," Jake replied. He took the satchel from the alien and tossed it to Angel. "Would you count that while I show our guests to the cargo hold?"

Angel deftly caught the satchel in her left hand, her right never wavering from the butt of her pistol. She backed up a few paces, never taking her eyes off the aliens and humans that worked for Frendlo'pan. Finally, she turned and made her way to the ship Jake had named the *Freelancer*. She keyed in her code and the Trillinden freighter's ramp descended. She disappeared inside.

The Trillinden freighter hummed to life and Jake turned to see Angel in the hammerhead cockpit, head bent down as if studying—or counting—something. She looked up and the ship's exterior lights flickered, bathing the scene in light and dispersing the shadows from the setting sun.

Jake smiled. "I'll need two of your guys to help me unload the merchandise." Two of Frendlo'pan's minions moved forward and Jake held up his hand. "Unarmed."

The two looked to their boss, who nodded. They removed their gun belts, passing them to the Traxillian sent to fetch Jake. The diminutive alien tossed the belts over his shoulders, the buckles dragging the ground.

"Satisfied?" Frendlo'pan inquired.

Jake nodded, peering into the crab-alien's eyestalks, pointing to the nearby freighter. "Oh. And if you do anything that Angel doesn't like, she will kill all of you."

"That is the last of it, boss."

The sun had long set, the freighter's lights, in conjunction with the spaceport's, created shadows from every angle. The spotlights blinded anyone who looked directly at the ship. Frendlo'pan nodded and the humanoid moved off, pushing an anti-grav cart full of boxes. The O'glenz, shielding his eyestalks with a raised pincer, watched as his men loaded a flatbed hover-truck, strapping the cargo securely. He nodded his approval before turning to face Jake.

"Delivered, *on time*," the O'glenz smirked, emphasizing the words. "Perhaps I will pay for the early delivery next time." The crab shivered slightly, the carapace scraping against itself like nails on a chalkboard. "I do not like the cold, night air."

Jake breathed in a lung full of the cool, crisp air. He exhaled slowly, watching his breath dissipate. The exterior lights of the ship faded and he turned to see Angel in the cockpit. She gave him a thumbs up before dousing the cockpit light.

"Payment received in full," Jake nodded. He took a step back to leave, trying to keep an eye on the O'glenz and his minions at the same time.

"I have another job for you, Captain," Frendlo'pan

said before Jake took two steps.

Jake smiled politely. "No thanks." He shook his head, thinking of Angel. "I have other matters that I must attend to."

Like who set me up! he thought.

Six months of researching the mysterious Secretary, of tracking every lead that he learned of in prison. Nothing. Even his ex-wife had disappeared. That had led to weeks of depression and, Jake suspected, the real reason for Angel's departure. Jake had stumbled across the freighter's log and found a reference to the 'Pan smuggling network.' Jake bribed his way into the organization and now ran freelance transport for Frendlo'pan.

The crab-like alien gave the equivalent of a smile. "I will make it worth your time, Captain. One hundred thousand. That's enough to overhaul that piece of *glech* you call a ship."

"A hundred thousand?" Jake repeated. He had never been a greedy man, but that amount would be very hard to pass up. *Offering that much means he is up to something, but what?* He kept his expression neutral as he thought through the offer.

"What's the job?"

"Simple transport," Frendlo'pan replied. "Local. If you left now, you would be back by morning."

Jake smiled, nodding as if thinking over the offer. He had cultivated a reputation of greed and recklessness over the last few months. A lesson learned from Grag. "Let your opponents underestimate you," the Blu'clic had said. "It gives you the advantage in negotiations, or fighting."

Definitely a setup. "If it's that simple, have one of your goons do it."

The crab shuffled his feet, clacking his pincers nervously. "I'm embarrassed to say, but none of my employees can fly."

Jake laughed. "That's hard to believe."

The crab shrugged, another grating sound as its chitin rubbed together. "They are creatures of the land." He offered another smile. "But perhaps flying lessons are worth considering."

"Half up front, half on delivery," Jake stated.

"Agreed."

Jake nodded. *No negotiation? No haggling? Definitely a trap. Fine with me*, he thought. *For a fifty thousand up front, I'll spring it.*

"Sounds great. Let's get started."

Chapter Fourteen

Jake boarded the ship after the meeting with Frendlo'pan and met Angel at the top of the ramp. She touched a panel, closing the ramp. He tossed the new satchel of coins to her and she caught the bag in one hand. She opened the bag and whistled. "What's this?"

"New job," he grinned.

"To do what, assassinate his competitors?" she asked.

He explained the conversation with Frendlo'pan and her jaw dropped. "You took that deal? Are you crazy? He is setting you up. Setting *us* up."

Jake nodded. "I know. But if he is willing to pay this much, I want to see who is paying him. And the only way to do that is to play along...for now."

Jake and Angel made their way to the hammerhead cockpit of the Trillinden freighter. The ship sat ready for departure, thanks to Angel's foresight. Jake took his seat, flipped two switches and pulled back on the throttle. He felt the ship lift from the tarmac. The chair's restraining harnesses held them in place as the

Freelancer roared over the countryside. Jake glanced at a screen to his left, watching the spaceport shrink in the rear cameras. Jake tapped a command into the control console and the ship nosed skyward, heading for space. Clouds gave way to a hazy, polluted, brown sky, that slowly morphed into blackness. The freighter achieved orbit, banked sharply to port, and left Kropple. In minutes, the planet was a small dot on the rear screens.

"Course set," Angel said, turning to Jake. "Are you sure about—"

A small tremble reverberated through the freighter, followed by a dull metallic clang somewhere in the bowels of the vessel. Alarms flashed red on the display and the ship pitched forward, hard. Jake unbuckled, found a solid foothold on the control panel and stood on the console, staring out of the open canopy, examining the exterior of the ship. "What the hell was that?"

"I don't know," Angel responded, apprehension filling her voice. "Jake, the weapons are offline."

The pilot sat back down, spinning his chair to engage the navigation panel and the auto-repair circuits. He cursed as the screen scrolled a list of the damaged circuits. "Shields down by half. Weapons down. Life support at eighty percent and falling," he muttered. He turned to face the controls and punched in a series of commands.

"Well, that didn't take long," he muttered. He grabbed the manual flight controller and found the controls sluggish, but responsive.

"Jake?" Angel asked.

"You were right, Frendlo'pan set us up." Jake admitted, shaking his head. The controls grew more sluggish. "I didn't think it would happen this quickly."

"Can we get back to Kropple?" she asked.

Jake studied the readouts and shook his head. "The controls are sluggish, engines are redlining. We hit an atmosphere, we are done." He double checked the sensor suite, focusing on an object at extreme range. He flipped a few switches, bringing the celestial body into sharper focus onto the screen on his left.

He motioned with his thumb towards the rear of the ship. "Go back and see what they did," he said without looking up. "My guess is some kind of explosive on the master circuits. Hopefully, they didn't do the same to auxiliary."

Angel rose from her seat as the ship rocked violently. She grabbed the communications panel behind the co-pilot's seat to steady herself. "And if they did take out the auxiliary, too?"

He changed course, turning to starboard where a distant, solitary planetoid slowly made its way through the system. "Well," Jake said through gritted teeth. His arms shook with the strain of trying to fly the damaged freighter. "Then we have much bigger problems than the weapons not working."

Another shudder through the ship and the artificial gravity failed. Jake felt his body lift from his seat, reminding him that he did not strap himself back into the seat. The backup generator activated a moment later, pulling him back into the pilot's chair.

"Get going," he finished with a motion of his head toward the rear of the ship. Sweat dotted his brow as he fought the controls. He never took his eyes from the controls even though most of the readouts were either confusing or dead. He tapped the rudder pedals and found them barely functional. His arms strained, holding the ship on course toward a small, rogue planet.

The sensors beeped for attention, Jake glanced at the screen and shook his head in frustration. A half dozen ships entered the system, followed by a handful more. The navi-comp identified them as TSA Picket ships and Corvettes, all heading for Kropple.

Jake released the controls with his right hand and flipped two switches on the center console between the pilot and co-pilot's seas, before returning his grip to the controls. His forearms and biceps burned with the effort of holding the ship on course.

The first toggle disrupted the transponder, hiding their sensor ID from the TSA ships in system. The second activated the internal comms.

"I'm heading toward a rogue planetoid, away from our previous course," he said, his voice echoing throughout the ship. "I've also dampened the transponder, but I don't know how long we have before the TSA finds us."

Angel ran down the stairs toward the main compartment. She grabbed the hand rails as the entire ship shook violently. The engines sputtered, adding more movement to the already swaying deck. She dodged items falling from storage lockers and cabinets as she made her way toward the engine room. The ship lurched and she jumped out of the way of the recreation console as it crashed to the deck in a shower of sparks and smoke.

She stepped around anti-grav chairs that had slid halfway across the ship. *They did a thorough job of mucking this ship up*, she thought. *All of this stuff should have been secured to the floor.* Another violent shudder and the engines died. The lights dimmed seconds later. The artificial gravity dropped by half and she found a new bounce in her step. Angel propelled herself through the ship, careful to control her speed.

"Angel," Jake's voice echoed through the internal comm system. Static filled the voice, the comms kept cutting in and out, but she heard most of the message. "...engines...dead. Life support is...about an hour left. We...the planetoid." The comm went dead.

The normal hum of the ship dropped, leaving a morbid silence except for...*What is that?* Angel thought.

A low whistling drew her attention and she followed the sound, creeping up to the engine room hatch like a lioness on the hunt. The hissing grew louder and she stopped at the hatch, peering through the porthole.

The engine room was in shambles. Papers and other debris raged in a maelstrom of vacuum. Two control panels showered sparks into the rapidly thinning atmosphere, the sparks dissipating quickly. Angel's eyes narrowed as she studied the room, looking for the hull breach. She finally spied a small hole right above the fuel cells. She could see the atmosphere venting out of the ship. She sighed, she had found the source of the hissing.

Footfalls announced the presence of Jake as he trotted down the narrow corridor. "Angel," he called, hurtling a pile of debris in the low gravity. He seemed to hover over the object before gently floating to the deck. Sweat covered his face and blood trailed down his arm from a long gash.

"I'm here," she replied. "Engine room is venting air. Whatever they did, they almost got it right. Three inches lower and they would have hit the fuel cells. We would never have made it out of orbit." She shuddered at the thought of her body raining down on Kropple.

"Everything's dead," he said. He peeked into the engine room before turning to face his partner. "I made a loose orbit around the rogue planet. I figure we have an hour, maybe two, before we crash."

Angel turned to stare back through the porthole into the engine room.

"Unfortunately, that's the good news."

Angel turned to face him. "And the bad?"

"We only have about a half hour of life support left." Jake reported. He pointed toward the engine room. "We need to plug that leak, fix life support, and get the engines back online."

He mentally calculated the oxygen left, silently

figuring on his fingers. "And we need to get into the EVA suits now."

"And then?"

"And then," Jake repeated, clapping his hands together. "And then, we go back to Kropple, find Frendlo'pan, and beat the *glech* out of him until he tells us who paid him to kill us."

Jake took a tentative step, ensuring the magnetic grapple of his boots held him to the hull, before letting go of the airlock hatch. He sighed heavily, his breath fogging the interior of his faceplate for a half-second. He hated EVA walks.

Jake had completed two previous space walks. The first during his pilot training. The TSA required all ship captains—military or civilian—to be certified in EVA. "You never know when you will have to go out there and fix it yourself," the instructor had said. Jake had shrugged at the time and went along with it.

It had not bothered him that first time. He was in a controlled environment, with two instructors with him, and a tether line to reel him in if he did something careless. He received his certification, bought the *Fortuna*, and headed out to open space.

The second EVA was different. He had been flying on his own for about a year when he received a distress signal. Jake responded and found an escape pod from a TSA Capstan Class Strike Fighter. He suited up, secured a tether, and leapt from the *Fortuna*. The sensation of sailing through nothing made his stomach churn and his head spin. Disorientation took control of him. He ended up banging into the small pod, almost cracking his visor glass in the process. After slowing his heart and his breathing, he scurried across the pod and peered into the control section. The entire adventure had been for nothing; the bloated corpse sitting in the pilot seat told the tale.

Jake Cutter swore he would never do another EVA unless his life absolutely depended on it. He stared at the thirty meters of ship he had to cross to get to the engine compartment and then at the endless sea of stars that surrounded him. He gulped, fighting off a wave of vertigo and nausea. "Well, I guess this does qualify as life dependent." He took another step.

"I'm sorry, can you repeat that?" Angel called over the suit's comm.

"Nothing," he replied. He picked up his pace toward the hull breach. "How long?"

"I'm suited up, entering the engine room now." she called. "Two hours of oxygen, but I estimated about forty minutes before we crash."

Jake stopped and turned toward the front of the ship. The gray, lifeless planetoid filled his vision, almost blocking out the stars. Eons of traveling its own path through space, the pock-marked surface told only a small part of the planetoids history. Jake turned and continued his journey across the hull of the Trillinden freighter. He had no desire to become a footnote in the planetoids biography.

A wisp of vapor announced the location of the

small hole in the hull. "Found it," he called. He made his way around the engine coolant tanks and other surface conduits, inspecting them for damage, before kneeling in front of the air plume.

Jake studied the quarter inch hole and the area around it. The metal curved inward from the impact of something small, but traveling at very high speed. Jake briefly thought it might have been a random meteorite instead of sabotage, until he inspected the metal.

The metal was not a jagged tear consistent with a meteor strike. The hole was almost perfectly circular. He ran a gloved finger around the interior of the puncture and felt no resistance. Smooth. It reminded him of the waterfall tunnel on Cla'nix. He pursed his lips together and nodded.

"Definitely sabotage," he said as he took out a small metal patch plate and micro-welder. "I'd guess they hit us with a rail gun as we made orbit. How are you doing?

"I have a patch in place," Angel replied, "started to weld now. Any other damage out there?"

"None that I can see," he said. His faceplate lit up as the welder came to life. The hole was small and Jake found it difficult to hold the small patch in place and weld it. He struggled, finally getting the edge under his left thumb. The micro welder touched the plate and flared in the residual atmosphere. Jake jumped, his finger slipped, and the small patch hurled passed his helmet and into space.

"Damnit," he said, extinguishing the welder and

digging out a second patch from his welding kit. He also grabbed a pair of spanners. He stole a quick glance at the planetoid, closer now. His heart pounded, he took a deep breath and placed the new patch on the hole. He took the spanners and held the patch in place. Reigniting the welder, he went to work. Three minutes and the patch was in place and holding. Jake fished a larger patch out of the kit and repeated the process. He doused the welder and stood up.

"The patch is in place," he called as he replaced his tools to the kit.

"Same here." Angel responded. "The engine core is fine. There is debris in one of the intakes, that's what started the shutdown. It'll take a few minutes to clear the debris.

"Any other damage?" she asked.

"Checking," he responded, surveying the area around the breach. He leaned down, peering under the coolant tanks. He ran his gloved hands along conduits, finding nothing but smooth dura-steel and titanium. Satisfied, he stood and began his trek across the freighter's hull toward the airlock. A loud clang sounded through the comm, followed by a low, steady hum under his feet.

"Engines are back online," Angel called. "Hang on, I'm engaging the retros to give us a wider orbit."

"Hold on," he said. He glanced at the planetoid, larger now in his vision. He quickened his pace, his magnetic books keeping his feet shuffling along the hull. He grabbed the airlock door. "Go."

The retros fired, blasting Jake toward the front of

the ship. He lost his grip, hurled over the hatch, and bounced twice along the hull before being catapulted, arms flailing, into space.

He screamed as he spun away, slowing watching the freighter leave his field of vision as he somersaulted from the ship. His tether grew taunt, halting his momentum, and spinning him to face the ship with a bone-jarring stop. He closed his eyes, and took several deep breaths. His heart pounded so loud in his ears that he missed Angel's frantic call for him.

"Jake? Jake!"

"I'm here," he finally managed. He took the tether in his hands and slowly pulled himself back toward the ship. He stared at the freighter from his new vantage and saw Angel race into the cockpit. She lowered her head in relief as he pulled himself toward the freighter. He breathed a sigh of relief as his feet planted on the hull, the magnetics firmly affixing him to the ship. He made sure he was secure in the airlock before unclipping the tether. The hatch closed and the air pressurized. The inner hatch opened and he saw Angel standing there, helmet off. She rushed to his arms.

Jake released her and collapsed on the floor, his back sliding down the bulkhead. Angel took his helmet off; his sweat stained face smiled weakly as he gulped in the air. He closed his eyes and let his head relax against the wall. "God, I hate EVAs."

Mark Dawson blinked as the star field

materialized, reverting from the opaque world of hyperspace. He sat alone in the cockpit of a scout designed for a crew of eight. His request for a hyper-drive compatible fighter denied—thank you Lieutenant Commander Aoffa—the scout was the only ship available. No weapons, low shields, and barely light speed capable, Dawson anticipated a long, arduous tenure under Aoffa's command.

Dawson banked the ship and the sleek, dual-winged ship slowly turned toward the distant planet Kropple. He pushed the sub-light throttle to maximum and the computer dutifully calculated his arrival time: thirty-eight minutes. He sighed, knowing that the fighter he requested could make it in twelve.

The communications panel beeped for attention and he leaned over to activate the comm. The cockpit filled with a monotone voice, devoid of emotion.

"The two escaped fugitives, last seen in the Kropple System, have been killed while trying to escape from TSA authority," the voice said. "A blockade of the system is now in effect until the remains of the ship and crew can be collected. Only persons authorized by special order of Parliament will be allowed into the system."

Dawson turned to stare out of the cockpit canopy as the message repeated. He listened to it again before flicking off the comm. He sat back in the pilot's chair, shaking his head. "Something's not right," he muttered, musing on why Parliament would get involved in the apprehension of two prison escapees. Then he remembered the Demoness and her admission of *The Secretary*.

The comm unit broke into his thoughts.

"TSA Scout *Overwatch*," a disembodied voice announced. "This is the TSA Frigate *Nocturne*. Power down your engines immediately or you will be fired upon."

Dawson pulled back on the throttle, cutting his speed, before actuating his comm. "This is Lieutenant Dawson, TSA Special Investigations Division, clearance level Epsilon Blue."

Silence.

He counted to ten and opened his mouth to repeat his identity when the comm cut him off.

"LT Dawson, you have no jurisdiction here," the voice said. "This system now requires Parliament level orders for entry. You are ordered to reverse course and leave the system immediately."

"I've been assigned to track the fugitives," Dawson protested, "by TSA Command. I should be part of the invest..."

"You are ordered to leave the system immediately," the voice repeated. The scout's control panel flashed, identifying a weapons lock. "Turn your vessel around or be fired upon."

Dawson sat still, silently contemplating the sudden course of events. The panel blinked its warning, lighting his face with an intermittent red light. He nodded and keyed the communications unit. "Wilco," he said.

He energized the engines, banking the ship around in a wide arc, the TSA Frigate matching his every move. He reached behind him, programming the nav-computer for a jump to the next system. The computer beeped ready and his hand found the throttle. He froze. A smile crossed his lips and he reached for the long-range sensor controls. He tapped the actuation sequence and the scout took a 'snapshot' of the entire system.

Warning lights flashed and the Frigate ordered Dawson to stand down. He smiled, threw the throttle forward, and felt the inertial dampeners activate as the engine's engaged. The scout slipped into hyperspace, leaving the Kropple system.

"The planetoid will pass by Kropple at its closest point in three hours." Angel pointed at the navigation station. The screen displayed a large brown mass, the smaller planetoid, and a dozen random dots. "The TSA ships have effectively blockaded the planet. I don't see a way through without getting into a fight," she continued. "And even if we do fight our way through, they will simply follow us."

The ship lay in shambles, but remained functional. Debris littered the deck and Jake felt a little déjà vu; it reminded him of the derelict sister ship left on Cla'nix. He adjusted the ship's attitude with a half-second burst from the thrusters. He knew that anything more could be detected by the TSA fleet now spread out through the system. So far, no one had bothered to scan the planetoid that currently hid the *Freelancer* in its gravity well.

"Then we ride out of the system with this planetoid," Jake said, studying the readout. "Frendlo'pan isn't going anywhere. We will bide our time and come back in a week or two. If they think we are dead, that gives us the advantage."

"And until then?" Angel queried. "This ship needs some major repairs. I know you have the fifty thousand, but I have a feeling we are going to need more."

"We'll send him the bill, personally," Jake fumed. He pointed to the small box that Frendlo'pan had contracted them to transport.

It lay open, revealing a simple note that read, "No hard feelings."

"I think it's only fair that Frendlo'pan pay for the damages," he smiled looking down at the note.

His voice ominous, "No hard feelings."

Chapter Fifteen

A strong wind whipped her brunette hair as Angel stood at the base of the *Freelancer's* ramp watching a four-man procession move along the walkway in between starships. *Four-man* was not entirely accurate; there was one human, two Blu'clics, and a Hazmora. Black trousers covered her legs, contrasting to the brown leather belt and cross-draw holster she wore. Her green shirt flapped in the breeze and she longed for a jacket to cover the thin material.

The group moved along a fifty-meter long suspended walkway that connected two elevated landing pads on the agricultural world of Hazmora. She felt the platform sway in the wind, thankful for the anti-grav system that suspended the platforms more than one hundred stories above the street below. Angel kept toward the center of the landing pad as much as possible, content in *not* standing on the edge and peering into the city below. She looked skyward for a moment, letting the sun warm her face, grateful to be in the sunshine again.

They had ridden in the shadow of the planetoid for eighteen hours, ensuring they were well out of the TSA's scanner range before Jake brought the *Freelancer* to life and headed for the nearest repair yard. Another day of travel brought them to a mining colony on a moon that Angel did not even know if it had a name. The repairs were extensive...and expensive. She watched Jake curse Frendlo'pan with every credit he paid. Thirty thousand credits later and the Freelancer's engines and life support reported green, but the weapons systems were beyond the miners' ability to repair.

Seeing an opportunity, the moon miners offered Jake a deal.

"We have a derelict ship in our possession," Tri'lo, the foreman began. Dirt smudged the Klan'do's face, his coveralls, and stained the dual-light helmet that he wore top his green-tinted head. "It crashed here a few months back. The crew is dead, the ship unsalvageable, but we do have its cargo, intact. Unfortunately, we have no way of off-loading the contents. Perhaps you could take it off our hands?"

Angel eyed the alien suspiciously. "What's the cargo?"

The Klan'do looked toward the ground, nervously shuffled his feet. He looked up, making eye contact with Angel and offering an innocent smile. "Weapons. Rifles, to be precise. From the ship's log that we salvaged, it was en route to Hazmora, to a Herozian named Klurian."

"Klurian?" Jake repeated.

"You know him?" Tri'lo replied, hopeful.

"Heard of him," Jake replied, offering no more.

"Will you take the rifles off our hands?" Tri'lo asked. "We have no use for such things here."

Jake lowered his head in thought and Angel took the opportunity. "How much?" she asked.

"A mere twenty thousand, for the entire shipment," the foreman stated.

"How many crates?" Jake inquired.

"Four, each containing twenty-five rifles," Tri'lo replied.

Jake nodded, but said nothing. He turned to look at Angel and she shook her head no. *Too risky,* she thought.

"Have you contacted the buyer?" Jake asked.

Angel rolled her eyes.

"I can," Tri'lo nodded.

"Do it," Jake said. "Tell him we will be on Hazmora in two days."

Hazmora. The green, fertile world used over ninety percent of its land surface for agriculture. Eighteen major cities took up the other ten percent. The cities tended to stretch vertical, not horizontal, and elevated landing pads littered the skyline.

Angel looked out over the city. Tall glass superstructures reached for the clear green sky. Hundreds of ships, of all shapes and sizes, scurried across the horizon. A local police cruiser passed nearby, watching a group carry their wares from ship to market. After a brief inspection, the ship moved on.

Angel turned her attention to the inhabitants, roughly humanoid with long legs and exceedingly long arms, perfect for growing and harvesting crops. Their skin, a reddish brown, blended in very well with the rich soil. Long manes covered their heads and neck to provide shelter from the twin suns. Most of the population lived in the flat farmland that stretched to the horizon, but some lived in the cities with the large off world population. The cities provided administrative services to the farmers including doctors, lawyers, and politicians.

The group of aliens and humans approached, stopping a few meters from Angel. The Hazmora of the group waved at her and she nodded in his direction while simultaneously unsnapping the strap on her laser pistol. "Jake," she called over her shoulder. "Company."

Jake appeared moments later, wiping the grease from his hands with a soiled rag. He paused at the top of the ramp. Contrasting Angel's clean, crisp appearance, grease covered his soiled, wrinkled clothes. "Who?" he asked, scanning the walkway.

"I don't know," she said, pointing to the group. "We were supposed to meet with a Herozian, right?" Jake nodded, dropping the rag and unsnapping the restraining strap of his laser pistol as well.

"Well, he brought friends," she concluded.

He nodded to Angel and she backed up the ramp, disappearing into the ship.

Jake heard a low hum from the ship as weapon systems came to life. A small, anti-personnel cannon dropped from a hatch on the bottom of the freighter, but did not swivel around. He waved his guests forward onto the *Freelancer's* pad.

"Captain Cutter," the alien began, spreading his arms as if greeting an old friend. The alien was average for a Hazmora, save for the long, ragged scar down the left side of his face. His normally flowing mane was cut short, barely blowing in the breeze. His low voice barely cut through the noise of the elevated spaceport. "Welcome to Hazmora. Your stay has been enjoyable so far, yes?"

Jake smiled, spread his arms in return. "It's a beautiful planet; fertile and vibrant. And you are?"

The Hazmora took a few steps closer to Jake, leaving his men standing on the edge of the landing pad. "My name is Pentwik." He lowered his voice conspiratorially and Jake had to lean toward the alien to hear him. "I understand that you have some, shall we say, rare artifacts for sell?"

Jake shrugged. "Sorry, friend, I have no artifacts in my hold."

Pentwik stared at Jake for a moment before nodding his agreement. "Shall we call them priceless works of art?"

"Sorry," Jake offered an innocent smile. "I have no idea what you're talking about."

"Come now, Captain," Pentwik replied. "You have been on my planet for almost three days. You have ordered parts for your ship that, from the looks of your clothes, are currently being installed. And you have been asking around for beings that might desire hard to obtain items."

Jake shrugged again, rubbing his chin. He looked down, noticed the grease still on his hand, and realized he now had a dark stain on his chin. He rubbed his chin with the back of his hand and was rewarded with a black smear. "Just idle chat, I assure you. I simply want to finish my repairs and move on."

"Surely, you were told that others would be interested in your cargo, Captain," Pentwik offered.

Jake and Angel left the miners a week earlier after a brief conversation with Klurian. The Herozian was indeed interested in the weapons, and gave them instructions on how to contact him upon arrival.

"Be careful," Klurian warned over the comm. "There are other parties that would be interested in the merchandise. Rest assured, I work alone. If anyone else approaches you, especially a Hazmora, they do not work for me."

A three-day space flight later they landed on Hazmora. They found Klurian on their second day on the planet. The pair took a ten thousand down payment from the Herozian with the promise he would meet them two days later—today—with the rest. Jake checked his chrono and realized that the buyer was ten minutes late. And now, the only Hazmora the buyer had warned him about shows up asking questions. *Not a coincidence...*

"Something may have been said in passing," Jake admitted. He stared at the Hazmora, "But as I said, I have no rare or priceless artifacts."

"I'm sure my information is accurate, Captain," Pentwik replied. "I was assured that you have four crates full of TSA rifles in your hold."

Jake stiffened, his eyes narrowing as he stared at the alien. His hand touched the butt of his pistol. Pentwik's minions raised their weapons, bringing them up and ready in Jake's direction. The belly turret of the *Freelancer* swiveled, targeting the three aliens. Jake eyed them for a moment, acknowledging the fear on their faces, before turning his full attention back to Pentwik.

"You seem to know quite a bit, Pentwik," Jake said. "Such knowledge usually ends up killing a being."

"Yes, I believe that a Herozian did meet an unfortunate end this morning for possessing such knowledge," the alien said with a hint of mock sadness. "Let us hope that we are more careful with whom we associate." He left the threat unfinished.

"I might know something about a crate or two," Jake nodded his understanding. "What did you have in mind?"

"The Herozian that you were negotiating with was a competitor of mine," Pentwik said. "I believe he wanted those rifles so that he could do me harm. Of course, I could not allow that..."

"Of course."

"So I wish to purchase the crates from you. To

ensure the safe keeping of the contents, of course."

"Of course," Jake repeated. "And your offer of compensation?"

"Double what he offered."

Jake made a show of rubbing his chin again, careful not to smudge more grease on his face. "Five hundred thousand." He stated, rewarded with a startled jump from the Hazmora. Apparently, he did not get all of the information on the agreement. The alien eyed the human suspiciously, before nodding his consent.

"And if I refuse?" Jake pondered aloud.

"Captain Cutter," Pentwik said with a humorous laugh, "such questions are better left unanswered. Wouldn't you agree?"

Jake returned the laugh, devoid of the humor. "Perhaps you're right. Five hundred thousand and we have a deal."

"I shall return before sunset for delivery," Pentwik said with a slight bow. "I will leave two of my men here to assist you with unloading the cargo."

"They can wait outside," Jake said. His tone turned icy, all business. "I know your reputation, so do not try to change the terms of our deal. You obviously know who I am, and I'm sure you've done your research." He paused, letting the words linger. "But you have no idea what I am capable of. Play it straight, and profit. You double cross me like you did the Herozian, and I will bring your little Empire crashing down around you."

Pentwik appeared shaken, his hand touching the small needle-beam blaster nestled across his chest.

Jake watched his eyes, and could feel the Hazmora sizing him up. Finally, Pentwik nodded, turned on his heal and left the landing pad. The human followed him, leaving the two Blu'clics standing on the edge of the pad, staring at Jake, who backed his way up the ramp and into the *Freelancer*.

"You aren't seriously going to trust him, are you?" Angel stood on the platform outside of the cockpit, staring down on Jake as he entered the main cabin. She placed her hands on her hips as Jake touched the button to raise the ramp. Jake glanced behind him, ensuring the ramp had closed completely, before replying.

"Of course not," he replied. "Once this new player was introduced, I had to stall." He shrugged. "I simply bought us time to figure out the double cross heading our way. It was either that, or start shooting."

"He owns half the planet," Angel said, descending the stairs to the main cabin. She stopped beside Jake before continuing. "He will call the local TSA enforcers on us. We'll be arrested with TSA munitions. They'll check our records and we won't even make it back to Cla'nix." Her tone was mocking, but worrisome.

"He won't bring the TSA on us until after he has the weapons," Jake stated, deep in thought. "He will wait until after the deal."

"We can't just *give* him the weapons," Angel countered.

Jake's smiled. "You're wrong. We can give him the weapons, and we will. Just not the way he wants to get them."

Jake stepped off the ramp and into the afternoon sun. He squinted against the harsh dual glare of the binary stars. Both suns were high in the sky; one directly overhead and the other halfway to the horizon. Jake slipped on a pair of sunglasses, took a deep breath, and stepped forward to greet his guests.

Pentwik stood a few steps off the landing platform, with his three minions from before, plus another half dozen for good measure. Jake noticed the mob was heavily armed with rifles, pistols and a few weapons that Jake did not readily identify. The entire consortium stood at ease, which gave Jake pause. *He has something up his sleeve.*

"Captain Cutter, I trust all is in order?" Pentwik began.

"It is," Jake replied with a smile. "Your crates are at the top of the ramp. All I need is the money and we can complete our business."

The Hazmora stepped forward and offered Jake a small satchel. "Five hundred thousand, as agreed."

Jake took the bag, quicly glancing inside. Credits upon credits glistened in the harsh sunlight. Jake ran his hand through the money, mixing it all up and verifying that it was all money and not a layer of credits on garbage. He was rewarded by more glistening money. He looked up at Pentwik and smiled.

"Four crates of TSA Police Mark IX rifles, as

discussed," Jake replied, pointing at the grey transport crates at the top of the ramp. "Please have two of your men drop their weapons and come retrieve your cargo."

The Hazmora motioned for two of his men. The two removed their weapons, handing them over to the others. They moved quickly across the landing pad, up the ramp and brought the first crate down, placing it before Pentwik. The crate sat almost a meter tall, a meter wide, and a meter long. The anti-gravity sled it rested on allowed for easy movement of the heavy crate. The two returned up the ramp three times, retrieving the remaining crates.

"Jake, the skies are still clear," Angel's voice sounded in his ear. Her voice was steady, but Jake could hear the underlying nervousness. Truth be known, he didn't like standing out here in the open either. He grimaced, cursing silently as he realized his mistake.

"Angel," he said aloud, "scan the surrounding buildings for energy signatures." Pentwik jumped at the sudden outburst and his two minions turned to stare at Jake. Jake locked eyes with the alien. "Scan for the energy signature of weapon power packs."

"Problem?" Pentwik asked. His hand drifted toward the pistol on his belt. Jake shook his head. *Don't do it.*

The recently repaired upper turret of the *Freelancer* sprang to life. Jake heard the servos groan as the cannon swung around, locking onto some distant target. Jake never took his eyes off the

Hazmora before him.

"Jake, I have two energy signatures, eight hundred meters away on that high-rise to your right."

Jake maintained eye contact with Pentwik, nodding to the building to his right. "Two beings, eight hundred meters out. Friends of yours?"

Pentwik gave an innocent look.

"That building," Jake pointed, "Sun to their back, clear field of fire. Good choice, but my partner has the main cannon trained on their position. I'm giving you exactly five seconds to call them off or you won't have any men to call off."

Pentwik touched his collar twice before nodding his head at Jake.

"Angel?"

"They are moving. Still on the roof, but moving from firing position."

"Now, if you will inspect your merchandise," Jake stated coldly, "we can conclude our business."

Pentwik motioned and the lone human in his employ opened the nearest crate. Twenty-five military grade rifles, five rows of five, sat gleaming in the container. The human removed a rifle from the top row and did a quick count before replacing the rifle. He replaced the lid of the container before moving on to the next. He completed the same procedure on all four crates before reporting to his boss. Pentwik patted him on the shoulder and the man rejoined his companions.

"A pleasure doing business with you, Captain," Pentwik smiled.

Jake nodded, backing his way onto the freighter's ramp. He never took his eyes off of the alien as he touched the panel to raise the ramp. The exit closed and he turned, sprinting up the stairs to the cockpit. "Shields!" he yelled as he burst into the cockpit.

Angel sat in the co-pilot's chair, watching both the group leaving the landing pad and the sensors. "Shields are up," she acknowledged. "The skies are still clear."

"They won't be for long," Jake replied. "Let's get out of here."

"What about the rifles," Angel asked. "We can't leave that much firepower in his hands."

The engines hummed as he lifted the freighter off the pad. He adjusted the trajectory and dove the freighter off the pad and down through the city. The heart stopping dive ended as Jake leveled off a few hundred meters from the ground. The *Freelancer* zipped through the city, banking over and around buildings. The freighter left the confines of the skyscrapers, roaring over farmland. He pushed the throttle forward, gaining distance on the spectacle behind him.

The sensors beeped for attention. A frigate appeared in orbit, closer to the planet than Jake thought possible. A half dozen others appeared a bit further away from the planet. Three TSA pickets detached from the frigate, heading straight for the spaceport. Jake read the screen as he sat in the pilot's chair.

"While you were calling in the off-world TSA," Jake

spoke as he flew, banking the ship to starboard to avoid one of the few mountain ranges on the planet. "I removed all of the power packs and firing actuators from the rifles." He looked at Angel and winked. "He has four crates full of non-functioning weapons that will get him twenty to life."

Angel laughed and Jake joined her, the stress of the encounter draining away. Jake pulled back on the controls, lifting the ship and heading for orbit. The maneuver pushed them both back into their chairs and an uneasy silence filled the cockpit. Angel broke it.

"What now?"

Jake stared out of the canopy as the *Freelancer* rose from the planet Hazmora, blending with other orbiting traffic. "We have half a million credits," he mused, rubbing his shoulders to reduce the tension in his neck. "It's time to pay a visit to Frendlo'pan."

"Jake," she began, tentatively, "we have a small fortune in the hold. The ship is fully operational," she paused staring at him. "Can't we just...live?"

Jake turned his head slowly, staring at her. She was more beautiful than the first time he saw her, tougher, yet...vulnerable. He shook his head, to both clear that line of thought and as a signal to the woman. "You sought revenge after Grag's death. We went back into the prison when we didn't have to. We killed the Demoness and the Sergeant. Grag was avenged.

"Now it's my turn. The Klan'do set me up, and someone killed him. Frendlo'pan was hired by someone to set me up. Not a coincidence." Jake turned to face forward, throwing the throttle to full. The freighter left the planet, heading for deep space. "I'm going to find those responsible. They cost me everything I ever cared about."

He turned back to Angel with menace in his eyes. "I'm going to find them. And then I'm going to kill them."

Chapter Sixteen

Frendlo'pan startled awake, his pincers anxiously clacking together. His body lay still on a bed of rock, surrounded by water. Ripples spread throughout the water bed with his sudden movement. He rotated one eyestalk, studying the room. Everything appeared to be in place. His bed composed one-quarter of the room, opening to a balcony where soft, translucent curtains fluttered in the breeze. A table, a small dresser, and a pair of chairs filled the remainder of the room. Small beams of light, residual illumination from the security field that surrounded his cavern fortress, streamed into the room. He scanned the room again, moving only his eyestalk, a throwback to ancient instincts where his body froze until the danger passed. Something had awoken him, and he needed to know what. *Nothing,* he thought, confidently. *Just my imagination.* The smuggler relaxed, willing his body back to sleep. No one could infiltrate this far into the planet without being noticed.

Kropple's only claim to fame, other than serving as

an intersystem commerce hub, was its abundance of natural caverns. Large caverns, some as monstrous as the biggest cities on the core worlds, littered the landscape. The government owned most of the caverns, which provided a high revenue as tourist attractions. One such cavern, outside of the capital, contained two amusement parks and a naturally flowing water-park.

Only a handful of the massive caverns sat in private hands, with corporations owning most of those. Stockholders, employee retreats, and extravagant parties were a near constant on Kropple. Two others rested solely in private ownership. The first, near the capital, was owned by Darién McHoliss, star of two dozen action holo-vids. It was a spectacular residence, nestled in a quarter kilometer cavern a dozen miles from the city. Fifty meter spires, a flowing river, and a wooden drawbridge gave the action star a literal castle. A castle he rarely visited and, due to a series of burglaries and intrusions, maintained a platoon of private security. Very few people had the opportunity to enjoy that cavern, or the castle.

Even fewer people had the pleasure of enjoying the largest privately-owned cavern on Kropple. It sat nestled in the largest mountain range on the planet, four thousand kilometers north of the capital. The quarter kilometer wide mouth of the cavern nestled halfway up a sheer cliff mountain, nearly impossible to get to from the ground. Burned out hulks of ships littered the area around the mouth of the cave, a portent to all to stay away. A warning that brought

Frendlo'pan the peace and security he desired.

For those who did venture inside, the tunnel opened to over a kilometer wide, traversing almost ten kilometers into the mountain. A sporadic artificial lighting system cast deep shadows throughout the ten-kilometer journey; shadows that hid weapon emplacements covering the entrance in crisscrossing patterns of fire. Burned-out hulks of starships sat on the cavern floor, attesting to the weapons' effectiveness.

The main cavern sat in the heart of the mountain, where it expanded into a two-kilometer-wide sphere. The artificial lighting of the tunnel gave way to natural light that flowed from a break in the cavern roof high above. The circular light created a halo spotlight on Frendlo'pan's fortress during the day. At night, naturally luminescent biospheres directed soft white light from the cavern roof. The castle sat on thirty-meter-tall stilts, glowing in the light day and night.

A rectangular superstructure perched atop the four supports, like legs to a chair. The main level contained housing, troop barracks, operations, and dozens of vaults containing a small portion of Frendlo'pan's wealth. Everything from priceless jewels, to rare paintings and antiquities, to cold hard credits lay secure within the superstructure. Twin panels, each the size of one of the support legs, created an "A" frame over the superstructure. Landing platforms, along with another array of offensive weaponry, covered the top of the structure between the "A" frame panels. A small nuclear reactor provided uninterruptible power to the complex.

The break in the cavern roof led to another series of weapons emplacements on top of the mountain. The wreckage of dozens of starships lay in concentric rings, identifying the no-fly zone on the plateau above. A ship had approached the day before. Initial reports indicated its hulk had been added to the dozens of ships lying there. Those initial reports proved inaccurate and Frendlo'pan, in a fit of O'glenz rage, killed the technician—a nephew—for allowing the ship to escape. "One day, the universe will learn not to encroach on Frendlo'pan!" he yelled.

The multiple layers of security afforded Frendlo'pan a sense of security he felt nowhere else. With that thought, he wiggled his body deeper into his bed, the water sloshing around the rocks. He drifted back to sleep, his body relaxed in the water and the ripples slowly spreading the length of the pool dissipated. He felt a slight breeze from the balcony as it caressed his skin. He snapped awake again. *There is no wind this far in the cavern.*

He rose from the bed, donned a robe from a nearby table, and moved toward the window. The curtains wafted lightly and he raised a pincer. He felt a slight breeze brush over his hard exoskeleton.

His eyestalks examined the room. Nothing was out of place. There was no one else in the room. As he edged closer to the window, he could feel the breeze grow stronger.

Something is wrong.

He opened his mouth to raise an alarm and froze

when a ghostly form materialized out of the darkness on his balcony.

Jake Cutter, dressed in a black skintight suit, appeared from the darkness. He snatched a pistol from a holster low on his right leg, a move so fast that Frendlo'pan couldn't follow, and pointed it at the smuggler's head. Jake snapped off the safety, as he put a finger to his lips.

"Pan, my friend," Jake smiled. "I think you and I need to have a little chat." He motioned to the two chairs sitting on the balcony. The O'glenz crab sat in the larger of the two chairs while Jake took the other. The pistol never wavered from its target.

Frendlo'pan stared at the intruder, his face a mask of calm. One eyestalk glanced at the controls near the door, the com-link and the alarm were only a meter away. He watched Cutter with the other and knew he would never make it to the alarm. *Better to bide my time and wait for my opportunity.* He spread his arms in a welcoming gesture. "Welcome to my home, Mr. Cutter. Are you here to talk, or do you intend to kill me?"

"That is entirely up to you," Jake replied.

Frendlo'pan nodded, his eyestalks bobbing with the motion. "I thought you were dead."

"Not yet," Jake shook his head. "Although many have tried."

The O'glenz looked thoughtful for a moment. "If you are not here to kill me, then why..."

"You still owe me fifty thousand," Jake interrupted.

Frendlo'pan paused, then remembered the last

time he had seen Jake. "But you did not complete delivery, Captain."

"Point," Jake observed. An uneasy silence filled the space between the two.

"I am curious," the O'glenz began, he needed to put his assailant at ease before making his move. "How did you arrive at my humble accommodations?"

Jake shook his head. "It wasn't easy…"

The *Freelancer* skimmed the countryside of Kropple as it flew north from the capital city. The trip from Hazmora had been uneventful, with both Jake and Angel contemplating their mission in silence. The ship made a quick stop at a salvage yard on Loren which netted a few modifications and additional repairs to cover some shoddy work from the miners. With the ship better than the day it left the assembly line, the duo headed for Kropple.

Jake and Angel sat quietly in the cockpit, watching the flatlands slowly give way to hills. He absent-mindedly rubbed his shaved face, the goatee gone as he flew. The mountains grew massive and the tiny freighter weaved in and out of large valleys, following the contours of the planet's surface. Jake kept the ship on manual, enjoying the twists and turns, the ship instantly responding to his touch. He let slip a smile, enjoying himself, as he kept one eye on the terrain following sensors (TFS) and one on the mountain of rocks outside the cockpit canopy.

Angel sat in silence, her body rigid as she watched the world zip past. Jake saw her cringe occasionally as he banked through the mountain paths at breakneck speed. Another maneuver; the freighter turned on its side to pass through a narrow ravine, followed by a quick dive underneath a rocky outcropping. Warning lights flashed and she grabbed the control panel as the shields flared and a harsh grating sound reverberated through the ship. She hurled a harsh look at Jake, accompanied by a string of obscenities. "Are you trying to get us killed before we even get to Frendlo'pan's cavern?"

"Killed?" Jake parroted. He banked the freighter to port, barely missing a large outcropping of rock. The TFS registered a hard right and Jake continued the barrel roll, rotating the ship and taking the turn in stride. The ship leveled out, roaring through a pristine valley.

"No, not killed. I want to get there before dark so I can get a good look at what the defenses are." He banked the ship up and starboard, rolling the freighter and wedging it between a narrow gap in the mountain. "Definitely not killed."

The two continued in silence as the valleys grew deeper and the mountains stretched to the sky. Long shadows infiltrated the valleys and Jake flipped on the running lights. The lights chased away the shadows, leaving Jake and Angel staring at an outcropping of rock. Jake inhaled sharply and yanked on the controls. The *Freelancer* stood on its tail as Angel gasped and grabbed her armrests. Warning lights rapidly flashed.

The freighter nudged the mountain, flaring the shields, and hurling a maelstrom of fractured rock into the air. The ship bounced off the outcropping, righted itself, and continued through the mountain pass.

Jake offered a sheepish grin and slowed the ship. He saw Angel relax, her knuckles no longer white on the armrest of the chair. He turned his attention more to the TFS and less on his vision as dark shadows began obscuring large obstacles. The sensors showed a clear path and Jake took a moment to look out of the cockpit canopy.

Darkness consumed the deep valley, but Jake's eyes were drawn to the sheer cliff-face mountain that towered over them. The sun may have set in the valley, but the mountain was still bathed in sunlight. Jake craned his neck to get the full effect of the largest mountain range on Kropple. "Wow," he said as he pulled back on the controls, gently this time. The freighter began to climb toward the distant mountain summit.

Jake gazed out of the canopy as the ship ascended. Snowcapped peaks littered the landscape as far as he could see. Occasional patches of open rock broke through the snow. The *Freelancer* exited the darkness and Jake squinted against the snow's glare.

Angel shifted in her seat to get a better view. She stared ahead at the snowy peaks and then out of the canopy at the darkness below them. The shadow of the valley revealed little detail. "Yeah," she replied. "Wow."

The freighter soared over the mountain ridge, only

meters above the snow. Jake pulled back on the throttle, slowing the *Freelancer* even more. Even at the slower speeds, they felt every turn and every stomach-turning drop as the ship maneuvered across the ridge line. "Remind me to check the inertial compensators," he muttered. Jake smiled as Angel sat way back in her seat, pulling the restraining harness tight. He turned his attention back to flying as they crested a mountain peak.

The ridge opened into a kilometers wide plateau. Jake leveled the ship, hovering at the edge of the ridge, hugging the flat and level terrain. A fresh layer of snow covered the plateau. Angel sat back in her chair, cinching her harness tighter as Jake nudged the throttle forward and the *Freelancer* moved slowly over the snowy landscape. A ring of ridges circled the entire area and Angel realized they were flying over the mouth of a volcano. Hundreds of rocky outcroppings littered the floor of the plateau, barely visible in the snow. *No, not rock...* she thought as the glare shields dimmed the cockpit canopy automatically against the reflective snow. *Destroyed ships.*

A flash of light on the horizon caught her eye and Angel scanned the snow for a moment. Nothing. She turned her attention to the sensors, but they showed clear. She turned her eyes back to the outside world as another distant flash caught her attention. She squinted at the blinding snow, daring whatever it was to show itself again. Another flash, sunlight reflecting off metal. She turned her eyes to the sensors in time to see a warning light flash.

"Jake," she began, "I think we are being scanned." She paused, her heart pounding as the warning light winked on, and stayed on. "Or we are being targeted..." Her sentence died off as the console beeped for attention and the red *WARNING* light began flashing rapidly in time with the beep. Alarms filled the ship with their ear-splitting howl.

"Target lock," Angel yelled above the klaxons. She found the button and turned the ear ringing noise off. She made a mental note to disable that alarm, if she lived.

"Multiple locks," she corrected. She turned her eyes from the sensors to look out of the canopy. "Oh, God."

Jake banked the ship hard to starboard as dozens of weapon emplacements opened fire. The shields flared and the freighter rocked under the impact of the laser barrage. Angel held onto her harness as Jake executed a barrel roll, giving the belly shields a break as the dorsal shields took a few seconds of pounding. Jake threw the throttle full and Angel was grateful she had tightened her harness as the ship dove over the ridge and back towards the valley below. Angel, now flying upside down, watched the ridge line pass over her head by only a couple of meters. She felt her stomach leap into her throat as the ship plunged into free-fall.

Laser bolts filled the sky behind them as the

Freelancer plummeted down the mountain. The alarm changed tone and Angel checked the sensors. "Missile lock," she called as a handful of objects crested the ridge in pursuit of the freighter.

"Lasers," Jake called and Angel actuated the cannons, turning them aft. The missiles closed on the fleeing ship and Angel opened fire without aiming. The random blasts connected with two of the missiles, erupting them into fireballs. The ship rocked from the blasts. The *Freelancer* dove into the darkness of the mountain's shadow and she blindly fired again.

The mountain exploded from her barrage, hurling tons of rock into the air. The missiles flew straight into the debris, detonating. The multiple explosions created an avalanche that followed the freighter into the valley below.

Jake sat in the pilot's chair, willing his heart to slow, as the *Freelancer* settled on its landing struts in the heart of the valley. He looked up through the cockpit canopy to see snow gently fall from the mountain. The ship popped as it cooled from the rapid descent and landing. He heard purging systems release pressure and steam somewhere in the back. He inhaled, shaking his head. "Damage?"

Angel released her harness, brushing her sweat soaked hair from her face. She toggled a switched on her right. "Minimal," she replied. "We were lucky." She pointed up the mountain. "That entire plateau was covered in dead hulks," she said.

He let out a long sigh.

"So, what now?" she asked.

Jake slumped in his seat, thoughtful. The snow fell heavier, adding a visual component to the gentle pops and pings of the cooling ship. He sat up, an idea forming. "When did they get a lock on us?"

Angel checked the sensor log. "We topped the ridge, moved across the plateau about, um, half kilometer." She turned toward her captain. "We didn't get far."

Jake rose from the pilot's seat, motioning for Angel to follow. The two made their way out of the cockpit, down the stairs, and into the main passenger dorm of the freighter. "Far enough," he said as they walked. "How wide is that plateau?"

The barrage and evasive maneuvers had littered the floor with a multitude of items from storage bins. Jake sighed as he picked up a few items and put them back. Angel followed his lead, answering his question. "Ten, maybe twelve kilometers."

Jake continued to storage locker 5N and began rummaging through the newly purchased cold weather survival gear. "Think you can get me to the top of that mountain and stay out of their sensors?"

"Yes, but—"

"Good." Jake opened another locker, this one containing a tripod mounted winch and hoist system. He crammed the equipment, including a roll of one-thousand-pound test wire into a high capacity, anti-grav backpack. Jake disappeared into his cabin, leaving the woman in silence.

His muffled voice drifted from his room. "Drop me off, and give me twelve-hours. If you don't receive my signal, run. Don't look back. Don't worry about me. Just run."

He returned to the main room carrying the pack in his right hand, large, overstuffed gloves filled his left. He wore a heavy parka, thermal pants, and snow boots. He touched a switch on the chest of his parka and felt the suit began to warm as the internal heating element activated. Satisfied, he turned the suit off.

"Jake, is Frendlo'pan really worth all of this?"

Jake turned, staring at the woman who had saved his life in prison, and a dozen times since. She meant more to him that he could ever say, but he could not...would not let his feelings for her deter him from finding out who framed him. And why.

"We've discussed this." He pointed to the bulkhead of the ship. "Someone out there is still after me and I don't know why. The TSA is after us, so we have to keep moving. Every job we take is a potential trap. The only person in the entire Tri-system I can trust is standing here with me. So yeah. If Frendlo'pan has information that can help me sort this out, then yes, it's worth it." He strapped on the pack and adjusted the anti-grav controls until it weighed almost nothing.

"And if he doesn't have any information?" Angel asked.

Jake smirked. He had no answer for the woman. "Get me up there, so we can get this over with."

Jake dropped from the ramp of the hovering freighter into knee deep snow. He offered a quick wave and saw the ramp retract. The *Freelancer* slipped sideways, disappearing over the mountain's edge like a wraith. He sucked in the cold air, shivered, and activated the heating coils of his suit. It took him a few minutes to moderate the temperature of the suit until he stood comfortably despite the frigid temperature. He donned the gloves, lifted himself out of the snow, and donned a pair of snow-shoes. He squinted against the blowing snow, adjusting the goggles over his eyes. He looked skyward, noting the sun was heading for the horizon. He had a few hours of sunlight. He shivered. He knew it would only get colder as night approached. With another deep breath, he took his first step toward the distant sun.

He passed dozens of burned out hulks as he traveled across the frozen no man's land. He recognized freighters, scouts, and fighters. Within a couple of hours, the anti-grav controls on the pack froze and Jake felt the full weight of the supplies, so he paused, seeking a few minutes of shelter in a downed TSA police scout. The burned-out hulk provided momentary shelter from the blowing snow. He checked his Chrono; nine hours until the deadline he gave Angel. He left the derelict scout, continuing toward his target.

The snow continued to fall, the wind chilling him to the bone as the sun set on the horizon. Jake donned a headlamp from his pack and activated the light. He lowered his head and trudged on.

His thoughts returned to Angel's final question: "And if he doesn't have any information?" *Is this all for nothing?* The thought thrust its way into his mind and he stopped his march across the plateau. *What if...?* Jake pushed the thought from his mind, willed his legs to move, and renewed his trip through the blinding snow.

Six hours into his journey and the burned-out hulks disappeared. Jake turned, but could see nothing in the darkness, his headlamp illuminating no more than fifteen or twenty meters. *Their defenses are obviously effective*, he thought. *No one has ever made it this far, at least not in a ship.* He adjusted the thermal setting on his suit, as the snow started falling with more enthusiasm. He checked a small tracker on his left wrist, homing in on the signal he wanted. He lowered his head and trekked on toward a distant, low level power source.

Forty pounds of equipment on his back began to feel like four hundred at the seven-hour mark. The snow fell harder and the wind howled over the mountain. His headlamp provided the only light on the plateau, even the stars were obscured by the blinding snowstorm. He stopped for a few minutes to eat a nutrition bar. His tracker showed another two kilometers to the beacon. Donning the pack again, he continued the journey.

Nine hours and the sun began to make its appearance on the horizon at his back. Wisps of color crept through the blackness as Jake dropped to his knees in the snow and allowed the pack to slide from his shoulders. He flopped onto his back, the cold icy tendrils of the snow seeping through his clothing despite the thermal coils. *Nine hours*, he thought. He rolled over, coming to his hands and knees, and face-to-face with his target: the beacon.

The beacon marked the mid-point of Frendlo'pan's cavern below the surface. He had read about the controls while researching the smuggler's home. Of course, the article did not mention the concentric rings of security, or the weapons emplacements that protected the marker. It did, however, mention the small shaft that provided light for the fortress below.

Jake brushed the snow away from the half meter tall protective surface and removed a panel that covered the electronics within. The snow fell away with ease, dull light from inside the control station giving Jake a view of the circuits within. He saw a small communications array, a sensor package, and primary and secondary computer housings. Control system: check.

He felt lighter without the pack as he came to his feet. Using his headlamp, he began a systematic search of the area around the dome. His foot kicked an object under the snow. Kneeling, Jake brushed the flakes away. He found the translucent shield that let the natural light into the cavern during the day. Entrance: check.

He returned to the control station, studying the complex electronics and wiring a few moments before shaking his head. He had no idea how to disarm the weapons system without setting off an alarm. He grimaced, shrugged, and pulled a small rectangle from his pack. He affixed the small explosive to the control system, molding it to the circuitry.

Leaving the station, he retrieved his pack and returned to the two-meter opening. Jake removed the three-prong winch and monofilament wire from his pack. He spent the next thirty minutes setting up the system. Jake double checked his equipment, testing the winch by lowering his pack into the darkness. He retrieved the pack with a touch of a button on a remote-control unit strapped to his right wrist. Satisfied, he turned off his thermal coils, and felt the cold creep into his parka as he strapped a harness around his waist. Clipping the harness to the thin wire, he felt a lump in his throat as he stared into the dark abyss.

"Now you start to think about this?" he admonished himself. Slowly, Jake eased himself out over the open hole. The winch slipped slightly as it accepted his full weight and Jake inhaled sharply. He stared at the contraption, his heart hammering in his chest as he waited for the tripod to slip and drop him into the cavern below. The winch held and he swayed over the two-meter wide opening. He closed his eyes and exhaled slowly as he oscillated in the breeze.

Opening his eyes, he looked down. Far below him, a well-lit landing pad beckoned him. Angel's words came back to him. "...is Frendlo'pan really worth all of this?"

Without another thought, Jake activated the winch and disappeared into the darkness.

"So, it was your ship that tried to land on my mountain yesterday," Frendlo'pan said.

Jake nodded.

The O'glenz wiggled in his seat and felt the breeze on his carapace. His eyestalks rotated, looking for the source. Finding nothing, he turned his attention back to his assailant. "I killed my nephew for letting you escape."

"My condolences," Jake replied dryly.

The alien watched as Jake stood and stepped to the edge of the balcony, leaning on the rail as he craned his neck upward. Frendlo'pan followed his gaze, staring at the two-meter hole in the roof high above his fortress and realized the source of the breeze. The O'glenz watched the human, calculating the moment to strike. Although Jake still had the pistol in his hand, they were still deep in the cavern. *His* cavern. While annoyed at the intrusion, Frendlo'pan still felt a sense of security in this place. "Are you expecting someone?"

Jake smiled at the crab-like alien. "Yes. But I'm not here to answer your questions. I'm here so you can answer mine."

"And if I refuse?"

Jake's smile grew cold and Frendlo'pan saw that his eyes, the window to the soul, were devoid of life. Frendlo'pan's castle suddenly felt like a prison.

Jake's voice held menace and the threat of unpleasantness. "You will answer my questions. It's simply a matter of persuasion. How much persuasion I use is up to you."

"I will not tell you anything." Frendlo'pan said with more bravado than he felt.

The human checked his chrono on his left wrist and nodded before sliding his hand out over the balcony. Frendlo'pan caught a glint of light off a thin, nearly invisible line and felt the first pangs of fear as he realized how the man entered his fortress. The crab's eyestalks turned skyward toward the two-meter wide hole at the top of the cavern.

"Perhaps not. At least, not here." Jake tossed a harness to the O'glenz. "Put that on. We are going for a ride."

"Captain," Frendlo'pan stood, "if you think I am willingly..."

He saw Jake raise the pistol, a flash of light, and darkness.

Angel startled awake in her chair when she heard the double click of the transmitter at the eleven-hour mark. "He made it," she said aloud, rubbing her eyes, trying to wake up. She brushed the hair from her face and stared at the comms. She stretched, listened to her joints pop, and slid her chair forward. She looked out at the dark valley beyond the cockpit canopy. The valley sat in the shadow of the mountain as the sky, high above, grew light with the dawn. Water streaked down the glass from a light drizzle. She thought the rain was a good omen. *Grag always said rain washed away the past, and your worries.*

The freighter, idle for hours, sprung to life as she tapped the console in front of her. With a renewed sense of hope, she lifted the *Freelancer* from the valley floor. Her stomach flip-flopped as she threw the throttle forward and the ship roared up the steep mountain. She smiled, knowing that she had scolded Jake for doing the same thing. Angel could see the sky begin to lighten as she crested the mountain.

She leveled off at the top of the ridge in the midst of heavy snow and eyed the scanner. Nothing tracked the ship. Testing the waters, she lifted the ship a little higher, edging the craft over the volcano's crater. No targeting computer, no barrage of lasers. Angel breathed a sigh of relief and, pushing the throttle forward, brought the freighter over the ridge and low across the plateau.

The *Freelancer* roared over the landscape, blowing snow in every direction, revealing the hulks of dozens of ships. Whereas Jake had spent hours walking across the snowcapped mountain, Angel traversed the route in minutes. A shower of sparks and a small fire marked the location of the beacon and weapons control station. The freighter's repulser engines steadied the ship at five meters above the winch. Angel goosed the throttle slightly, blowing the snow away and she got her first glimpse of what Jake had done. She saw the burning debris of the control station, the winch, and a two-meter hole that led to darkness.

Angel rotated the ship, lowered the landing gear, and settled the *Freelancer* a few meters away, with the winch on the ramp side of the freighter. She felt the freighter settle into the snow and, activating the lateral cameras, saw that the landing struts were half-buried in the snow. She powered down the engines, set the sensors to automatic, and switched the weapons and shields to computer control. Thanks to Jake's explosive charge, the fortress security system was down, and she expected company soon.

Angel donned a heavy parka, boots, and goggles and made her way to the ramp. It took several minutes of lowering and raising the ramp to compact the snow enough for her to leave the ship. Holding on to the bulkhead and the frame of the hatch, she made her way cautiously down the ramp.

The wind howled, sweeping through her, and she almost lost her balance. She planted her feet in the compacted snow and shivered. She did not wear the thermal coils like Jake, and she felt the cold immediately. She lowered her head against the blowing snow and trudged toward the winch as the snow fell. A green light on the winch flashed intermittently, indicating the device was on and functional. She stood in the cold, bouncing from foot to foot for almost five minutes when she heard the sound of a ship's engine above the wind.

Angel turned to see a small three-meter long skimmer approaching from the far side of the plateau. Long, outstretched wings drooped, almost touching the snow as it weaved and dodged its way through the destroyed hulks. Angel glanced at the *Freelancer*, now covered in snow, and wondered if the skimmer's pilot would recognize the strange outline in the snow. *Doesn't matter*, she thought as the computer controlled forward cannon rotated, acquired its target, and fired.

The repair skimmer was one hundred meters away from the control station when the T'Traxi pilot realized that something was not right. His short trunk twitched with anticipation and he brought the skimmer to hover. He rubbed a tusk with his left hand as he stared at his sensor monitor.

The screen indicated the cover to the cavern was open. He lifted his gaze and could barely discern something covering the shaft. He shook his head, returning to the sensor screen and the image of a large patch of snow that stood out from the surrounding countryside. He saw movement and zoomed in on a human bouncing from foot to foot near the bulky patch of snow. He cocked his head in amazement and his finger moved to the communications button.

He froze, his finger hovering over the alarm button, when he saw a man dressed in black and his boss, Frendlo'pan, appear from the open maintenance shaft.

The man's mind screamed *call it in* but he simply sat in bewilderment. He moved his gaze from the monitor, staring out of the cockpit window at the distant scene. "Boss?" he voiced aloud. Then he saw the large patch of snow move. Well, not the entire patch, but a small section of it near the front. The pilot saw the laser cannon spin and lock on. *Its pointing right at me*, was his last thought as the *Freelancer*'s computer opened fire.

The winch whirred, pulling Jake up and out of the maintenance shaft. He crawled into the snow on his hands and knees, unstrapped himself from the line, and reactivated the winch, drawing the unconscious Frendlo'pan out of the two-meter hole. Jake saw Angel and started to wave when the *Freelancer's* weapons opened fire. Jake involuntarily ducked at the sound of an explosion. He looked up to see a fireball plummet into the snow a hundred meters away. He turned his face as the blast of heat washed over him.

Angel appeared at the winch before the debris stopped falling from the sky. She embraced Jake momentarily, before assisting him in pulling the O'glenz onto the snow and unhooking the alien from the winch.

"I can't believe you did that!" She pointed to the hole in the floor of the mountain. Jake shrugged as he tugged the unconscious crab-like O'glenz away from the shaft, dropping him into the snow. Frendlo'pan groaned awake and curled up tight in the frigid air.

"Me neither." He grabbed his parka and goggles

from where he had stashed them near the destroyed control station. He slipped them on, activated the thermals, and shivered as the heat radiated. He grabbed his pack and started to disassemble the tripod. "Would you escort our guest to dorm C?"

She nodded, and moved to the nearly frozen O'glenz and, with a grunt of effort, helped Frendlo'pan to his feet. He shivered, offering little resistance as she led him toward the warmth of the freighter.

Jake paused for a moment, looking across the snow-covered plateau in the daylight. The burning skimmer was one more burning hulk to add to the collection. The plateau looked and *felt* different in the daylight. The snow had stopped, and Jake could see about a kilometer in the early morning light. Jake shook his head in amazement at the distance he travelled over the last twelve hours. His body slumped with exhaustion, his stomach growled. He looked at the maintenance shaft, and kicked a clump of snow down the hole, as he tossed the refilled pack on his back.

He shook his head. "I will never do that again..."

Chapter Seventeen

Knee-high beige grass waved gently in the breeze. Birds circled tirelessly overhead, floating on the warm breeze, as they hunted for their next meal. One of the carrion eaters dove, the wind whistling in its near silent descent. The bird raced toward the ground as its shadow raced across the grassy plain on an intercept course. At the last moment, the bird flattened its descent and met its shadow. With a flash of claws, the bird lunged the last few feet toward the ground. Emitting a shriek of victory, the bird lifted away, a small, struggling prairie rat in its grasp.

A distant rumble filled the prairie as the bird attempted to gain altitude. The hum grew into a dull roar as a hover-car raced through the grassy field, startling the prey-laden bird. It released its meal, flapping hard to escape the path of the screaming car. The prairie rat landed hard, rolling end over end in the tall grass; bruised, but alive. The carrion bird banked sharply, reacquiring its target and dove for the rat as it raced for the shelter of a nearby hole. The bird's shadow followed the rodent, growing steadily larger until the rat ran into its shelter. The bird flapped its wings frantically, stopping its downward dive. The animal paused in midair, wings beating in a blur, before rocketing high into the sky, shrieking in anger. The hover-car continued, undaunted, across the prairie.

Angel sat behind the controls of the open-air hover car, her long hair flowing behind her. She craned her head upward, watching the bird take to the sky. She smiled, shaking her head at the shrieking animal, before returning her attention back to piloting the car. She brushed a stray strand of hair from her face and checked the controls. She looked forward and tensed, knuckles white on the steering console, as she swerved around a clump of small boulders. The twin-engines of the car roared with the sudden attitude change before returning to their normal throaty growl.

"How long?" came a voice behind her.

"Three minutes, maybe less," she yelled, the reply lost in the wind.

"What?"

She held up her left hand with three fingers extended. Turning her head slightly, she yelled again, receiving a mouth full of hair for her efforts. "Three minutes!"

Jake nodded his understanding, waving her long hair out of his face, before ducking back to stare at the O'glenz trader lying in the back floorboard. Jake pinned Frendlo'pan with a knee on his chest. Jake's wind-blown face wore a mask of impatience and malice. He adjusted his right hand on the seat for stability while his left hand pushed Frendlo'pan a little lower out of the side of the open car door.

"You should have talked to me on the ship," Jake yelled. " Now, you have two minutes to tell me what I want to know." Jake left the threat unspoken. The fear in Frendlo'pan's eyes was tangible.

"I want to know why the TSA is hiring thugs like you to frame me!" Jake pushed the O'glenz a little further out of the open door of the hover-car. "Why?"

Jake felt the sting of the grass on his hand and could only imagine what Frendlo'pan felt on his hard carapace. The O'glenz trader's pincers flailed in an attempt to grab the hover-car, but found no purchase on the car's slick exterior. Jake pushed him out of the car a little further, careful not to lose his grip on the car or the alien. The O'glenz thrashed harder in panic. Jake's smiled broadened.

"Tell me!"

"I don't know," Frendlo'pan screamed into the wind. "I don't know, why!"

Jake raised his head when he felt the hover-car turn sharply. He closed his eyes as Angel's hair caught him full in the face. He ducked, shaking the hair from his face. He moved his right hand to brush the last strands, lost his balance, and pressed harder on the alien's carapace with his knee. The O'glenz screamed in panic.

Jake's glance revealed that Angel now piloted the hover-car parallel to The Cliffs of Garmul; a thousand-meter sheer rock face that ended at the salt ocean below. The cliffs were featured in hundreds of holo-movies and served as the official diving site for the Pan-System games. It was one of the most spectacular scenic spots in the Tri-System; unless you were hanging out the side of a hover-car.

Jake felt his own stomach flip and could only imagine the sheer terror the O'glenz felt. Jake reacquired his grip on the seat in front of him and shoved the crab-like alien out the door a bit more to emphasize his point. They were very close to the teetering point where Frendlo'pan would slid out of the air-car.

"Why am I being set up? Who wants me out of the way?"

The O'glenz screamed. "I DON'T KNOW!"

The hover-car lurched and Angel's faint voice could barely be heard over the wind, "Hang on!"

Jake gripped the seat back and steadied himself for what came next. He had plotted the route carefully and knew what was coming. That gave him little comfort now that he knelt on top of an alien crab hanging out of the side of a racing hover-car. He kept his own fear in check and, leaning down into the crab-alien's face, flashed a wink at Frendlo'pan. "You're going to love this," he said with a nod toward the cliff.

Frendlo'pan involuntarily turned his eyestalks in the direction of the nod. The alien screamed as the cliff dropped away and the hover-car sped over a chasm. Jake looked past the O'glenz at a river hundreds of meters below. Jake felt the tremble of panic from the alien as the crab's eyestalks rotated to take in the view.

Frendlo'pan sucked in another breath and screamed again.

Jake's pleasure in the alien's scream disappeared as weightlessness lifted them up and off of the floorboard of the hover-car. Jake scrambled for a new grip as his body lifted high enough that he could see over Angel's shoulder. Her long hair now stood almost straight up as the hover-car plummeted from the cliff, arching over the chasm. Jake saw their destination coming up to greet them and mentally counted the seconds. He secured his grip on the back of the pilot's seat.

The hover-car roared, straining past red-line as Angel applied full power to the engines. The retro-thrusters flared, bouncing Jake into the back of Angel's cushioned seat as the hover-car landed on a large cliff on the other side of the chasm. His head slapped the seat and recoiled as the hover-car stopped its plunge with a bone jarring rebound. He heard Angel curse at his impact on her chair. The hover-car ground to a halt a few meters away from the cliff wall amid screaming engines. A herd of terrified quadrupeds, resembling mountain goats, stampeded away, disappearing up the rise in a thunder of hooves and panicked yelps.

The engines wound down, leaving only the heavy breathing of the humans and the whimpering of the alien O'glenz, to fill the air. High above, a carrion bird screeched.

Jake stood and shook his head before kicking the O'glenz the rest of the way out of the car. Frendlo'pan rolled out of the open door into knee-high grass. Jake stepped from the vehicle, towering over the alien, and tried to catch his breath. He looked at Angel, still sitting behind the controls. "Nice driving."

He looked down, watching his shadow play over Frendlo'pan's shaking carapace. "I'm going to ask you one more time," Jake said, pointing at the car. "If you don't answer me, we are going to do that again. Maybe you make it over the chasm," he shrugged, "maybe you don't. So, for the last time, who is setting me up?"

Frendlo'pan remained silent for a moment, breathing in ragged gasps and shaking uncontrollably. The alien looked past Jake at the open door to the hover-car before lowering its eyestalks. "The Klan'do you want is named Caboraa, on Dikorn."

Jake knew of the merchant, but had never worked for him. "Why?"

"I...I don't know," the alien replied. "He paid me handsomely to call the TSA when you arrived. That...that's all I know."

Jake knelt on one knee and grabbed the alien's eyestalks. He stared into the eyes of the O'glenz and spoke slowly, clearly, enunciating every syllable. "Take that money and buy yourself a nice funeral. If you ever cross my path again, I'll kill you on sight."

Jake stood and brushed himself off. He exhaled slowly before walking around the vehicle and climbing into the hover-car. He ran a hand through his hair, looked at Angel, and nodded.

Frendlo'pan struggled to his feet, his knees weak and wobbly. "You're just going to leave me here?"

Angel turned her head slowly, staring at the alien. She produced her pistol, aiming the weapon at Frendlo'pan's head. "I could shoot you." Her voice was cold, menacing.

The O'glenz fell on his carapace, raising his arms to ward off the shot.

Angel returned the pistol to her cross-draw holster. "That's what I thought."

She fed power to the engines and the hover-car lifted. Jake sat back in his seat and saw Angel wave before throwing the throttle forward. The vehicle tore up the mountainside, following the paths of the quadrupeds a few minutes earlier.

Frendlo'pan, alone on a rocky cliff, watched the car disappear over the rise. The hum of the hover-car faded, replaced by the crashing of waves. The O'glenz stepped to the edge of the cliff and stared down at the waves a thousand meters below. He stood there several minutes, lost in the hypnotic swells and sounds, his body rocking in time with the waves.

Vertigo made him nauseous and he withdrew from the edge of the cliff. Although a water creature, he had no desire to fall a kilometer. He breathed a sigh of relief when he touched the solid rock of the mountain. His gaze followed the trail of the animals and the hover-car and he shook his head. His chest tightened with anxiety and he found it hard to breath.

"I'll never make it up that cliff," he said aloud.

A shadow cast over him and he looked skyward.

His eyes followed a single, solitary bird as it circled high above. Frendlo'pan's knees gave way and he sat down heavily in the shade of an outcropping of rock.

Chapter Eighteen

The three-piece band in the corner of the bar played a sad, tormented tune. Jake Cutter sat with his back to the bar, his elbows resting on the fake wood. He leaned back, closed his eyes, and let the sounds wash over him. There were few patrons in the bar, but he expected that in the early afternoon hour. The bar offered a few secluded corners; a bit of privacy for clandestine business or romantic interludes. A dozen small, round tables filled the majority of the room, the bar and the stage occupied the rest. One of the musicians struck a sour chord, ruining the moment, and Jake turned back to face the bar, motioning for the bartender.

Jake raised his eyes as the bartender brought him another drink. He thanked the robot, it acknowledged, turned, and whirled away on two wheels to assist the next patron. Jake's eyes roamed over the diorama behind the bar. He smirked: *The Busty Ostrich.*

Again? I had no idea it was a chain.

The painting was similar to the one on Kropple; a

large breasted, feathered bird standing on skinny legs. This one, in a bar on Dikorn, a sector away from Kropple, held not so subtle differences. The bird's head dipped down into the sand at its feet, while its neck snaked through its large, over-exaggerated breasts. One wing offered a half salute to the patrons of the bar.

Not as good, Jake thought and turned his attention to the drink before him. He watched as a puff of smoke wafted from his glass. His head and eyes followed the smoke as it rose and dissipated. He reached for the glass, removed the piece of fruit from the rim, and tossed it onto the bar before gently swirling the drink. The three different colored liquors mixed into one almost yellow concoction. The smoke gone, he lifted the drink to his lips.

"Don' do that," came a gruff, slurred voice from his elbow. "You don' mix a Krilmar Sunrise like that.

"If you buy me one," the voice continued, "I'll show you the proper way."

Jake sighed and downed the drink in a single gulp. It was his third in an hour and the warm liquid did not burn like it did when he started. He shook his head, it still stung enough so that a thin sheen of sweat formed on his brow. He wiped his forehead with his sleeve before turning to stare at the humanoid sitting next to him.

The creature was the typical green of the Klan'do, with oversized eyes, small ear slits, and a bald head. Jake examined the alien, noting the fancy clothing, expensive knee-high boots, and a necklace that almost perfectly matched his skin. Jake raised an eyebrow during the inspection, a thin smirk touching his lips. "Why not, Mister?"

The Klan'do swayed slightly on the stool. Apparently, he had already had a few. "Caboraa," he slurred.

Jake motioned for the bartender. "Two more."

Caboraa licked his dark lips as the bartender sat down two Krilmar Sunrises less than a minute later. The two men observed the smoke that drifted from the glasses and melted into the air. Jake watched as Caboraa pulled the sliver of Darlencko fruit from the edge of the glass and squeezed the juice into his drink.

The juice mixed with the liquors, turning the three-colored drink into a bright red sangria that popped as the chemicals mixed. "You don' swirl it," Caboraa said, mesmerized by the crackling of the drink. "You let the fruit mix it.

"Listen to that," Caboraa said, holding a hand to his ear slit and turning his head to listen. "Dat's the sound," his voice took on a dreamy, almost trancelike feel, "dat's the sound of a Krilmar Sunrise."

Jake discarded the fruit as before, and swirled his drink. He took a sip. "I've been to Krilmar," he said humorlessly, "sunsets don't crackle."

Caboraa looked hurt as he straightened up in his chair. "They mos' certainly do. I was there years ago for the winter solstice celebration—the Krilmar New Year." He took a sip, belched slightly, and looked Jake straight in the eyes. "I distinctly remember *crackling*."

Jake smiled innocently. The winter solstice

celebration included a lot of fireworks, most of which crackled as they exploded. "That must be it. I wasn't there during the winter."

Caboraa finished his drink in one long shot and placed the glass on the bar. He swayed on the stool and Jake reached out a hand to steady the Klan'do. Caboraa shoved the hand away with a swipe of his green arm. His eyes were half closed as he smiled. "I' fine."

Caboraa's grey-pupil eyes rolled into the back of his head. Jake caught the Klan'do as he passed out and gently laid the alien's head down. The alien let out a gentle snore.

Jake downed the rest of his non-alcoholic sunrise. Even without the alcohol, the chemicals warmed his body. He motioned to the bartender as he flipped a coin at the robot. "Now, bring me a real one. I want to see what all of the fuss is about."

Caboraa woke to an incessant pounding in his head. He opened his eyes, light flooded in, and he immediately shut them. He groaned, tried to rub his temples, and felt rough restraints bite into his wrist.

"What?" He opened his eyes again and battled past the bright, stabbing light. Fear and alcohol induced numbness fought for supremacy of his system. He shook his head to clear it. *What was the last thing you remember?* a voice in his brain asked.

The bar! he answered the voice. The *Krilmar*

Sunrise!

And where are you now? The voice questioned.

A human approached, pulled up a chair, turned it backwards, and sat down, propping himself on the back of the antique wood. Caboraa ignored him for a moment, looking past him into the depths of an abandoned warehouse. Old, discarded boxes littered the floor of the open bay. Support columns collected trash at their base from the breeze through broken windows. Sunlight flooded through the windows. *How long have I been out?*

"I spent three weeks and several thousand credits tracking you down," the man's tone was cold, echoing off the barren walls. Caboraa stopped his inspection to listen. "Now you're going to tell me who set me up and why."

"Who are you?" the Klan'do asked, confused.

"Jake Cutter."

Caboraa's eyes widened as he recognized the name. Fear triumphed over the hangover and the numbness subsided, replaced by a sense of impending doom. Caboraa wished he was still drunk as he stared into the cold eyes of the human. He struggled, found his hands securely bound by taunt ropes that bit into his skin, and began to tremble.

"I-I don't know what you're talking about," Caboraa stammered.

"Now, why don't I believe you?" Jake shook his head. "You obviously recognized my name. And since Frendlo'pan told me that you hired him to frame me..."

"Frendlo'pan lies." Caboraa struggled against the

ropes.

"He had no reason to lie to me." Jake flashed a smile. "Especially after I let him live."

Caboraa stopped struggling as a wave of desperation washed over him. "Frendlo'pan is alive?" Caboraa blurted, confused. "No one has seen him in a month."

"I left him alive, although, I admit, his chances of survival were slim," the human confessed. The look in the human's eyes sent a chill through Caboraa and he began struggling against the restraints in earnest.

"If you want the same courtesy I gave to him," the human continued in a low voice, leaning forward in the chair, "then you will tell me who hired you. Why. And where I can find him." The man patted Caboraa on the knee.

Caboraa flinched, recoiling at the touch.

The human sat back. "I gave Frendlo'pan a chance to survive. You also have a chance. One." He held up one finger to emphasize his point and his voice grew sinister. "That's more than any of you gave me when you sold me out.

"Now, for the last time: who hired you and why?"

Caboraa felt sweat—a milky substance with the faint smell of cinnamon—slide down his back. He struggled another moment at the ropes, felt the sting as they bit deeper into his wrists, and weighed his options.

Refuse, and be killed now.

Lie and escape immediate death. But if the human survived? Caboraa shuddered at the thought of a slow, painful death at the hands of the human.

Tell the truth and hope that the human kills those responsible.

The first two options did not appeal to the Klan'do, especially since they involved his death. *There is only one option.*

"The contract originated from the Heroz system. The package used to frame you came from the same system."

"A name?"

"I- I don't have the man's name," Caboraa replied nervously. He rushed the rest, spilling all he knew in rapid release of words. The stench of cinnamon filled the room. "He was well connected. Some high-ranking official. I don't know his name. He hired Jorchlo'pan, and Jorchlo'pan hired me. That's all I know."

The human sniffed the air. When he spoke, his voice held a low, soothing tone. "Who is Jorchlo'pan?"

Caboraa heard the human's change in tone and relaxed. He stared into the man's eyes and saw, for the briefest of moments, a hint of compassion. "He is Frendlo'pan's brother."

Caboraa felt a presence at his back. He struggled to turn and look behind, found the restraints held him firm, and panicked. Fear consumed him. Firm hands gripped his shoulders and he froze.

The smell of cinnamon was overwhelming. Jake sat backwards on a chair, leaning on the back of the seat toward Caboraa. He looked past the Klan'do at Angel, standing behind the alien, her hands on his shoulders.

Jake shook his head. "Frendlo'pan's brother. I should have thrown that crab off the cliff."

Angel nodded, her dark hair bobbing with the movement. It was shorter now, a little past her shoulders instead of down her back. She wore a light blue, form fitting body suit and her customary cross-draw holster. Her hands squeezed Caboraa's shoulders. The alien squirmed and attempted to shrink down in his seat, recoiling from the woman's touch. The restraints held him firmly in place.

"He wouldn't give up his brother, so he gave up Caboraa," Angel pondered. "I guess he figured we would kill Caboraa and his brother would be safe."

Jake stood, moving the chair behind him, out of the way. He stared down at Caboraa as Angel cut the ropes that bound his hands. "This is what's going to happen," he said, addressing the Klan'do. "I'm going to find Jorchlo'pan. He is going to tell me who the official is, and then I'm going to kill him. And then, I'm going to find Frendlo'pan and, if he is still alive, I'm going to kill him."

Caboraa rubbed his wrists as Jake knelt on a knee, looking the Klan'do in the eyes. Caboraa shrank back. "If you warn them in any way, then I will make their deaths seem painless and quick compared to what I will do to you. Do you understand?"

The Klan'do gulped audibly. "I—I won't tell anybody. I swear I…"

"Good," Angel said from behind Caboraa, cutting

him off. "Now leave."

The Klan'do bounded across the warehouse, tripping over the litter, and out of the door. The lingering of cinnamon the only proof the Klan'do was ever there.

Angel turned her attention to Jake and saw the look on his face. "What's wrong?"

"Heroz system," he said. His voice no longer held the icy tone, but was downtrodden and apprehensive. His face morphed to match his tone as he spoke. "I used to live in the Heroz system. I had forced myself to forget about that part of my life." He sat down heavily on the chair and sighed. "It's been so long..."

Angel knelt before him. "That part of your life is behind you. You said you wanted to find out who is behind all of this. And why." She took his hands in hers and pulled him to his feet. "Do you still want to see this through?" She stared into his eyes, willing her strength into his suddenly vulnerable eyes.

He pondered the question as images flashed through his mind of the last two years of his life. The pain, suffering, and loss. Each memory capitalizing on the last, building his resolve. He needed answers. He knew he would never find any peace until he confronted his unseen enemy. "Yes."

"Then it's time to visit your home system and put all of this to rest." She led him toward the door of the warehouse.

He paused at the warehouse door. "First, we need to find an O'glenz and his brother. Time for them both to die."

"We need to have a plan this time," she countered. "Let me buy you a drink and we can discuss."

Jake opened the door, bright sunlight filled the warehouse. "Have you ever had a Krilmar Sunrise?"

Chapter Nineteen

Angel and Jake took a hover-cab back to the Busty Ostrich Bar. Jake sat behind the robot driver while Angel sat beside him. They each stared out of their own window, traveling in silence, lost in their own thoughts. The driver, there purely for aesthetics, was of hominid design, but with the ears of a Chandrillian, the green-tone of a Klan'do, the mane of a Hazmora and features from a dozen other races. Jake shook his head, wondering if it was by design, or if they ran out of spare parts and cobbled the amalgamation together. A few minutes into their journey, it began a countdown of blocks remaining to their destination. Jake sighed and returned to staring out of his window.

A steady downpour began falling halfway to their destination, which fit Jake's mood. The cab arrived at the bar and Angel left the cab first on the curb side. Jake tossed a handful of credits into the receiver and followed Angel. A quick sprint and they huddled under the awning covering the door to the bar.

"Think anyone will remember that we took

Caboraa out of here yesterday?" Angel asked, as Jake opened the door.

"We'll find out in a minute," he replied, unsnapping the restraining strap on his holster. Angel heard the sound and paused. Jake smiled. "Better safe than sorry."

She unsnapped her holster and led the way into the Busty Ostrich.

The robot bartender recognized Jake as he and Angel approached the faux wood bar. "Another virgin Krilmar Sunrise, sir?"

Jake tossed a couple of coins on the bar as he sat in the same seat he sat in the day before. Angel took the seat next to him, in Caboraa's previous spot. "Two," Jake replied, holding up two fingers. "Real ones this time."

"Make it three," a voice called out behind them.

Jake's hand went to his sidearm. He stared straight ahead, wishing for a mirror behind the bar, but all he saw was the diorama of an Ostrich with its head in the sand. Jake smirked, as he slowly turned to face the newcomer.

The robot bartender wheeled away. "Three Krilmar Sunrises coming up!"

Jake saw a man dressed in a dirty brown TSA flight suit, pistol holstered and slung low on his right leg. He held up his arms non-threateningly as a huge grin split his face. Jake instantly recognized him.

"You are a hard man to track, Jake," Mark Dawson smiled, offering his right hand.

"By design." Jake slid off the stool and shook the

offered hand.

Dawson released his grip and turned to Angel, who leapt into his arms, embracing him in a hug. "Thank you for all of your help," she said. Tears welled in her eyes as she released him. "I don't think we would have survived without you."

The bartender arrived with the drinks and the three moved to a secluded table in a dark corner of the tavern far from the entrance. All three sat, Jake facing the door, Angel to his left with a good view of the back, and Dawson to his right, watching the bar. Each removed the fruit and squeezed its juices into the beverage. Crackles filled the air as the three sat in contemplative silence.

"So, what brings you to Dikorn?" Angel asked, looking at the TSA Officer.

"My new assignment," Dawson replied, taking a sip of the drink. His eyes bulged and he swallowed hard before smiling at the others. He leaned over the table and whispered, "I've been tasked with finding all of the escapees from Cla'nix."

"How many escaped?" Jake asked, throwing back the shot and letting the alcohol burn through his system.

"Including you two?" Dawson asked.

Jake nodded.

"Two."

"How many were relocated to other facilities?" Angel inquired.

Dawson shook his head. "You don't understand. The three of us are the *only* survivors. Everyone else—

prisoners and guards alike—died when the prison flooded." He shrugged. "If my team had not arrived when it did, I probably would have died, too."

"Team?" Angel asked. She tasted her drink for the first time, crinkling her nose at the concoction. She passed the Sunrise to Jake.

Dawson nodded. "Introductions are probably in order. My name is Lieutenant Mark Dawson, TSA Special Assignments Branch. I was assigned as a guard to infiltrate the prison to investigate a possible connection to the slave trade."

"I guess you found it," Jake replied.

"And more," the TSA Officer replied. "The smuggling operation was a bit of a surprise, especially when we traced the funds."

"Oh?" Angel asked.

"The Secretary of Commerce has been implicated, but, there is no direct link." He shrugged. "We can't prove his involvement."

Jake perked up at the mention of the Secretary. "The Secretary of Commerce?"

Dawson nodded. "Dante Terra."

"On Heroz?" Jake inquired.

Dawson nodded. "Does that mean something to you?"

Jake and Angel exchanged glances. Jake looked Mark in the eyes, leaning forward. "Before I say anything else, I want to know what your intentions are. Are you going to take us back to prison?"

Dawson shook his head. "No. I know you're innocent, Jake. The Sergeant confirmed that much in between the beatings." Jake saw the man rub his ribs. "But again, no proof."

"And Secretary Terra may have been behind your arrest, but I haven't found a motive. Have you ever had a run in with the Secretary of Commerce?"

Jake shook his head. "No."

Dawson smirked. "His possible connection was what led me to enlist Grag and Angel's assistance when you arrived. I needed you alive to hopefully trace back to him."

The TSA Officer turned to Angel. "My condolences on his death. I never meant that to happen."

She lowered her head. "Thank you."

Dawson turned to face Jake. "As for my intentions," he leaned back in the chair, "they are to find a way to report you as dead so you can move on."

Jake shook his head. "I'm not moving on." He finished Angel's discarded drink in one gulp and banged the empty glass on the table. "I'm going to find the person responsible for framing me, for wrecking my life. I'm going to find him, and kill him."

"And you think that Secretary Terra may be responsible?" Dawson asked.

Jake nodded. "Both the Sergeant and the Demoness referenced a man known as the Secretary. Now you tell me that this guy—Terra—was running a smuggling operation at the prison."

"There is no proof," Dawson cautioned.

Jake continued, unimpeded. "It's another piece of the puzzle and it fits."

"But why?" Angel interjected. "Why would the

Secretary of Commerce for the TSA want you out of the way?"

Jake waved to the bartender, indicating another round. "That is what I intend to find out."

Empty glasses filled the table. The late afternoon regulars began arriving and the Busty Ostrich showed signs of life. A second robot bartender appeared behind the bar as a robot hostess began working the tables. The three-piece band arrived around sunset and began dishing out their slightly out of tune harmonies. Thick smoke filled the air.

Angel guided her two inebriated charges out of the door and hailed a cab. The two men leaned against the exterior wall of the bar as the rain continued to fall. The cab arrived, a different driver with the same mismatch of alien physiologies, and Angel dumped the two men into the back. They slid down in the seat, each one propping their head on a window. She climbed in the front and, with a sigh, ordered the driver to the spaceport.

Of course, they would try to drink each other under the table, she thought, sitting beside the driver. *And I'm the one to clean up the mess.*

The cab ride was quiet except for the gentle snores from the back seat. Angel shook her head before offering a small laugh. "At least he made a new friend," she said to no one, referencing Jake. She worried about him.

He was right about things, in a way. She did have the opportunity to avenge Grag. But the closure she longed for never coalesced. There was still a hole in her life. She missed her mentor, the man who had saved her from a fate worse than death.

She saw the same desire for revenge in Jake and wondered if he would find his closure once the Secretary was dead. Somehow, she doubted it. She wanted to tell him that her revenge was not worth it. They had nearly died going back into the prison to kill the Demoness. If she could do it again, she would have left Cla'nix that first time in the orchard.

The cab arrived at the spaceport and Angel tried to awaken her charges. Neither man stirred. She told the robot driver to hold on a minute and ran to the *Freelancer*, returning a minute later with two anti-grav carts from the cargo hold. She muscled the men onto the carts, flirting with the idea of leaving them on the plasti-crete pavement after banging her head on the cab door. Her task complete, she paid the cab and watched it speed off before pushing the carts, one at a time, onto the freighter.

"You two better be worth it," she said, closing the ramp. She left them floating on the carts in the main cabin and made her way to her room. She collapsed onto her bed, exhausted.

Jake rolled over, felt a brief sensation of falling, and landed hard on the metal deck of the *Freelancer*.

"What the hell?" His head pounded from the burgeoning hangover.

He sat up on an elbow. "Where am I?" he asked. His eyes focused and he recognized the interior of the freighter. He heard a deep sigh and turned to look behind him. Mark Dawson sat cross-legged on the deck, holding his head.

Jake sat up, smacking the anti-grav cart hovering above him. He cursed and began rubbing his head. He shoved the cart out of the way, watching it float effortlessly across the cabin.

"Morning," Dawson said, rubbing his temples. "Where are we?"

"Aboard the *Freelancer*," Jake said, rising unsteadily to his feet.

"How did we get here?" Dawson asked, also rising to his feet.

"I brought you here," Angel said, appearing from a side corridor. She yawned, brushing her tangled hair from her face in the same motion. "After you two drank yourselves into a stupor..."

"Sorry," Mark said, embarrassed. "It's been a long time since I've had friends to just sit and talk with."

Jake clapped him on the back before looking at Angel. "I'm sorry, too." He rubbed his temples. "What can we do to make it up to you?"

"Make me breakfast," she said. She turned to head back the way she had come. "I'll be ready in twenty minutes."

The men served breakfast—protein and carb supplements with hot java—twenty minutes later as Angel emerged from her room, brushing her hair. The three settled around a table in the galley, eating in relative silence. Breakfast worked wonders to dispel the hangovers and bring the two men back to life. The meal concluded and the men put away the dishes.

"What's your next move?" Dawson asked as they returned to their seats.

"We have to find a smuggler named Jorchlo'pan," Angel replied. She propped her elbows on the table, cradling her chin in her palms.

The Lieutenant nodded. "I've heard of him. Do you know where he is?"

Jake leaned back on the padded seat. "We were going to start on Kropple, track him through the family network." He smiled. "Besides, I want to see if Frendlo'pan survived his vacation."

"He survived," Dawson confirmed. Jake raised an inquisitive eyebrow and Dawson held up a hand to ward off the question. "I don't know how, only that he did. May I make a suggestion?" Jake nodded. "Jorchlo'pan has an operations center on D'rik. That might make a better location for your...interrogation."

Angel sat back, rubbing her elbows to return circulation to them. "We don't know if he's there."

"And if I can arrange for him to be there?" Dawson inquired.

"What's in this for you?" Jake furrowed his eyebrows, suspicious.

Dawson spread his hands. "This coincides with something I discovered during my investigation on Cla'nix. The smuggling was only one part of the operation. Slave trading was the other. Did you know that a rebellion is brewing on the rim worlds of the Tri-System?"

The two shook their heads.

"The government on Arbra, a moon in the outer section of Quadrant Three, is seeking its independence from the TSA," Dawson explained. "Other planets are watching. If Arbra is successful, there will undoubtedly be other governments that try to secede."

"What does this have to do with slave traders?" Angel asked.

"The TSA is conscripting prisoners to fight the rebels to keep their own losses to a minimum," Dawson replied. "It's a public relations coup. Win a war with few losses and cut costs of operating the prisons. That's the kind of thing that gets politicians re-elected. And there are three more prison planets like Cla'nix, still sending prisoners to fight."

"Three more?" Angel asked. "I thought Cla'nix was the only prison in the TSA."

"That is exactly what the TSA wants you to believe," Dawson replied.

"Wait. Why would the prisoners agree to this?" Jake asked.

"Pardons," Angel said. Dawson nodded a confirmation and she continued. "That's high motivation. Especially to prisoners who have been underground for a while. Think about your own time at Cla'nix. What would you have done to get out of there?"

Jake recoiled at the thought of living underground again. "Anything."

"Fight. Survive. Get a pardon," Dawson confirmed.

Jake sat back, astonished at the new information. "This isn't a simple framing anymore," he said. "This is way bigger than I thought. And we still don't know how I fit into all this."

Dawson nodded. "You are the wildcard, Jake. Everything else appears to be interconnected.

"The 'Pans are known to smuggle anything and everything, including slaves. My sources tell me they are in deep."

Jake went silent for a moment, lost in thought. The chess board of his life was much bigger than he realized, with many more players than he imagined. He was not even the King of his own game, merely a pawn. The thought infuriated him. He looked at Angel. She smiled and nodded. He turned his head to Dawson and smiled. "You get Jorchlo'pan to D'rik and I'll take care of the rest."

The Jake Cutter Conspiracy

Chapter Twenty

Mark Dawson smiled as he bounded up the ramp and entered the main cabin of the *Freelancer*. He waved to Jake and Angel as he sidestepped a crate of supplies and ducked under a sheath of wiring under repair. He dropped himself into an overstuffed faux-leather chair across from the woman. He sank deep into the chair, letting the suction drain the last vestiges of stress from his shoulders. He ran a hand through his short blonde hair.

"It's done," he said. "I've called in my report, speculating that you would be on D'rik in four days. I've requested an armed party to raid Jorchlo'pan's warehouse. That should draw him out. Once the TSA leaves, you can sweep in. "Simple."

"And to bring a little credibility to your speculation," Angel chimed in. She sat in an identical, overstuffed chair, her legs tucked under her, her hair pulled back in a small ponytail. "I've put the word out that we are looking for work taking us in the direction of D'rik or one of the other moons of Crescalt."

"Any leads?" Jake joined in the conversation. He sat on the edge of a small, round table facing the two chairs. The table doubled as both a holographic projector for briefings and a gaming console. The system sat dormant as the pilot folded his arms listening.

"One," Angel replied. "It will get us to D'rik a few days early."

"You don't need to be on that moon when the TSA gets there," Dawson cautioned, shaking his head. "They will turn that place upside down looking for you."

"We'll take the job," Jake stood. "Deliver whatever it is, and ask around about Jorchlo'pan. That should add some fuel to the fire. We'll find another job to get off world for a day or two, and then come back after you," pointing to Dawson, "let us know the TSA has gone."

"Me?" Dawson asked, pointing to his chest.

"Yes," Jake confirmed. He reached out and helped Angel out of her chair. "You need to be there. It's your case. We are your fugitives. If you are not there, it might raise suspicions."

Dawson struggled with the chair for a moment, before rising with them.

"And," Angel smiled, continuing Jake's train of thought, "if they do get on our trail, you can point them in another direction."

The three of them stood in silent contemplation for a moment. A broad smile stretched across Dawson's face. "I'll see you on D'rik in seven days.

Accommodations were made at the *Spacefarer*, a low-key hotel on D'rik that provided surprisingly good security and the best boar-beast steak on the moon. Their goods delivered and payment received, Jake and Angel ate that night in relative peace. The dinner was excellent, the conversation lively, and the wine expensive. Jake left an exorbitant tip and word spread quickly that the two TSA fugitives had arrived.

Finding a job to get them off D'rik before the raid proved a bit more difficult.

"The word is out about you, Captain," an old merchant said the next day. He smiled, offering a shrug. His wrinkled jowls jiggled when he spoke, his skin like leather against the cold of the moon. He wore his hair long, scraggly and grey, in a ponytail that stretched past his shoulders. An old, faded cowboy hat topped his head. His sharp, piercing blue eyes took in every detail as he scanned the man and woman before him.

He was the fifth importer/exporter Jake and Angel had talked to after their night out. Each of the previous four—reputable and disreputable alike—turned them away without explanation. The old man was the first to even carry on a conversation with them. Jake pulled his leather jacket tighter against the cold, northerly wind, his frustration growing with every person that turned them away.

"The TSA is out for your blood, in a big way. Funny

thing is, no one really knows why." The old man smiled, leaning in conspiratorially and lowering his voice. "I hear they are on their way here. Should arrive in a day or two."

He adjusted his hat against the wind and rubbed his whiskered chin. He grinned, "There is that story about your transporting contraband," he waved a dismissive hand, "but everyone knows that was a setup." The old man jerked his thumb towards a distant high-rise; high-rise on D'rik meaning three stories tall. Jake followed the thumb to the tallest building in the spaceport.

"Those idiot 'Pan brothers kept bragging about some poor bloke they set up...got paid a fortune, so they tell." He scratched his chin again. "They got real quiet after the rumors that you broke out of Cla'nix. How'd you manage that anyway?"

"Long story," Jake smiled. The old merchant went from the only person on D'rik that would even talk to him to the one that would not stop. "Maybe some other time."

The merchant looked at Angel and gave her a wink. "Would it be worth the story for a job? Maybe get you off world for a couple of days?"

It was Angel's turn to smile. "How much and where to?" She winked at the old man.

Jake held his left hand. "Maybe..."

The old man nodded and offered a knowing smile. "I have some, uh, artifacts, that need to be moved from here to Panz. That's about a four-day round trip in that freighter of yours.

"I'll give you twenty-five thousand for the trip. You give me your word that the goods will be delivered or you'll die trying..." the old man's eyes twinkled, "...and the story of your escape."

Jake rubbed his chin and felt stubble. He smiled, briefly wondering if he would live long enough to grow a grisly beard like the old man before him. "The story, twenty-five thousand, and you tell me where I can find Jorchlo'pan."

The old man extended his hand. "Deal."

Jake shook the offered hand. The trio moved to the spaceport café, sat down at a corner table away from the other handful of patrons, and ordered a round of stim-caff. Once settled with the hot beverage, Jake and Angel took turns telling the old man of their escape from the prison planet.

"That's quite a story."

Jake took a sip of caff. "It was quite an escape."

"You really drowned the entire valley?"

"Yep. Everything," Jake smiled.

The old merchant smiled. "The TSA denied everything you just said, by the way. No one has ever escaped from Cla'nix." He laughed. "But, those of us in the business know that something happened, and since the focus is on you..."

Jake dropped a few coins on the table. He stood and changed the subject. "Angel will oversee the loading of the cargo."

The old man rose, giving a half bow to Angel. He handed her a small bag of coins. "Payment, in advance." He turned to Jake. "And the last part of the deal..."

"Where does Jorchlo'pan clean his pinchers?" Jake asked.

The old man pointed to the three-story building. "Good luck."

"The raid...as planned," Dawson's voice sounded tired over the comm. Static interrupted the report. "The team came...empty, but did find...order Jorchlo'pan to...appearance...He...arrive tomorrow."

Jake ran a hand through his hair. He felt as tired as Dawson sounded. Two days through a static-discharge nebula to Panz, and now returning through the same nebula. The four-day trip—usually a restful stint on autopilot—turned into a constant monitoring, fly on manual, nightmare. Jake relaxed his shoulders, staring out at the maelstrom of colors beyond the cockpit canopy. Purple, green, red, interspersed with yellow flashes of discharge created a mesmerizing display.

"We are on our way back," Jake replied to Dawson. "Eighteen hours."

"What?"

"Eighteen hours," Jake repeated.

"Roger," Mark replied. "We will...gone."

The comm went dead and Jake turned his attention back to the nebula. Eighteen hours and he was one step closer to finding out who wanted him dead. And why.

A trio of laser bolts slammed into the wall near Jake, each one closer than the one before. He dove behind a crate with TX983-MACHINERY stenciled on the side and felt the vibrations of the laser bolts hitting the crate. He sat, his back against the wooden box, and felt the steady *thump, thump, thump* of the impacts. The steady beat almost drowned out his adrenaline-charged heartbeat.

Almost.

"Stop, dammit!" he screamed over the incoming volley. The fire stopped abruptly and Jake felt a glimmer of hope.

"There is no one to assist you, Captain Cutter," came an unfamiliar voice in the low baritone of an O'glenz. "There is only you, me, and ten of my men. I suggest you surrender before someone gets hurt."

Jake scanned the warehouse. Intervening catwalks overhead provided a sniper's paradise, metal cylinders and superstructure beams offered great cover. The glimmer of hope faded quickly. *No easy way out*. Jake shook his head. *She did tell me to be careful.*

"You must be Jorchlo'pan," Jake called, staying low behimd the crate as he rose to his feet. He fumbled around in a small pouch on his side and pulled out two small cubes. The ten-centimeter, crystalline cubes resembled diamonds, except for the small dial on one side. Jake gave the dial a twist and held down a button with his forefinger.

"Yes, Captain Cutter," Jorchlo'pan replied. "My brother told me to watch my back. That you would be coming to find me sooner or later."

"Talked to him lately, have you?" Jake responded. His thoughts flitted briefly to Angel. *Where is she?*

The head of a Hazmora appeared on the catwalk above Jake. He snap-aimed a shot and was rewarded by a scream, followed by the sound of something squishy landing on plasti-crete. That warranted another volley of fire. Jake ducked, but not before catching sight of the muzzle flashes. *Three distinct locations, roughly at twelve, two, and ten o'clock.*

He crinkled his nose against the smell of smoldering wood as smoke filled the air. The laser barrage stopped and the O'glenz continued the conversation.

"Not ten minutes ago, Captain," Jorchlo'pan called out. "We sat in my office and wondered if you and your lovely assistant would ever make it here."

"He made it off that cliff," Jake nodded, admiring the tenacity of the O'glenz. "I didn't think he had the will."

"My brother has become quite resolute since you abandoned him to die." The voice was moving from left to right. "So resolute, in fact, that he took it upon himself to discipline Caboraa, who was quite surprised to see us.

"That reminds me," the alien crab continued, "I want to thank you for the little raid on my warehouse. The TSA has been looking into my operations for quite some time. Now that they have found nothing, their case is diminished. You have done me a great service, Captain."

"Shoot yourself and we'll call it even," Jake responded. He snuck a peek and ducked quickly. They were well hidden, but he could hear their movements in the quiet warehouse. He judged the voice to be to his right, so he adjusted his aim a little left. He wanted the smuggler alive.

"You killed Caboraa?" Jake inquired, changing the subject. He released his finger and, with an overhead toss, launched both crystal balls high in the air.

"He died a tragic and horrible—"

Twin explosions rocked the complex as the small thorium bombs exploded.

Jake heard the explosions, felt the heat and twin shock waves wash over him, and counted to three before rising from his hiding spot. A quick scan showed seven men and aliens crouching, holding their ears, and screaming. The pilot took a breath, released it, and methodically shot each of them, one at a time.

He moved quickly, hopping over crates and boxes and dodging debris, moving across the open warehouse toward a platform where Jorchlo'pan's henchmen lay dead. He checked each, ensuring they were dead, before turning the weapon at the screaming and crying Jorchlo'pan. The O'glenz lay on his side, holding his carapace. Jake could see the blood seeping through the cracks in his chitin, sliding down his pinchers. The pilot took a step forward.

"Cutter!" The scream echoed through the complex and Jake froze. "Drop the gun, now."

Jake, exposed on the metal platform, slowly turned his head to see Frendlo'pan, the alien's carapace cracked and sunburnt. The O'glenz stood on a catwalk a few meters above Jake, holding a rifle. The crab-like alien stood shakily, leaning against the railing as he stared down at the scene below. The alien gestured with the rifle. "Lose the gun."

Jake slowly opened his fist and let the pistol fall to the floor. Out of the corner of his eye he saw Jorchlo'pan struggle to rise from the floor. The O'glenz partially stood, before falling back to the platform floor, stunned and disoriented, writhing in pain. Jake turned his attention back to the catwalk, staring at Frendlo'pan.

"You left me to die," the alien stated. "I spent a week on that cliff before an archeologist and his family found me." He moved his left pincher up and down his body, showing off the cracks and burned areas of his carapace. "I'm told I may never properly heal."

Frendlo'pan made his way down a spiral staircase, his huge bulk barely able to navigate the confined space. The rifle never wavered from Jake's midsection. The O'glenz made it to ground level, leaning against the wall in obvious pain. "I don't have the means to strand you to die," he continued, out of breath. "But I will make you suffer until you beg for death, and I will wipe that stupid smile from your face."

"It's not stupid," a female voice answered. "It's confidence."

Frendlo'pan turned an eyestalk toward the speaker. Angel emerged from the shadows and stepped onto the catwalk above the O'glenz, a pistol held at the alien's head. "He's confident that you'll never get the chance to hear him beg.

"Now, drop it!"

Frendlo'pan dropped the rifle. It clattered off the platform, landing unceremoniously onto the duracrete floor below. The O'glenz leaned heavily on the wall to steady himself.

Angel kept herself well out of the alien's reach as Jake retrieved his pistol from the floor and made his way over to the still crying Jorchlo'pan. Jake was still a few steps away when he realized the alien's wounds were more severe than he thought. The hard-shell carapace around his abdomen sported an oozing crack.

"Bring Frendlo over here," Jake called, as he knelt on one knee beside the wounded O'glenz. "If he wants to help his brother, he will answer my questions."

Jorchlo'pan tried to speak, but only spittle and something akin to blood came out. Jake shook his head as he quietly spoke. "You know, that much blood isn't good. If you want to live, you need to answer my questions quickly." Angel and the slow moving Frendlo'pan arrived to hear, "If you don't, the pain you feel now will pale in comparison to what I do to your brother."

Angel pushed Frendlo'pan to the floor, her pistol replaced with a short-barreled rifle. Jorchlo'pan lay in the spot where the thorium bombs had deposited him. His pincers tried desperately to hold in his entrails, as he slowly bled out. The red tint of his carapace had turned pale from the loss of fluids.

"My attention isn't on you, Jorchlo'" Jake corrected. He stood, and stepped to hover over the sitting Frendlo'pan. "You are already hurt and dying. But Frendlo'...Frendlo' is only hurt. He is still *very* susceptible to pain." He tapped the alien's carapace near a crack, rewarded with a recoil and quick intake of air against the pain.

"So, Jorchlo', I'm going to ask you a question," Jake slowly drew his laser and pointed it at Frendlo'pan's knee joint. "You are going to answer," he clicked off the safety, "or you will watch your brother suffer and die before your eyes."

"Don't tell him any—" Frendlo'pan croaked.

Jake fired. The bolt missed the knee, scorching the platform near his thin leg. Jake imagined the shot was close enough that the O'glenz felt the heat from the blast. Silence filled the room.

Jake nodded. "First question. Who set me up?"

More silence.

Jake sighed. "I need a name." Jake looked from Frendlo'pan to Jorchlo'pan. "Last chance."

More silence.

Jake, still watching the pale O'glenz, squeezed the trigger. The bolt blasted through the bone and cartilage of Fendlo'pan's knee, searing and cauterizing as it destroyed the joint. Frendlo'pan's scream echoed in the abandoned facility. Jake let the pain run its course, allowing the alien to get himself under control before speaking again.

"I need a name," Jake said, low and menacing.

The sound of Frendlo'pan's sobs filled the building, but neither O'glenz spoke.

Jake shook his head, frustrated. He holstered his weapon and produced a magna-blade from his belt. He held the small cylinder in his palm and let the two crab-like aliens see the device. He activated the heated blade and waved it toward the left eyestalk of the O'glenz. Jake could feel the heat from the knife and imagined the fear of having it that close to your eye. The freighter pilot looked at Jorchlo'pan. "The name?"

Jorchlo'pan remained silent.

A piercing scream cut the ensuing silence as the magna-blade sliced through the eyestalk of the Frendlo'pan. Jake watched the organ fall to the floor as the wounded alien fell over on the platform, thrashing on the floor. Jorchlo'pan tried to turn away but his own wounds kept him on his side, watching his brother suffer. It took several minutes for Frendlo'pan to stop screaming.

"Tell me the name and all of the pain goes away," Jake said. "It's not too late to end the suffering. But..." he let the word hang in the air for several seconds, "...I'm about to lose my patience."

"I don't have a name," Jorchlo'pan screamed. He broke down, sobbing, defeat in his voice. "All I ever heard was *The Secretary*."

"You met him? What does he look like?"

Jorchlo'pan twitched, pain racking his body. "I never met him. Contacted..."

"Who contacted you?" Jake pressed.

"The TSA," came the reply. Jake could see that the

alien was weaker. He did not have long. "A TSA patrol...on Panz... contacted us." The words took effort. "A bar...the Panhandler." The O'glenz stared at his brother who was weaving in and out of consciousness. "Don't hurt him anymore, please."

Jake moved over to kneel beside Jorchlo'pan. "Why would the TSA contact you to set me up if they are investigating you?" Jake asked. "Did they offer you a deal?"

"Frame you...clean record," O'glenz croaked.

"A TSA Patrol in a bar called the Panhandler on Panz," Jake repeated. "That's all you have?"

The O'glenz nodded his head in a fair imitation of a human. "Please...don't hurt him. You...you promised not to hurt him..."

"No," Jake said, drawing his pistol. "I said I would make the pain go away."

Jake Cutter shot each one in the head before leading Angel away from the carnage.

Chapter Twenty-One

Jake felt the binds *tighten around his wrists, cutting into his flesh as he tried to free himself. A cold sweat chilled his spine, as footsteps approached from behind. He tried turning his head, to see who was there, but the bindings kept him from turning. Adrenaline flooded his system.*

All he could see were the shadows playing on the walls around him. The only sound he heard was his own ragged, panicked breathing. He struggled again, tugging at the metal cuffs around his wrists and ankles. A cold hand grabbed his forehead and he froze.

He heard the click of a button and the hum of magna-blade. Jake felt the heat of the blade as it neared the back of his neck. He tried to put his chin on his chest, but the clammy, rough hand pulled his head backwards. The overhead light blinded him. He could not see his attacker and the panic rose.

The magna-blade moved from the nape of his neck to his face, hovering over his left cheek. Jake flinched away from the red glow of the hot metal and tried to break free again. The rough, callused hand held his head still. His eyes locked onto the knife as he struggled, careful to keep his face away from the blade. The cold hand moved from his forehead to his chin, cupping it roughly. The hand pulled and Jake's head arched backward, exposing his neck. He closed his eyes tightly, feeling the heat play over his skin as the blade neared his left eye.

Jake screamed, leaping from the cot in his quarters aboard the *Freelancer*. He frantically searched the room, ready to fight.

His cabin door opened and Angel appeared at his side calling out to him. "Jake. Jake!"

Jake backed against the wall, eyes wide in panic. He gasped for air, placing his hand on his chest to try to calm his racing heart. He took several deep breaths and watched Angel approach, her hands outstretched placating. She led him back to the bed and slid behind him. He felt her hands on his shoulders. Warm and soft, not cold and clammy.

"I'm okay," he said and knew that she would not believe him. He was not sure he even believed it. He retrieved a canteen of water from his nightstand and drank heavily. "Just a nightmare." He dropped the empty canteen on the floor.

"That's one every night for the last three nights," Angel scolded, "ever since we left D'rik. Tell me what is going on."

"Nothing," he responded. "Just..."

"Just what?" she persisted.

"It was...Frendlo'pan," he began, "only it wasn't. I don't..." Jake took a breath and told Angel of the dream; the same dream he had had every night since the warehouse. He shivered when he told her about the knife. He could see the image of the red, glowing blade inching closer to his eyes. He put his head in his hands and willed the dream to the recesses of his mind.

"Finally," Angel said.

Jake looked at her quizzically. "Finally, what?"

"Finally, you're showing signs of a conscience again."

"What?"

"Jake," she slid around on the bed, facing him. She took his hand in hers and began slowly, carefully choosing her words. "When we met, you were an innocent man." She held up a hand to ward off his interruption. "Just listen.

"You were innocent, a decent man. You could not, would not, hurt anyone. Prison changed you. It changes everyone. But you...you shed off your innocence and did what you needed to do to survive, including killing. Once we escaped, I thought that some of your," she paused, "humanity might return. But it hasn't. You've gotten more inhumane.

"That was one of the reasons I left a year ago," she continued. "I wasn't sure if I wanted to travel with you in that state."

"Then why did you come back?" he asked.

"Several reasons," she confessed. Her shoulders slumped as she continued. "Grag, before he died, told me to watch over you. That I would need your strength, and you would need mine. I didn't know what he meant at the time, but he was right, as always. Now I understand what he meant. Your quest for revenge has blinded you to compassion."

"You want me to show compassion to the very people who framed me and wanted me dead?" Jake asked incredulously.

"No," she said. "But you could show them some mercy."

"I killed them quickly."

"Not what I meant, Jake." Angel shook her head. She stared at him and wagged her finger at him as she spoke. "These dreams...these dreams are showing you that you are on the wrong path."

"They are just dreams," Jake countered, waving off the conversation. "I'm fine." He stretched, yawning.

Angel stood, towering over him as he sat in bed. She took his head in her hands, staring into his eyes. He saw hurt, anger, and fear. "No, you're not," she said, her voice full of sadness. "These dreams are sending you a message."

"What message?"

"That is something you must figure out for yourself," she said. She walked to the door and paused. "Maybe you should start with what you did to Frendlo'pan and his brother, and what the figure in your dreams did to you." She exited the room, leaving him in silence.

Jake lay down and pulled the bed-cover around him, the gentle hum of the engines the only sound in the room. He recalled the dream, examining the images not as Jake, but as an outsider looking in. He rolled over onto his side, drifting off to an uneasy sleep, with the sadness of Angel's eyes forefront in his mind.

Chapter Twenty-Two

"I know where the fugitive, Jake Cutter, is," the caller said.

The Tri-System Authority Police Dispatcher on Panz touched the record button on her console, activating the automated record and trace function. The Hazmoran female saw a short trunk under the dark hood, but not much else. Rain fell in sideways sheets behind the caller, as pedestrians ran down the soaked sidewalk. The passersby paid no attention to the caller as they scurried about their business.

T'traxi, the dispatcher thought, making a note on the log. The caller turned, watching two giggling Traxillian females pass, their clothes clinging to very wet skin, accentuating their curves. The T'traxi turned back to face the vid-screen, face still in shadow from the hood.

"Is there a reward for information about him?" the caller asked.

"What is your location?" the dispatcher replied, ignoring the question. "I can have a team there in less than four minutes."

"The fugitive is in the *Panhandler*, a bar near the spaceport."

"And your name is...?" the dispatcher asked. The line went dead, ending the trace four seconds before complete. The dispatcher sighed and typed in a query for the name Jake Cutter. The screen flashed with a long list of offenses ending with CAPTURE IMMEDIATELY-ALPHA TEAM NOTIFICATON REQUIRED. The dispatcher bristled, in all her years she had only seen that order once. She shuddered as she keyed the microphone.

"Alpha Team. Priority Green Epsilon. Proceed to the *Panhandler*. Arrest and detain Captain Jake Cutter, wanted for murder, theft, smuggling, conspiracy, treason..." and the list went on.

Jake Cutter leaned on the bar, nursing his drink in silence. He stood between a Chandrillian and a Crendoshian, both of which towered above him. The Crendoshian jostled him, issued a soft growl in apology, and waved to the bartender for another drink. The human bartender, a rarity in the age of robotics, slid a quart sized jar down the bar's smooth surface. The Crendoshian caught it with practiced ease, stopping the glass without spilling a drop. The alien grunted his thanks, tossing a coin toward the human.

Jake observed the spectacle and surveyed the bar's countertop. Scratches, stains, and burns in the wood grain affirmed years of use and abuse. He raised his eyes toward the large mirror behind the bar, the view obscured by dozens of bottles of liquors. He looked above the mirror, looking for the drawing of an ostrich, before remembering he was not in a *Busty Ostrich Bar*. He felt somewhat diminished at the realization, smirked, and took a sip of his drink. Staring at his glass, he turned his attention to the conversations around him, listening for anyone showing more than a casual interest in the pilot.

The bar bustled with activity in the early afternoon with females of several species working the place for tricks. He felt a gentle tap on his shoulder and turned to see a Hazmora, her long, faux-blonde mane braided and decorated with flowers. She leaned in and whispered her proposal. Jake smiled, but politely declined. He took his drink and moved from the bar to a secluded corner table, hoping a less public place would dissuade further offers.

A large Chandrillian, her rabbit ears decorated with dozens of piercings, saddled over, and proved how wrong he could be. He declined her offer and sighed as a Blu'clic and a Klan'do lined up to take her place. The blue-skinned Blu'clic was very attractive in her tight-fitting shorts and a shirt that left very little to the imagination. Jake waved both off with a shake of his head, scooped up his empty glass, and returned to the bar, away from the Chandrillian and Crendoshian.

Jake ordered another drink, amazed by the non-robotic bartender, and turned his attention to a pair of old freighter pilots sitting nearby. They sat at a wooden table covered with empty glasses. Each man looked ancient; scars, tattoos, and leathered skin displayed to the universe that these men had seen it all, done it all, and lived to tell about it. Neither was drunk, but they were well on their way in the afternoon hours.

"You couldn't 'a flown with him," the first man pleaded with a vigorous shake of his head. "That was two hundred years ago."

The second man smiled, wagging his finger at the first pilot. "I didn't say I did." His words came out slightly slurred. "I said that my great-great grandfather led the mission that discovered the wreckage."

"I had a great-great uncle on that mission," the first man replied. He downed his drink and motioned to the Hazmora barmaid for another. "He was the one that found the voice recorder left by Captain Panz."

Jake turned back to the bar, leaving the two men to their conversation. He had learned the story of Captain Robert J. Panz in school twenty years earlier, just as every kid in the Heroz system did. He downed the shot in one gulp and ordered another drink, wondering how long it would take for the TSA to arrive. He had paid the T'traxi one hundred credits and a drink to make the call. He felt the alcohol light a fire in his belly and hoped it would not take too much longer.

Jake's thoughts drifted from the TSA, to the pilots at the nearby table, to his history lessons about Captain Panz. The story had inspired Jake to become a pilot, dreaming of someday leading an expedition across the stars to explore beyond the Tri-System. Jake shook his head, that dream was over.

Dreams. Jake recalled the last few restless nights, dwelling on Angel's words. *These dreams are sending you a message.* He was loath to admit it, but she was right. He had become cold, distant. Revenge was the focus of his life, and he knew that he would pay a heavy price. He vowed to do better; to be the man Grag knew him to be.

He slugged back the drink, *I just don't want Angel to pay that price as well.* There was enough heartbreak in his life, he did not want to add to it. Jake shook his head, erasing the morbid line of thought, and ordered another shot, and turned his attention back to the two old men still discussing the ill-fated flight of Captain Panz.

The Captain's life ended in tragedy. *He may have a planet, a city, and spaceport named after him, but he died in a freak accident of nature. Don't know if that's a fair trade.* Jake drained his drink.

"What do you think, young man?"

Jake turned to the two old freighter pilots. "I'm sorry, what?"

"Do you know the story of Captain Robert J. Panz?" one of the men asked.

Jake nodded. "Yes, sir. I remember the story from school."

The man let out a derisive laugh. "School? Book lernin' is fine, but you gotta get out there and *live*, son!"

Jake glanced at his watch, wondered briefly if the TSA would *ever* show up, and ordered another drink. The bartender prepared the non-alcoholic drink with a wink and slid it down the bar. Jake caught it like the Crendoshian, only spilling a drop or two. He smiled, leaned back against the bar, and turned to the two pilots. "Yes, sir. Get out and live."

The old man smiled, holding up his drink in salute. Jake returned the gesture and watched as the pilot downed his orange concoction in one gulp. He waved to the barmaid for another as his partner began the tale.

"Captain Panz changed the course of history. How many men can say that?" the second man asked, his bald head shone dully in the bad lighting of the bar. The bald crown accented the short cropped blonde hair encircling his skull. He wore a van dyke that matched his hair in both color and length. His blue eyes sparkled.

Jake smiled realizing that he had, against his will, been pulled into their world.

"Captain Panz, you see, he was the first man to volunteer for the deep space program." The first man chimed in. The old man wore his long white hair in a ponytail that trailed down his back. His grey beard came to a point halfway down his neck and his brown eyes held a treasure trove of knowledge and adventure.

The men took turns, each telling a part of the story and Jake realized that these two had told the story so many times that, in their minds, they *were* Captain Panz. Jake checked his watch again, shrugged, and settled in to listen while he waited.

"He launched about three hundred years ago," white beard said, his voice drifting as if he were recalling his own memory. "His course would have taken him to Zar'got. Of course, he didn't know that at the time," the man chuckled. "That old ship barely made system speed. You know, the trip was expected to take months."

"The first problem he encountered was a rogue comet," the bald man entered with his part of the story. He swirled his drink as he spoke. "That old ship got caught in the gravity well of that comet, you know. Pulled him right in and then slung him out the other side." His arms flailed as he spoke to emphasize the story. His half-full drink sloshed on the table but neither man noticed. They had an audience and they were not going to let him go.

"He ended up crashing here on Panz," white beard picked up the story. "No more than thirty kilometers from this very spot. You know there is a monument there?" The old man leaned over the table as if telling a secret. "Of course, it wasn't there when he got here, they put it up afterwards..."

Jake suppressed a smile and took a sip of his drink as the man continued.

"Even though he survived, his ship was a wreck, never to fly again." The man's voice held a hint of both storyteller and historian, with enough suspense to keep you on the edge of your seat. Jake was caught up in the moment despite himself. "Captain Panz knew that a rescue was months away, if ever. So, you know what he did?"

Jake shook his head involuntarily.

"He made a voice log of what had happened," baldy interjected, his voice all business. "Declared the planet in the name of Heroz and named it Panz."

"What happened to him?" Jake asked, enjoying the story.

The first man pointed a crooked finger at Jake. "I thought you lernt this in school?"

Jake nodded. "I did, but you tell it much better than my teachers."

The barmaid brought another round as the first man eyed Jake suspiciously for a moment, before filling his face with a huge grin. He continued with a flourish of hand gestures. "I'll tell ya what happened next. A piece of that darned ol' comet broke off and followed him down here." The old man tapped the table vigorously to emphasize the story. "Figure the odds of that."

The second man slapped the table lightly. "Boom! It hit right here! A hunk of rock half the size of a standard escape pod. Smacked down right here," he slapped the table again, harder this time, rattling a couple of the empty glasses. "The shock wave and dust storm killed everything within fifty kilometers, including the good Captain." His eyes sparkled as he pointed to the floor. "They built the spaceport in the impact crater."

"That was years later," grey beard interjected. "Almost a century after Captain Panz crashed. Another team of explorers, led by one of my ancestors..."

"And one of mine," the bald man added.

"...found the crater and created the first settlement off of Heroz. They named the spaceport 'Panhandler Port' and the city 'Panz City', after Captain Panz."

"They found the wreckage a month after they landed," baldy continued when grey beard stopped to take a drink. "They listened to the voice recorder and realized that they now had a spaceport, a city, and a whole damned planet named Panz."

Grey beard laughed. "They couldn't decide on anything else to name it, so they just left it." His contagious laughter infected his partner and Jake laughed despite himself.

The laughter died as the TSA team arrived. The door to the street slid open and the four-man team, dressed in black TSA armor with weapons drawn, stormed through the door. The policemen entered in standard breach formation. Left, right, left, right; they covered the room in seconds. Everyone in the bar froze, slowly turning their heads towards the TSA agents. The women working the bar moved into the shadows as the officers stood silently, slowly scanning the room. The third man in their formation locked eyes with Jake.

"Got him," the officer said, pointing his off-hand in Jake's direction.

The two old pilots turned their heads to stare at Jake. Jake downed his drink, smiled, and gave the men a wink. "Hold that thought, I'll be right back."

"You in some kinda trouble, son?" grey beard asked. He started out of his seat, pushing up his sleeves. The second old man also began rolling his sleeves up, a mischievous grin on his face. They froze as the nearest TSA officer turned his rifle in their direction.

Jake motioned for the two men to stand down as one of the TSA Officers started toward him. "Nah, this will only take a minute." He turned and faced the officer that had identified him.

"About time you got here," Jake said, holding out his empty hands. "I called a half hour ago."

The officer stopped a few feet away, obviously confused. He raised the armored mask to look at his prey eye to eye. The file reported the fugitive to be armed and extremely dangerous, not sarcastic. "You called?"

"Well, not me personally," Jake replied. He took a moment to look around before pointing to a drunk T'traxi at the end of the bar. "He did it."

The officer, along with two of his team and most of the bar, turned to look at the T'traxi at the opposite end of the bar. The crowd around the snouted-alien parted, leaving the T'traxi exposed. The drunk paused in mid-drink when he noticed that everyone stared at him. He lowered his drink and smiled innocently, before offering a timid wave.

Laser fire brought everyone's attention to a dark, corner booth.

A tall Hazmora with a long, braided mane, back-peddled away from the shadowy booth, blue electric currents ravaging his body. He yelped in pain, stumbled a few steps, and crashed into a table, sending the occupants and their drinks flying.

A second blue bolt blasted from the dark shadows near the front door of the bar, hitting the officer watching Jake in the back, sending electrical bolts arcing across the officer's body. He screamed as his body shut down, his knees buckled, and he collapsed on the faux wooden floor of the bar.

The other three officers turned at the scream. A third bolt appeared from the shadows, striking the man nearest the door. Blue electricity engulfing his body. He collapsed without a sound.

The TSA Officer nearest Jake turned in time to see Jake's fist. The punch connected and Jake was grateful the man had raised his visor. Blood flowed as the blow sent the man reeling backward, crashing into the last goon still standing. The corner booth fired a forth time. The stun bolt connected, electrifying both men. The man Jake had punched collapsed in a heap, his armor clanging as he hit the floor. The last TSA Officer spun and staggered a few steps before sprawling across a nearby table. The sturdy wood held as the officer twitched with electricity.

Jake shook his fist and grimaced. "I have got to stop hitting these guys!" He nodded his thanks as Angel emerged from the shadows. She nodded before holstering her pistol. Jake turned his attention back to the two old pilots. He waved to the barmaid and held up three fingers, nodding to their table.

Jake sat down at the table with the two freighter pilots as the drinks arrived. With a smug smile, Jake looked at the two storytellers and raised his glass,

"Here's to living!"

The two looked at the four TSA agents, then each other, before raising their glasses. "To livin'!'"

The wooden table gave way and the unconscious officer crashed to the floor.

Body armor and weapons lay strewn about the warehouse. Gentle sobs, punctuated occasionally by muffled cries, echoed in the vast, empty structure. To one side of the warehouse sat a trio of offices. The center room exhibited the only movement; shadows playing on the walls in the waning sunlight.

The far wall depicted the scene; a shadow hovering over a smaller shadow. The taller shadow raised an arm filled with a half-dozen limp tentacles, bringing the arm down sharply. The tentacles disappeared into the form of the second shadow with the sound of leather on flesh, followed by a muffled whimper.

"Where did the diplomatic pouch come from? The silver box you used to frame Jake." Anger and frustration permeated the feminine voice. "Who sent it?"

Silence met the question. Angel threw the leather cat of nine tails across the litter strewn room. She grabbed the man's shoulders, shaking him violently. He rocked side to side, his hands bound behind him as he slouched in a chair, but remained silent. "What the hell is wrong with you?" she screamed, her spittle splattering the man's bloody face. "All I want is a name!" The policeman, stripped naked and vulnerable, said nothing. He wore the bruises and cuts of a beating; ugly and misshapen, but nothing life-threatening.

Angel backed away as Jake entered the room from the left and, without preamble, grabbed the man, pulling him to his feet. The man wore his hatred for Jake like a cape. The fugitive pilot smiled, offering a look more menacing and deadly to the TSA operative. The man started to protest, to say something, but Jake shook his head, "Too late for you."

He turned to Angel as he shoved the man toward the door on the right side of the room. "Grab the next one. This one just died."

Angel nodded and retraced Jake's footsteps, entering the left-hand room. She grabbed the third TSA Officer who lay sprawled, semi-conscious, hands bound behind his back, on the floor. Dried blood stained his face from where Jake had punched him in the bar. She lifted, then escorted the man to the center room, dropping him into the chair as a laser shot echoed from the other room.

The woman smiled at the man in the chair as she retrieved her rolled leather strap. "That's two," she said, retracing her steps to stand before the chair. The Officers panicked eyes told her he was fully conscious now. "By now, you know what I want, and that you will take a beating if you don't tell me what I want to know. So, save us both the trouble and give me the name."

Angel saw the man's lip quiver. *Good, now we are getting somewhere,* she thought. She placed her hands on her hips. "I'm waiting."

"We were simply hired to pass the case on to the smuggler, Jorchlo'pan. We didn't know what was in it." The man's voice cracked. "Please," he pleaded. "I have a family." A tremble coursed through his body as Angel took a half step closer.

Angel's voice was ice. "Who. Sent. It?"

"The Secretary."

"The Secretary of what?" The man jumped at the sound of Jake's voice behind him.

"The Secretary of TSA Commerce," the officer murmured, his head hung low. "Dante Terra."

Angel looked at Jake. Confirmation.

Jake walked around to face the man in the chair. "Why? Why would this man be after me?"

"I don't know!" the agent screamed and began struggling with his bonds. "I don't know why. I don't know what was in the case. I don't know, I don't know, I DON'T KNOW!" Exhaustion overcame the panic and the man slumped, sobbing. "I don't know," he murmured.

"Please don't kill me," he pleaded over and over. "Please don't kill me."

Jake shook his head and sighed. "I'm not going to kill you." He drew his pistol and shot the man in the chest. He abruptly turned and shot the last TSA Agent who sat tied up in the next room. The man's eyes, wide in shock, closed as the stun bolt shut down his system.

"Let's get out of here before the rest of the TSA tracks these four down," Jake said as he gathered his jacket from a nearby chair. Angel nodded, packing her belongings.

"Bruised, but alive," she smiled looking at the four men spread out in the three rooms. "Thank you, Jake."

He nodded as they walked to the warehouse entrance, but said nothing.

"And we have confirmation of what Mark told us," she continued.

"Dante Terra," Jake confirmed. He shook his head. "But I still have no idea why he wants me dead."

Chapter Twenty-Three

"We are twenty-three minutes from the edge of the nebula," Jake said, spinning his chair around from the navigation console and facing forward. The purple and green illumination of the nebula cast eerie shadows in the cockpit. He squinted against the odd light and checked the calculations on his screen. Nodding, he turned toward Angel sitting in the co-pilot's chair. She stared out of the cockpit window at the mesmerizing light show. "Can you send a message to Mark?" he asked. "Make sure our exit vector is clear?"

The two had contacted Dawson before leaving Panz two days earlier. His image looked haggard on the screen, tired. He waved off their concerns.

"You two need to leave Panz immediately," he warned. "The TSA knows you captured their retrieval team. They have dispatched a Corvette and two Pickets in support. They will be at the nebula's edge in sixteen hours.

"If you take an elliptical course," he continued,

running a hand through his unkempt blonde hair, "you can pass them in the nebula and they'll never know. I'm transmitting the coordinates for rendezvous. I'll be there in forty hours. That'll give you plenty of time. Contact me when you're close." The line went dead.

The coordinates arrived as promised, along with a dossier on Secretary Dante Terra. Jake set a looping course for the coordinates before opening the data-pad with the biography of the TSA Secretary of Commerce. The biography contained the standard information, nothing that Jake could exploit.

Raised by a wealthy family, Dante Terra was destined to follow in his mother's political footsteps. He started small—district council—before moving up the ladder to regional governor. Terra was appointed to the Department of Commerce after negotiating a successful trade deal for his region. Married two years earlier to Dari, no children.

Angel nodded her acknowledgement of Jake's request and reached for the controls on the headset she wore. She adjusted the comm to the secure frequency the TSA Officer had provided and touched the toggle button. "TSA Scout *Overwatch*, this is the *Freelancer*. Do you copy?"

Static.

"TSA Scout *Overwatch*, this is the *Freelancer*. Do you copy?" she repeated.

The comm chirped with Dawson's distorted, undecipherable message. Angel touched a series of buttons on the console behind her and the comm emitted an ear-splitting whine. She winced, adjusting the gain. The whine subsided and Dawson's message came through, broken but clear.

"At rende..." the message began. "...Corvette led...one beh...waiting...trouble...trap."

"Mark? Mark!" Angel yelled, adjusting the controls again. "Repeat your message."

Mark Dawson banked to starboard, guiding his unarmed scout out of the line of fire of the TSA Picket. The picket, designed as a quick interdiction vessel, sat nearly twice the size of the scout and while the two ships were roughly the same shape, the scout counted on superior speed and maneuverability to ward off its enemies. The picket simply obliterated them with state-of-the-art particle cannons and missiles.

Mark executed a barrel roll to escape the red laser bolts bouncing off the shields. The energy barrier flared into existence with each impact. He straightened out his course and stomped on the left pedal at his feet. The scout slid through space losing velocity, and turned to face its pursuer. Dawson slammed the throttle forward, rolling the scout and flying underneath the larger vessel. Another dozen laser impacts rocked the small scout before it left the picket behind.

"I'm at the rendezvous," he answered Angel's message. Her message was garbled, but it sounded like they were only a few minutes out. "The Corvette led one Picket into the nebula, but left one behind. It was waiting when I arrived. I'm in trouble. Do not leave the nebula, it's a trap!"

A warning light blinked and Dawson checked the rear screens. Two missiles streaked from the picket as it began a wide turn to pursue the scout. The warheads appeared to pause for a moment before finding their target, locking on, and zipping toward the fleeing ship.

"Not good." Dawson wished for the thousandth time he had been given a fighter. It would have been more uncomfortable and cramped, but at least he would have a better chance to survive an attack. He shook his head and reached to his left, activating the only weapon the scout possessed. The high-tech jamming system.

The TSA designed their scouts to infiltrate a system undetected. That required a sophisticated jamming system that rendered the scout invisible and, in the event of discovery, squelch all communications. He had jammed the picket's comms the second he saw it on the edge of the nebula, sitting, waiting. Now, he hoped to jam the missile targeting system. He flipped the switch.

The missiles maintained their lock, gaining on the scout.

"Not good," he repeated and changed course toward the nebula. The missiles followed, gaining. The TSA Picket *Audacity* adjusted its course in an attempt to cut off his escape. Mark mentally calculated the converging lines on his sensors and saw the lines converge in his mind. He would make the nebula.

In pieces.

The lines converged a few kilometers short of freedom.

The comm crackled to life and Angel's voice filled the cockpit. "Hang on Mark, we're coming."

Sensor distortion cleared and warning klaxons filled the air as the *Freelancer* exited the nebula. Angel winced, remembering that she was going to disconnect that circuit. She hit a button on the panel beside her and the noise faded. She felt the freighter bank sharply.

"Angle the shields forward," Jake ordered.

Angel complied before looking out of the canopy. She gripped the arms of her chair tighter as Jake flew directly over a TSA Scout. She saw Mark Dawson in the cockpit window, ducking as the freighter roared overhead. He disappeared from view in a flash, the scout behind them.

Explosions engulfed the *Freelancer* as Jake fired the freighter's cannons, destroying the missiles in one pass. Angel cringed as brilliant flashes of light and expanding fireballs replaced the warheads. The ship rocked violently as it passed through the shock waves, coming nose-to-nose with the TSA Picket. The two ships rivalled each other in size. The picket maintained the edge in firepower, the Trillinden freighter in maneuverability.

And the *Freelancer* had surprise on its side.

Angel's knuckles dug into her chair as Jake nosed the *Freelancer* down, flying underneath the TSA Picket. She watched as the freighter's dorsal cannons—one forward and one aft—rocked the *Audacity* from stem to stern. Explosions of light and shield impact flares activated the *Freelancer's* cockpit glare shield.

The *Audacity* opened fire on the freighter. Bright red energy bolts traced behind the fleeing freighter, never making contact. Jake flipped the *Freelancer* over and reversed course in one motion while the picket was still making its turn to pursue. He activated the belly cannons; the freighter's bolts striking the TSA ships shields in a second strafing run. The shields flared, but held, and the *Freelancer* streaked away into open space. The canopy flare shield returned to normal.

"Missile lock," Angel called out as her screen registered two launches from the TSA Picket. The missiles acquired their target and streaked toward the *Freelancer*. Jake rolled the freighter, changing course back toward the *Audacity* as it emerged from its turn. Angel, seeing a target of opportunity, trained the freighters weapons on the TSA vessel's bridge, and opened fire.

The *Audacity's* shields flashed with the impacts of the focused energy beams. The TSA Picket returned fire and the *Freelancer* rocked from multiple impacts. Jake maintained his course directly toward the enemy vessel. Angel cinched her seat harness a little tighter and continued to fire.

"Jake, the missiles are closing. Jake!"

The missiles flew directly into the path of the *Audacity's* fire and exploded underneath the TSA ship. Powerful, dual explosions rocked the ship, blasting through the weakened shields protecting the bridge. Angel turned the *Freelancer's* cannons aft and fired.

Explosions rocked the picket, dispelling atmosphere and crew from the fractured bridge. The engines stuttered and failed. Lights flashed on and off. The ship stalled, hanging silently in space, before ripping in two as the reactor core breached. The *Freelancer's* glare shield reactivated as a rolling fireball engulfed the *Audacity*.

The explosion dissipated, leaving a small debris field as the only sign the picket was even there. Angel let out a breath as Jake sat back in his seat. She saw him grin before movement caught her eye. The TSA Scout *Overwatch* wove into view, coming alongside starboard. Dawson waved and Angel returned the gesture.

The comm crackled to life. "I see you didn't get my message," Dawson's voice filtered through the speaker. Even metallic and disembodied, Angel heard the relief in his voice.

"Yes," Angel replied. "Good thing you left that one comm line open."

"We got it," Jake interrupted. "But I ignored it."

"Thanks," came the reply. "I owe you one."

"We still owe you," Angel interjected. "You kept us alive on Cla'nix."

"What next?" Dawson asked, changing the subject.

"We head to Heroz," Jake said. "Your dossier was helpful, but we need more intel before the plan can be finalized."

"We have a plan?" Angel asked. "First I've heard of it."

Jake smiled. "I'm working on it." He turned to look through the cockpit canopy at Dawson. "I'm transmitting an address to you. Meet us there in two days.

"In the meantime," Jake said, "I need you to do something for me..."

Chapter Twenty-Four

The city skyline stretched to meet the distant curve of the hazy horizon. Towering buildings reached toward the cloudy sky as a multitude of brightly colored air cars zig-zagged in between them. Lights winked on and off in apartments and businesses. Strobes flashed at frequent intervals on top of the tallest buildings; a warning to approaching craft. The roar of a starship occasionally blanketed the usual city noises.

Large electronic billboards, some the size of entire city blocks, jutted from the tallest buildings, broadcasting news, and civic alerts. The citizens of Heroz filled the streets, walking shoulder to shoulder in the congested capitol of the Tri-System Authority. A few would occasionally glance up at the large flashing panels to be informed, entertained, or warned, depending on the circumstance.

Jake Cutter watched the spectacle, including the massive advertisement billboards, from his vantage point across a flowing river along the northern boundary of the city. He stood, arms crossed, his attention crossing from billboard to billboard. The wind whipped his shirt, but he paid it no mind, his focus elsewhere.

Memories invaded his conscious.

Jake worked construction before getting his commercial pilot's license, installing billboards like these all over the planet. He briefly pondered which of the massive panels he had worked on and shook his head, realizing it did not matter. His mind wondered, trying to recall the life he once had in this city; a wife, a burgeoning family, and a career he mostly enjoyed. Specifics escaped him, only brief images of faces and fleeting remnants of emotion remained.

Angel stood beside him, shivering in the damp, cold, early evening breeze. She pulled her leather jacket tighter. Jake caught the movement out of the corner of his eyes but said nothing. He turned his attention to a police cruiser patrolling along the river, spotlights playing along the shore. His eyes followed the air-car as it continued its course downstream, until he lost contact with it as it turned sharply, activated its siren lights, and raced back into the city.

Jake turned his back to the water and faced the dilapidated house that he had once called home. The house sagged on its foundation, the roof sat partially caved in. Half of the windows were cracked and broken. He stared at the fire ravaged front porch and he imagined the worst possible scenarios for his family.

He shook his head. Former family.

Jake put his imagination aside, recalling instead many nights sitting on the porch and tracing the city skyline with his eyes. The memories, momentarily clear, made his heart ache and he shook his head again. *You've got work to do,* he admonished himself. *No time for what-ifs or sad memories. Get to work!*

Jake's eyes focused on the holographic sign in the front yard as it cycled between *NO TRESSPASSING* and *CONDEMNED*, its yellow glow shining in the dim light of dusk. He watched the words flash for several minutes before he felt a tap on his shoulder.

"Jake," Angel called, her voice a distant call to the recesses of his mind.

He stepped into the yard and carefully examined the remains of his former home. Angel tried to call to him again, but the roar of an arriving freighter drowned out her words. He looked up, watching the freighter cross the sky; a dark shadow against the overcast dusk. His thoughts drifted to the last time he had sat on the porch with Pamela. Almost three years ago. Jake felt a tear slide down his cheek.

"Jake," Angel called again as the rumble of the freighter faded. He motioned for her to stay on the edge of the street while he took another step toward the house. He needed to find out what happened. Another step. *Was Pamela home?* Another step. *Did she survive the fire?* Another step closer. *Where was she now?*

Soft hands gripped his shoulder and spun him around. Reflex and instinct took over; he batted the hands away, took a step back, and raised his fists to counterattack. He paused when he saw Angel stepping away from him, her hands up ready to defend. She lowered her fist, offering an open hand to her partner. "Jake," her voice barely above a whisper, "it's time to go."

"I'm not done here," he replied, lowering his own fists and ignoring her hand. "I need to find out what happened." He turned back to the dilapidated house.

"What happened is that she left you," Angel said, her voice cold and harsh. "The house is destroyed and she is gone." The woman shook her head. "How did I let you talk me into coming here?"

Jake slowly turned to face Angel, pain and anger in his eyes. His words were slow, deliberate, and pained. "Because I need answers. I need to know why my life went straight to hell." His voice drifted, searching for words.

"We know that Dante Terra did this to you—" Angel began.

"But *why*?" he cried.

She touched his face, lifting his sad eyes to stare into hers. "Those answers won't be found here," she replied with a warmer tone. "Those answers lie with Dante Terra." She pointed to a well-lit complex of buildings on the horizon, "and Parliament."

Jake sighed and his shoulder's slumped. His eyes lifted from her face, drifting across the city. He squinted to focus on the distant billboards as all of them displayed the same message. A chill coursed down his spine. Angel turned to follow his stare.

The city billboards showed an image of Jake Cutter

in a prison jumpsuit. Jake's hologram rotated, showing his profile, as a list of charges scrolled to the side. The writing was too small to see, but the length of the list left little doubt to the extent of the criminal activity. Jake's image was replaced by a man with a dark complexion, well-groomed mustache, and smooth, slicked back, black hair. A caption in bold letters underneath the man read *DANTE TERRA, SECRETARY OF COMMERCE*.

The man spoke for several moments, but the sound did not carry across the quarter-kilometer wide river. Jake turned away from the image as anger burned its way through his body. He clenched his fists and stared at his fire ravaged home. He heard Angel muttering to herself and turned to see her staring at the billboard.

"The man is traveling with an unknown woman," she said and Jake realized she was lip reading. He faced the billboard, watching as she narrated. "He is considered armed and dangerous, an enemy of the state. There is a substantial reward for his capture, dead or alive."

A woman joined Secretary Terra on the screen. She was slender, elegant in a black dress. Brunette hair spilled over her shoulders. Jewelry adorned her neckline and fingers. The caption read *DARI TERRA*.

"This man must be brought to justice," Angel read the woman's lips. "He has threatened my husband's life, and mine. We need your help to stop him."

Jake stared at the billboard, his mouth open. A wave of anguish washed over him. His vision blurred. He gasped for breath, every cell in his body burned in agony. He collapsed to his knees and vomited.

"Jake!" Angel called, rushing to his side. She lifted his head and stared into listless eyes. Tears streamed down his face. "Jake, what's wrong?"

He attempted to answer, tasted only the bile in his mouth. He shook his head. He felt the weight of the universe squarely on his shoulders. He pointed a shaking finger at the distant billboards. Angel followed his hand and saw the woman smiling as she stood arm-in-arm with her husband. Angel turned her eyes back to Jake. "Jake, that's Dari Terra, his wife."

Jake shook his head. "No," he choked. He wiped his mouth with his sleeve, forcing air into his lungs. He forced his voice to function. "Not...his...wife." He shook his head, sucking in another breath. "Mine."

Angel turned to stare at the hologram for several seconds before facing Jake again. "Pamela?" she asked, confused.

He nodded and, with Angel's assistance, slowly staggered to his feet. Pain etched each word he said. "He framed me. He framed me to get her." He closed his eyes and leaned on Angel, who supported his weight and kept him upright. His breathing came in ragged gulps as if each was a struggle. "Why?"

Another police cruiser made its way down the shoreline, spotlights lighting the way. Angel pulled Jake away from the burnt-out house, back in the direction of the spaceport. "We need to leave, Jake. There's nothing else you can do here."

"Nothing," he murmured. He stood straight, steadying himself by force of will. He heard Angel sigh in relief as his weight lifted. "Nothing left to do here…" he mocked her earlier comment.

He turned, leading them deeper into shadow, moving in the general direction of the spaceport. "We need to get back to the ship and contact Dawson," he said. He quickened his pace as a distant freighter lifted into the night. "We are going to need his help to get to the Secretary."

Chapter Twenty-Five

"This is reckless," Mark Dawson admonished, staring at Jake Cutter. The two, along with Angel, stood at the base of the ramp to the *Freelancer*. The ship, under false transponder codes and docking papers, sat nestled on a landing platform in Heroz spaceport. Flood lights dispelled the darkness around the platform, chasing shadows away from the trio. Jake pushed his arm into an open plate above the ramp. He peered into the panel, squinting against the darkness, standing on his tiptoes.

"You are going to get yourselves killed," Dawson finished.

Dawn lit the western sky. Streaks of emerald and ruby strobed the darkness, pushing the stars to the east. Sounds of an awakening city permeated the new light, punctuated by the sound of another freighter lifting from the spaceport that seemed to never sleep. The roar of the engines drowned everything as it lifted from the next pad over. Jake, Angel, and Mark each lowered their heads and shielded their eyes as the exhaust, dust, and debris washed over them.

Jake yelped and jerked his hand free of the ship in a shower of sparks. The freighter's lights dimmed for a count of two before returning to normal. Jake dropped the transponder circuit board onto the tarmac and shook his hand before bringing it to his mouth. He sucked on his index finger and turned to face the TSA Officer. "It's a distraction."

"That is going to get you killed," Dawson reiterated.

"Boys," Angel chimed in. "Parliament is in session in two hours. Do you think you two will have this out of your system by then?"

The two men looked at each other, then to Angel. "No," they said in unison.

"Then I officially take command," she placed her hands on her hips, defiantly. She smiled, hoping that her attempt at levity would break up the tension they all felt.

The men smiled, nodding their acceptance of her leadership. They looked at each other, and then stood at crisp attention.

"Awaiting orders, ma'am," Dawson said.

Angel laughed despite herself, not sure to be angry, frightened, or relieved. She nodded, staring each in the eye as she spoke. "Jake, finish with the transponder. We need all of their attention on the ship."

Jake nodded.

"Mark," she continued. "You probably need to get moving. It'll take a while to get in orbit. Once you are in position, send the signal."

"Yes, ma'am."

"Parliament begins their session in two hours," she finished, feeling her hands begin to shake. "We hit them in three."

"Lieutenant Dawson, a word."

Dawson froze at the mention of his name, turning slowly to face his commanding officer, Lieutenant Commander Dagon Aoffa. The Lieutenant Commander stood in his dress uniform, medals dangling over his right breast pocket. He carried a large bag in his left hand, his right hand empty. Mark snapped to attention, rendering a salute. "Sir."

"You should know that I have filed a report highlighting your gross negligence concerning the apprehension of the fugitives," Aoffa said, returning the salute. "I recommended that you be formally reprimanded, and then discharged immediately." He dropped the bag and stepped closer to Dawson.

"We have lost a squad of officers, and a ship and crew of fifty-three due to your incompetence," he explained. "And do you know what I received for my recommendation?" Anger filled his voice. "I have been reassigned, because I apparently cannot tell incompetent officers from good ones."

His fists clinched and Dawson half expected Aoffa to swing at him, but the officer's demeanor changed, his shoulders slumped, and a look of sadness filled his face.

"Command feels that if I had assigned a different

officer, this matter would have been put to rest already," he voiced trailed off.

"I'm sorry, sir," Dawson said sincerely.

"I don't want your pity," Aoffa spat. "Your fate is yet to be determined, but I'd wager it will take a miracle to salvage your career." Anger flashed in his eyes, as he wagged his finger at Dawson. "You have made an enemy, Lieutenant. You better pray our paths never cross again."

The man turned, grabbed his bag, and left Dawson standing on the gantry leading to the pad and his scout.

Mark watched him leave. He shook his head, turned, and hurried to his ship a few hundred meters away. *If they transferred him, my recall can't be far behind.*

He boarded the scout and made his way to the single person cockpit. He dropped into the seat and began flipping switches to add power to the systems of the craft. A vibrant hum filled the scout. Mark strapped himself into the pilot's chair and wondered briefly what lay in store for him.

The odds were against them, he knew. Jake's scheme held too many moving parts; too many variables that could lead to disaster. Add to that the threat from Aoffa that Dawson's career would soon be over. He scoffed. *If I survive today, I'll worry about my career.*

With green lights across the board, he applied power to the thrusters, lifting the scout off the pad. He verified his clearance and set course for low orbit. He had a lot of work to do and time was running out.

"Angel," Jake said, "it's not too late to back out."

The two sat in the *Freelancer's* galley, half-eaten plates on the table between them. A long, sullen silence permeated the ship, neither had spoken during the entire meal. Jake tugged at the collar of his suit shirt as he waited for Angel's reaction.

"Yes." Angel countered, her face flushing. "Yes, it is."

"No, it's not," Jake protested. "You don't have to do this. I...I don't *want* you to do this. You can run, hide," he shook his head. "Go and live your life. Mark can help you find a—"

"I cannot survive on my own," Angel interrupted, shaking her head. "Not if I'm on the run. I've always had someone there with me. My father, Grag, you." She stared into his eyes. "I need you as much as you need me."

"I don't want you to get hurt," Jake said sadly.

"If I do," she smiled, "it'll be standing beside you."

The comm chimed; a single, long burst of static.

She stood, adjusting the long coat she wore. "The wheels are in motion. We will never get this opportunity again." Jake felt her gaze bore into his soul. "So, what's it going to be?"

He slowly stood. He swept the tales of the long coat he wore over the back of the chair. Her confidence—her loyalty—affirmed his resolve. "Let's go."

Spaceport Control Systems Computer 387-M9 registered the Trillinden freighter *Freelancer* requesting clearance to lift from the Heroz Spaceport. The computer attempted to verify the transponder code and produced an error. The ship launching from pad ninety-four broadcasted a different signal than the one that had landed two days earlier.

The computer ran a trace on the new code and produced another error. That transponder was registered to the TSA as a transport freighter from Cla'nix prison. Cla'nix prison raised another error and the computer immediately denied clearance.

Ensign Torem Klorig joined the TSA to see the universe, or at least get out of the hovel he had grown up in on the outskirts of Heroz city. He had worked hard, studying engineering, astrometrics, navigation; anything to make him valuable to a space bound freighter. When he could not book passage on any freighter leaving his home world, he enlisted in the TSA.

Thanks to his studies, he excelled in his training and was selected into the Officer Corps. Months of hazing, studying, and physical training paid off and he graduated as a TSA Officer. He recalled opening his assignment orders with shaky hands. All of the months and years of training and study all led to this moment. He opened his orders and felt his spirits sink.

"Ensign Torem Klorig," he read, "You are assigned to Spaceport Authority, Heroz Spaceport." Less than five kilometers from the hovel he grew up in.

Eight months and he still sat in a cubicle, in the corner of a server farm four stories beneath the spaceport. He propped his feet up, leaning back in his chair as he played a computer game on his data-pad. His thumbs flew over the screen, guiding his holo-character through a maze of underground tunnels. A computer-generated monster leaped from behind a tangle of vines and swallowed his character in one gulp.

Torem jumped at the sudden appearance of the monster and cursed as the holographic characters dissolved, replaced with the floating letters YOU LOSE. He tossed the data pad aside and looked at his surroundings. He smirked, and said aloud, "Yeah, I lost. But at least I can't *see* Heroz." The computer banks that ran the spaceport remained silent save for their near constant beeps and whirs.

His desktop computer beeped, displaying a message about an anomaly on an outbound freighter. Torem casually scanned the message and the computer's hold on the lift. He approved the hold and the screen went blank. He picked up the pad to start a new game, trying to remember where the monster was hidden, when the computer beeped again. He read the message, sighed as he put down his data-pad, and keyed the comm.

"*Freelancer*," he said, boredom filling his voice. "You are not authorized to lift. Shut down your engines." He read the readout and perked up. Something was not right. "TSA Officials are en route to your location."

Silence filled the comm and the Ensign reached for the transmit key to repeat the message when it crackled to life. The computers automatically recorded the message, analyzing voice patterns.

"I'm not going back to prison," the voice said. "We are lifting. You tell anyone above us to get out of the way!"

The computer beeped a warning as voice ID confirmed the voice of Jake Cutter. His information— a picture and the charges against him—rolled across the screen. The Ensign keyed the mic. "You are not authorized to depart, *Freelancer*," he read. "Stand down or be..." he gulped, "...or be destroyed."

"I'm not going back!" the voice repeated.

The Spaceport computers declared the ship was lifting.

The pilot applied thrust, lifting the ship off the tarmac in a cloud of dust and exhaust. The computer blared a warning as a disembodied voice on the comm called for the ship to power down. The *Freelancer* rotated, setting a course over the city in the hopes they would not shoot them down over a populated area. Warning klaxons blared as weapon emplacements locked on.

The pilot threw the throttle forward and the engines flared. The freighter roared from the spaceport, banking on its starboard side to sideslip an incoming tug. The pilot leveled the ship, only to stand it on its side again to slip between a pair of thousand story skyscrapers.

The first rounds impacted as the ship emerged from between the towers. Shields flared with the hits, faded blue energy dissipating the bright red laser bolts. The ship righted itself again and dropped, flying low over the city. Missile lock alarms added to the cacophony of warnings already sounding through the ship. The pilot ignored them as he banked the ship starboard, toward another high rise. The ship rolled to port, flying so close to the building that the pilot could see the occupants through the cockpit window.

"Bad idea," he muttered and leveled out the ship. "No civilian casualties." He nosed the ship skyward, applying full thrust. More missile locks sounded, adding another layer to the already deafening chorus of klaxons. The pilot ignored it all, changing course and diving toward the outskirts of the city.

A missile impact jarred the controls and the pilot rolled the ship, taking the next four missile strikes on the dorsal shields. Those shields failed and sparks showered the cockpit. The pilot rolled the *Freelancer* in time to absorb the next half dozen impacts on the ventral shields. They collapsed as well, leaving the ship vulnerable, and the last missile in the salvo struck the hull.

Fire raged through the interior of the freighter scorching everything in reach. The missile blew a three-meter hole in the hull, depressurizing the main cabin. The pilot heard the whistle of wind as he tried to pull up from his dive, the controls sluggish and heavy in his hands. The *Freelancer* leveled off a dozen meters over a busy hover-car transit. The engines flared, exhaust knocking a few cars out of their assigned lanes.

Lasers streaked across the sky as the freighter entered the target range of the city's southern batteries. Red laser bolts impacted the ship, jostling the ship in a continuous barrage. The pilot pulled the nose up, sending the freighter skyward, and making it more of a target. Another volley of laser bolts, followed by a salvo of four missiles, robbed the *Freelancer* of thrust. The ship reeled, stalling in mid-air, as red bolt after red bolt impacted the ship.

A final missile streaked from a hidden weapons emplacement ten kilometers away. The computer controlled missile locked onto target, speeding skyward. The freighter sat, stalled with engines toward the ground, suspended in mid-air. The missile covered the ten kilometers in seconds, impacting the ship aft, right above the pair of dorsal engines. The missile detonated, rupturing the reactor core.

The *Freelancer* exploded in a flash of blinding light, scattering debris for a dozen kilometers in the grasslands south of the capital city.

Chapter Twenty-Six

Chaos gripped Heroz City. The *Freelancer* roared overhead, missiles exploding against the freighter's shields. Sirens wailed. Aliens and humans paused their routines to look skyward, watching in horror the firefight above their heads. The flash of laser bolts and the zip of missiles overcame the initial shock, sending the residents scurrying for cover. Screams of terror and panic filled the city, reverberating off the tall glass and steel skyscrapers. Hover-cars, their drivers distracted by the firefight, crashed into each other, creating more confusion and gridlock in the crowded city.

Security forces scrambled. Fighters and pickets launched from the spaceport to pursue the freighter. TSA Officers filled the streets in an attempt to protect key facilities: financial institutions, government buildings, and key infrastructure—utilities—the top priority. Panicked crowds engulfed the officers, halting their advances. Humans and aliens filled doorways, alleys, and rushed hardened buildings. The peace enforcers found themselves swept along by the flow of the crowd seeking shelter against the raging firefight overhead.

Jake and Angel ran for the guarded doors of Parliament as the first sirens filled the city. Among the first to arrive, they pushed their way through the growing throng of people. The crowd parted as security forces deployed out of the government building. Jake used his proximity to the entrance to get to the nearest guard and flash documents provided by Dawson. Jake and Angel were ushered inside. Seeing the two let in, the citizens rushed the gate. Jake watched as security lowered a metal gate from the ceiling, effectively locking him inside and the rest of the city out. The panicked crowd pushed against the blast-proof glass façade of the building, screaming.

Four TSA Security Officers stood at the entrance, each more interested in the crowd outside than the two humans with credentials in their midst. One guard, her visor open and hand resting on the grip of her rifle, turned to Jake and Angel. "Sir, Ma'am," she said with a nod to each. "I'm afraid you'll have to stay here until the incident is over."

"What's going on?" Angel asked. She wore a red shirt with a black skirt that hung down to her ankles. Her dark hair was tied in a small ponytail that hung down past her shoulders. She gripped a small handbag in her hands as her eyes shifted nervously from the crowd to the TSA woman.

"I'm not sure," the TSA Officer replied. "Radio chatter indicates some kind of fugitive tried to escape the city in a stolen freighter." She pointed to a screen on the wall. Distant security cameras captured lasers and missiles pummeling a Trillinden freighter. The ship nosed up, hovering in a stall, before additional impacts forced an explosion. Debris rained down as the screen went blank.

Jake winced at the sight of his ship exploding.

A resounding boom echoed through the city, sending already panicked citizens diving for cover. Shock waves from the *Freelancer's* explosion rocked the city, swaying the tallest buildings, and shattering windows throughout the metroplex. Everyone ducked as the shock wave washed over the Parliament Building.

The lights flickered twice before winking out. Emergency batteries actuated, providing minimal lighting in the foyer. Two guards watched the crowd swelling against the gate, but the security structure held. One guard approached the security desk, flipped a few switches, and shook their armored head.

"Comms and cameras are out." Jake thought the muffled voice male, possibly Hazmora. "EMP?"

The female TSA Officer standing next to Jake shrugged. "At least the chemical backups are working," she said, pointing to the emergency lights. She turned and offered a reassuring smile to her two charges. "I think that it's over. But, as you can see, the power has been compromised. Once it has been restored, you will be allowed to go to your offices."

"Thank you," Jake said, reaching underneath the long trench coat he wore. He drew a pistol from his right hip, flicking off the safety as he raised the weapon. He fired as the pistol came even with the woman's chest.

The TSA Officer's eyes bulged as she saw the weapon and opened her mouth to yell. The stun bolt, delivered at near point-blank range, cut her warning short. She flew backwards, sliding several meters on the slick, waxed floor before stopping against the security checkpoint desk.

Jake spun and dropped to his left knee as he acquired his next target. The closest TSA Officer, a Blu'clic with a confused expression, took the next blast. He folded as the electric current overloaded his system. Jake acquired his next target and tightened his finger on the trigger as Angel fired. The male human screamed as the stun bolt hit him in the groin. Jake shifted to the final officer.

The fourth member of the checkpoint team was a small Traxillian. The small, blue alien dove for cover behind a chair in the posh lobby, firing a shot blindly as she flew through the air. She landed on her shoulder and tried to roll to her feet. The waxed floor caused her to skid and she slid into the wall head first. She slumped and lay on the floor, unmoving.

Angel leapt over a chair, careful not to lose her balance on the waxed floor, and moved to the TSA Officer's side. She removed the helmet and checked for a pulse. Finding it strong and steady, Angel stood and breathed a sigh of relief. She turned to Jake and nodded, before firing a stun bolt into the sleeping officer.

Jake offered her an inquiring look.

"Just in case," she shrugged. Angel checked each officer in turn as she made her way back to Jake, finding each had a strong pulse.

Jake holstered his pistol and checked his chrono. He expected to feel more anxious, but found a calm resolve embraced his body. "Ready?"

Angel took a deep breath and exhaled slowly. She nodded.

"Three stories up and six hundred meters east," Jake recited, recalling the route from memory.

"I hope Mark made it," Angel mused as the two started moving down the pristine corridor.

"We'll find out soon enough," Jake nodded.

Mark Dawson felt the impact of each missile and laser as he maneuvered the *Freelancer* across the Herozian sky. The tap into the city's security feed provided an exterior view of the ship, and he watched the impacts like an out of body experience. The controls grew sluggish, heavy in his hands as the freighter took damage. The system warned of another missile lock and he watched the final missile strike the freighter. He threw his hands in the air as the controls went dead.

He exhaled a long, ragged breath as he watched the debris rain down on the plains south of the city. He lowered his head, knowing he had completed his mission; the freighter exploded outside of the population center. He slid his chair from the remote-control station onboard his scout and into the pilot's position.

The Scout sat in low orbit, among a cluster of orbiting satellites that provided security and communication to the capitol city. Dawson verified his position and tuned into the security traffic of the city. As expected, everything revolved around the destruction of the freighter, but he knew that would soon change. Once the alarms rang out in Parliament, the *Freelancer* would be forgotten, and he would begin phase two.

He turned up the volume and sat back in his chair. All he had to do was wait and then jam the system at the appropriate time. He sighed, exhaling slowly. Waiting was the hardest part.

And he hated waiting.

Lieutenant David Derez watched the freighter explosion from his fifth-floor vantage point of the security annex building. Although technically assigned as special security to Secretary Terra—a job he hated— he had unofficially been placed in charge of fugitive retrieval, with the primary focus on apprehending Jake Cutter. *That* job he cherished, and felt confident that he would soon capture the fugitive. His brown eyes watched the debris fall with little interest.

Would have.

He shook his head, his brown, longer-than-regulation hair waving with the motion. "Something's not right," he muttered. He left the wall of windows and crossed the sparse office to his computer desk. He recalled the profile compiled on his target. He leaned forward, fists propping him up as he hovered over the desk. His eyes skimmed the screen and he shook his head again. "Cutter is intelligent," he read, "resourceful, blah, blah, blah, but not suicidal." He stood, brushing the hair from his eyes. He tapped the intercom on his desk as he grabbed his coat from the back of his chair.

"Sir?" the intercom asked.

"Prepare a shuttle," Derez ordered. "I need to get to the Parliament Building."

"Sir, TSA Air Control has grounded all aircraft except for CAP," the voice responded.

"I don't give a damn about combat air patrols," Derez announced harshly. "I want a shuttle on the roof in five minutes or I'm throwing you off the roof. Understand?"

"Sir," the intercom gulped.

"Give them my priority clearance code," the fugitive retrieval officer commanded. He opened a drawer and removed a belt with a holster and laser pistol. He strapped on the belt, tying the holster to his left leg. He removed the pistol, inspecting the weapon to ensure a full charge. He nodded as another thought struck him.

"They had to have help," he said aloud.

"Sir?" the intercom asked.

Derez smiled, pounding his fist on the desk. "They

had to have help!" he repeated before addressing the intercom.

"Have the CAP look for other craft in the vicinity. They are looking for a ship with remote capabilities; an interceptor, corvette or..." He returned to the computer screen and read more details in Cutter's file.

He stood straight, smiling. "...or a scout. Have the CAP check orbital ships as well."

"What are they looking for?" the intercom voice inquired.

"Traitors," Derez said, sliding the pistol back into its holster. "Now where is my shuttle?"

Jake and Angel had traversed almost a third of the ground floor of Parliament before finding a set of stairs to the second floor. The first floor typically served as a front for visitors with posh furniture, rich tapestries, and famous works of art. They saw no one as they made their way along silent corridors.

The lights flickered as they climbed the stairs to the second floor and they hastened their ascent. Main power failed leaving the chemical emergency lights the only source of illumination.

The second floor, a place that few non-political entities ever saw, displayed even more opulence. Rare statues and archeological relics from dead cultures added to the already aristocratic accommodations. Main power returned as they walked toward a second-floor checkpoint. Bright lights activated in sequence, lighting the corridor in a wave. Computers chirped and whirred as they rebooted.

"I'm sorry, sir," the TSA officer held up his left hand. "Parliament is still on lock down. You'll need to return to your offices."

Jake stopped his forward momentum less than a meter from the outstretched hand. Angel arrested her movement, crossed her arms and began tapping her foot impatiently. The officer lowered his hand, his right palm resting on the butt of the pistol holstered on his right hip. Two other checkpoint officers stood a few meters away, rifles cradled in their arms. The barricade consisted of two stations—one on either side of a metal gate—which divided the corridor. The guards spread out in a rough triangle around the gate. A walk-through weapons scanner sat between the stations, the only way through the barrier. A small green light indicated the machine was active.

The Officer's visor was down, but the nasal voice and squat armor led Jake to believe he was dealing with a Klan'do. Jake placed his arms on his hips in exasperation.

"I thought the emergency was over?" Jake inquired.

"A ship was destroyed, yes," the Officer said. "But, we are still on lockdown until Command is certain the threat has been neutralized and the power has been fully restored. Now please, sir, return to your office."

Jake sighed. He had hoped to get a little further before running into another security detail. Every encounter and firefight reduced their chances of getting to the politician's offices. His eyes studied the weapons scanner and he shook his head. He also did not count on that kind of security this far into the building.

"Of course," Jake said, taking a step back. "Do let me know when we are free to move about again."

"Of course, sir," the TSA Officer replied, relaxing his stance. His right hand dropped away from the butt of his weapon.

Jake dropped his trench coat to the floor, revealing a dark suit and two pistols strapped to his waist. The Klan'do's armored helmet looked down and hesitated, before reaching for the pistol. Jake's first shot hit the officer in the chest, stopping the alien's draw and propelling him backwards into the weapons scanner. The scanner emitted a high-pitched tone as it detected the Klan'do and its pistol.

Jake ducked behind the checkpoint station as the other two TSA officers raised their weapons and fired. Bright red lasers flashed down the corridor, exploding against the barricade. Jake fired a couple of un-aimed shots back at the guards, missing wide. Jake rose from cover, fired two shots, and ducked as a hail of return fire zipped overhead. He moved to the edge of the desk and repeated the maneuver with similar results.

Angel entered the fray, springing to her feet from behind the left side barrier, two pistols out and ready. She fired both weapons simultaneously, blue bolts blasting the nearest guard. The double stun bolts lifted the officer into the air as electrical charges played across their armor. A reflexive trigger pull sent a red bolt into the ceiling. The officer dangled in the air for a heartbeat, before crashing onto the waxed tile floor.

The remaining guard turned his weapon toward Angel. She ducked as bolts rocked her position. Jake, taking advantage of her distraction, rose from behind the barricade and fired. The TSA Officer took the bolt on his left side, shaking as the electrical shocks shut down his body. He dropped his weapon as another bolt hit him in the chest. The guard half spun and paused midair, before collapsing in a scene that would make any holo-vid director proud. Jake checked both ends of the corridor for reinforcements, relieved when none appeared.

Silence filled the corridor except for the incessant beep of the weapons scanner. Jake grabbed the first officer's boot and pulled him from the machine, ending the noise.

Satisfied, he turned to see Angel stripping out of the long skirt she wore. She dropped the garment on the floor, kicking it to land next to Jake's discarded coat. The skirt gone, she now wore a pair of black, skintight pants and a pair of cross-draw holsters.

"That should get someone's attention," she smiled, nodding to the numerous cameras around the checkpoint.

A buzz at his side signaled an incoming call and Jake removed a headset from his belt. He slid the lightweight comm on his head, adjusting the small boom mic. He saw Angel adjust an identical device on her head. "Cutter."

"I don't know what you did," Dawson's voice filled

his ear, "but you stirred up a hornet's nest."

"We took out checkpoint two-oh-four," Angel replied, reading a small sign on the weapons scanner.

"The TSA is on alert," his voice sounded distracted, pained. "They have a fugitive retrieval specialist en route."

Jake nodded. "Then we better get moving before reinforcements arrive."

"Hurry," Dawson replied. The sound of overheating engines filled the comm before it died.

"Mark?" Angel called. No answer.

A shadow filled the corridor and the two turned to see a low flying shuttle blocking the light from the windows. The ship's nose flared as it came even with them. Jake stared at the ship, but the dark tint of the shuttle's windows hid the occupants. He felt the intense gaze of a predator on him and the hairs on the back of his neck stood for attention. Jake watched as the shuttle cut speed, crawling past the conquered checkpoint.

Jake led Angel down the corridor, passing through the weapons scanner which beeped dutifully. The shuttle matched their pace, hovering a few meters from the windows.

"You said reinforcements?" Angel mocked.

"We need to move," Jake countered, a feeling of doom enshrouding his soul.

David Derez stared out of the shuttle's windows as

it aligned with the second-floor checkpoint. The reflective windows of Parliament revealed nothing except the reflection of the shuttle. Derez could not see his target, but knew he stared at him. A quick check of an infrared scanner confirmed his instincts. He raised his hand, finger and thumb extended like a pistol. "Bang."

He turned to the pilot. "Get us up to the pad. Now."

The shuttle lifted into the clear sky and executed a tight loop that brought it in line with the landing pads on the roof. The craft touched down with barely a nudge and the retrieval specialist released his harness. The hatch opened and he descended the ramp into the bright sunshine of afternoon. A squad of armored guards met him at the base of the ramp.

"Sir, they are on the second floor. We believe they are heading for level three," the Officer in Charge (OIC) reported as Derez strode even with him. The OIC executed an about face and matched the Lieutenant's long stride, the rest of the squad filing in behind them.

They entered the building and Derez felt the cool shade wash over him; relief from the blazing sun. He nodded as the OIC finished his report. Derez abruptly stopped and the OIC continued walking, only to backtrack to face the officer. "Secure Parliamentary Hall," Derez ordered. "I will go to the offices. With both ends of the corridor secure, we will have them in a crossfire."

The officer saluted, turned, and ordered his team to move out. The armored squad double-timed it down the pristine corridor, passing priceless sculptures, paintings and tapestries, their armor clanking as they ran. They disappeared around a distant corner, and Derez turned down a junction toward the Parliamentarian's Offices.

Mark Dawson edged the nose of his scout toward the planet, watching the heat shields glow red. He felt the heat rise in the cockpit as turbulence buffeted the small ship. He pushed the control pad to the right, feeling the controls jerk in his hands as the scout skipped across the atmosphere. Lasers flashed past his canopy and he pulled hard on the control yoke. The pursuing fighters roared past as the scout rebounded into space, out of danger for the moment.

The trio of fighters slowed, making wide turns in the upper atmosphere. Dawson glanced at the rear screens and saw the fighters turn on his tail and immediately open fire.

"Hurry," he said to Angel, ducking involuntarily as another volley of fire strafed his shields. The scout vibrated with each impact. He changed frequencies and tried to contact the TSA for the fourth time.

"TSA fighters, this is the Scout *Overwatch*," Mark called. "Do you copy?"

"Scout *Overwatch*," a voice answered in a less than friendly tone. "Power down your engines. Now!"

"The last time I did that you opened fire on me." Dawson banked the ship to port around a collection of derelict space junk. "Fool me once..."

"You are aiding wanted fugitives, Lieutenant," the voice replied. "You are under arrest." Another volley of bolts hit the scout, the shields glowing with each impact. Dawson fought the controls. "Keep flying in circles," the voice said smugly, "I've got all day."

Dawson ducked the scout under an orbiting dreadnaught, rotated the ship, and skimmed the fuselage belly to belly. His sensors beeped and he saw two additional fighters directly ahead, in addition to the three on his tail.

"I'm doing what?" he asked.

"You are aiding and abetting fugitives," the pilot repeated.

"No...no," Dawson exclaimed. "I'm cutting engines, cease fire!"

He turned the *Overwatch* away from the dreadnaught and powered down his engines. He kept his hand on the throttle, anticipating another barrage of laser fire, and relieved it never came. He watched as the lead fighter sped past, slowed, and maneuvered nose-to-nose to the scout. The pilot flipped up his visor and stared into the larger vessel. With only meters separating the ships, Dawson knew he had nowhere left to run.

"If you are not aiding the fugitives below," the pilot said, "then why did you run?"

Mark shook his head, pointing at the pilot through his window. "You fired on me without provocation." He wondered if he could talk his way out of the predicament.

"Someone in orbit is jamming TSA transmissions to recall security forces to Parliament," the pilot said, pointing a gloved finger back at Dawson. "And we found you in orbit in a ship designed for that very thing."

"Well, it isn't me," Dawson stated.

"Lieutenant," the fighter pilot replied, "you are the only scout in orbit..."

"Is the jamming still active?" Mark interjected.

The pilot looked down at the readouts in his cramped cockpit. He raised his hand and tried to scratch his head, his helmet blocking the action. "Yes," he looked up, confused.

"Well, then it can't be me," Dawson explained. "A scout has to—"

"—be stationary to be effective," the fighter pilot concluded. He looked down again, and flipped a switch. The scout's weapons lock indicator flashed green.

"Sorry, Lieutenant," the pilot said. He lowered his visor and the fighter inverted, flying underneath the scout and disappearing from view. "You may return to your duties." The comm went dead as all five fighters roared past, the light from the engines fading into the stars.

Dawson slumped, breathing a long sigh of relief. "That was close," he said and set a course for a group of distant satellites. The flight took less than five minutes and the scout assumed its original orbit. He checked the dials, ensuring the jammers he had placed on the orbital bodies still functioned. As he watched, the preprogrammed switches relayed the jamming signal from one satellite to another, masking their origin. "Try to track that down," he muttered.

He opened a secure channel. "Angel?"

"A little busy right now," came her terse reply. Laser fire filtered over the comm. "On third level, near Parliament Hall. Heavy resistance..."

The Jake Cutter Conspiracy

Chapter Twenty-Seven

Angel and Jake left the checkpoint on level two and crossed more than half of the remaining Parliament building. They moved quietly, encountering only minor resistance during the journey and leaving a handful of stunned TSA Officers in their wake. Approaching footfalls encouraged them to bypass the first set of elevators and stairs they encountered. The pair continued to a second stairwell, well off the main travelled corridors. They climbed the stairs, weapons ready, hugging the walls, and exited onto the third floor only a few hundred meters from their objective. To their left sat Parliament Hall, a vast, three-tiered meeting hall where politicians, dignitaries, and honored guests met to discuss the complexities of the Tri-System. To their right lay the political offices.

Angel poked her head around the corner and ducked back quickly. She motioned for Jake to look for himself, pointing around the corner and mouthing the word *trouble*. He nodded, moved up beside her, and glanced around the corner. A squad of armored guards had taken up positions around the entrance to the Hall. Overturned tables, chairs, and marble and bronze statues provided cover for the squad. Jake withdrew, shook his head, and pointed toward the offices. She nodded and, hugging the wall, took a step to her right.

A door marked RESTROOM directly opposite the stairs opened and Angel froze, staring at a Hazmora exiting the lavatory. His helmet hung from the butt of his pistol, a rifle slung across his back, his hands busy adjusting his mid-torso armor. He looked up from his armor and froze at the sight of her. He stared at Angel, eyes wide, before opening his mouth to shout a warning.

Angel fired, the blue stun bolt striking the Hazmora in the groin. The alien screamed as the bolt slammed him into the wall, his armor and weapons clattering on the polished floor. She turned, picked a second target, and fired. The guard ducked behind a statue, untouched.

Jake joined in, edging around the corner and firing both of his pistols as fast as he could pull the trigger. A maelstrom of bolts roared down the corridor at the TSA sentries. The stun bolts impacted tables, chairs, two artificial plants and one guard, who fell twitching in blue energy. Jake retreated behind the wall as the squad returned fire.

Her headset buzzed, "Angel?"

The firing slowed and Angel took advantage of the lull to sneak a peek around the corner. "A little busy right now," she answered. She fired, rewarded with a guard flying backwards, blue electricity ravaging his body. "On third level, near Parliament Hall. Heavy resistance..."

The squad began advancing and she snapped another quick shot. She heard a scream and the clatter of a weapon. The attackers took cover and opened fire again.

She felt the thump of laser blasts into the wall at her back and wondered how long the structure would hold. She looked at Jake. "Any ideas?"

He holstered the pistol in his right hand, dug into a small pouch, and produced two small crystalline balls. "One," he nodded, twisted the timer on the first bomb and tossed it toward the far side of the corridor. He activated the second and looped a side armed toss down the near side of the hallway. Jake ducked, clamping his hands over his ears. Angel stared at him a moment before mimicking her partner.

The first explosion rocked the third floor of the Parliament building, shattering windows, upending TSA officers, and tossing furniture about the corridor. The second stun grenade followed on the heels of the first, knocking over statues and flinging armored guards around the hallway like ragdolls.

Angel heard a loud ringing in her ears and felt the shockwave wash over her, knocking her to the floor.

"Move," she felt Jake's hand pick her up, "now!"

Angel watched as the TSA guards rose slowly, shaking their heads to rid themselves of the concussive blasts. They fired, their shots wide. Angel felt Jake push her in the direction of the offices and she ran as her hearing returned. She heard the whine and felt the heat of the energy bolts as the armored TSA Officers' aim improved. The laser fire edged closer to the two retreating fugitives.

Angel heard a grunt and a weapon skittering across the floor behind her. She turned to see Jake fall backwards, his left shoulder smoldering from a hit. He grimaced in pain, but continued to fire with the pistol in his right hand. Angel fired both of her pistols as she retraced her steps. She holstered the pistol in her left hand and grabbed Jake by the collar. She grunted with exertion as she dragged him behind the cover of a statue. She glanced over her shoulder; they were only meters from the political offices.

She fired again, hitting an armored trooper. The man fell, tripping his companion that followed. The firing lulled for a moment.

"Go!" Jake ordered.

Angel ignored him, shifted the pistol to her left hand and reached down to the pouch on his belt. She felt a small orb, pulled the thorium bomb out of the pouch and, with a flick of her finger, activated the device. She hurled it down the corridor toward the regrouping squad. As soon as the bomb left her hand she clasp her hands over her ears and snuggled next to Jake on the floor.

"That's not a stun—" Jake began.

An explosion rocked the hallway, toppling priceless statues and destroying works of art in a wall of fire. A table rocketed skyward, flipping end over end, before crashing onto a potted plant. Three of the assault team took the brunt of the explosion point blank, vaporizing instantly. Two others, their armor scorched and cracked, flew through the air. Their impacts left body outlines two meters up the wall. The explosion propelled one guard out a broken window, his gurgling scream trailing off as he fell to the street below. Flames scorched a thousand-year-old tapestry hanging along the corridor.

Angel ducked and felt the heat of the blast wash over her. The shock wave pushed them another meter closer to their objective. She rose, scanning the corridor with her pistol as she grabbed Jake's collar again. "Come on!" she yelled and hauled him to his unsteady feet. He wobbled for a moment, but stayed up right.

He checked his pistol and nodded to the door. "Let's go," he murmured, fighting through the pain of his shoulder. Angel scanned the corridor behind them, saw no movement, and pushed Jake toward the Parliamentary offices. She pushed the heavy oak door open and shoved him inside. She backed in, watching the destroyed corridor for movement.

"Angel!" he cried.

She turned at his warning, allowing the door to close behind her. She saw Jake lying on the floor, staring to his left. Her eyes followed his gaze and she saw a reception foyer with a rich mahogany wood desk, three large, leather couches, and portraits of past politicians adorned the walls. Thick carpet made the reception foyer as lush as the corridor beyond. Her stare locked eyes with Secretary Terra standing three meters away, next to his wife.

Movement caught her eye and she turned, raising her weapon at a TSA Officer with a rifle in his arms.

She saw the energy beam discharge from the man's weapon and felt the impact throw her against the door, knocking the breath from her. Blue swirls of electricity engulfed her body and she felt millions of ants crawling across her skin. She slid to the floor, her pistol falling from numb fingers. The world closed in around her and she fell into a dark abyss.

Jake pulled himself into a sitting position as the TSA Officer who stunned Angel collected his pistol. The man removed Angel's sidearm before returning to his spot beside Dante Terra. Jake scooted over to the slumped form of Angel, ignoring the pain in his shoulder as he checked on her. He breathed a sigh of relief as he found her pulse strong. A small blinking green light drew his attention to Angel's headset and he realized the comm line was still active. With a glimmer of hope, he pulled himself to his feet and turned to face the man who ruined his life.

"Mr. Cutter, I presume," Secretary Terra began. He wore a dark grey suit, an olive shirt, and a black tie. His black mustache appeared recently trimmed, as did his hair. He smiled as if greeting an old friend. "I've heard so much about you." The Secretary motioned for the TSA Officer to lower his weapon as he spoke.

"Don't worry about the young woman, she will be fine. Lieutenant Derez used the lowest stun setting, per my orders.

"Now, what brings you to my office today?"

Jake watched the officer lower the rifle, but keep it at the ready. He touched his shoulder and felt sticky, wet blood. He looked down at Angel before addressing the politician. "Information," he said before nodding to the woman standing beside the Secretary, "and to see my wife."

"Ex-wife," Dari Terra corrected, her tone disgusted.

"Ex-wife."

"And what information can I provide for you, Mr. Cutter?" Dante Terra asked.

"Why you framed me would be a good place to start," Jake said. The room spun momentarily, and he reached out for the wall. The wave of nausea subsided and he stood tall.

"Why I..." the Secretary began. He offered his best politician smile. "Mr. Cutter, I believe you are mistaken." He shrugged, holding his empty hands out innocently. "I had nothing to do with your criminal activity."

"You deny that you framed me?" Jake inquired. The politician nodded. "Then why did *everyone* in Cla'nix say you offered them pardons for my demise."

The politician lost his smile, as confusion filled his features. "I offered no such thing." He looked to Dari and Derez, neither said a word, their faces emotionless.

"You don't have to lie," Jake said, fighting off another wave of nausea. He checked his wound and found the sleeve of his coat wet. The bleeding slowed, but Jake knew his vertigo would only worsen with additional blood loss.

"I assure you, Mr. Cutter," Dante Terra explained, "I offered no such thing. Do you know what such an accusation would do to my career?"

"Your career?" Jake asked, astonished. "You ruined my life!"

Angel groaned and Jake bent over to tend to the woman, the sudden movement bringing on a bout of dizziness. His vision narrowed and he took several breaths until his eyesight returned to normal. "Angel?" he croaked, shaking the woman lightly. "Angel?"

She opened her eyes, blinking rapidly for several seconds. "I'm...I'm alright," she said shaking her head to clear it. She struggled to her feet, leaning against the wall. She stared at Jake for a moment before her eyes surveyed the room, locking onto the other three in the reception area. She reached for her weapons and found the holster empty.

"No need for that, Miss," the politician said, motioning to Lieutenant Derez, standing at his side. The man turned, exposing her pistols tucked into the belt at his waist. The Secretary turned back to Jake. "Now, Mr. Cutter. I believe you accused me of ruining your life. I can assure you, I had nothing to do with your descent into criminality."

"Perhaps I can provide the answers he seeks," Dari interjected.

Dante turned to look at his wife, shocked. "Oh?"

"Yes," she smiled, before turning to Jake. "You may want to sit down for this."

"I'll stand, Pamela," he refused, crossing his arms. He winced from his wounds, but gritted his teeth through the pain. "Now what the hell is going on?"

Dari Terra sighed before turning and nodding at Derez. Secretary Terra jumped as Lieutenant Derez flicked the fire selector switch with his thumb and fired, striking Jake in the leg. The bolt burned through flesh, destroying muscle and bone while it cauterized the wound. Jake collapsed, screaming in pain. Angel slid across the floor to Jake on all fours. She covered the wound with her hands as he writhed in agony. She released the leg, tore off a piece of his suit, and tied it above the wound as a tourniquet.

He looked up and, with his eyes, motioned toward the headset she wore. He mouthed *intercom* and she nodded.

She cinched the tourniquet tight and Jake yelped in pain.

"Mark," she whispered into her headset, "get down here. Now!"

Dawson leaned forward in his ship, listening as the events on the planet below spiraled out of control. Jake screamed as someone shot him. He heard the tear of cloth and Jake's cries of pain worsened as Angel administered aid.

"Mark," came Angel's whisper, "get down here. Now!"

The TSA Officer paused, listening to the drama play out over the comm. The pair were in deep trouble; wounded and unarmed. The secure frequency remained active and the plan continued to unravel. He flipped the record button and continued to listen.

"What are you doing?" a voice asked. Dawson identified it as Secretary Terra. "I gave you no order to fire."

"Lieutenant Derez works for me," Dari Terra's voice said, followed by laser fire.

Dawson flipped to the emergency channel, broadcasting planet wide. "The Parliament building is under attack. All units return to Parliament." He scanned the sensors noting that none of the dozens of ships in orbit moved.

"Jammers!" he yelled, realizing his message could not get through due to his own handiwork. He pushed the throttle forward and the *Overwatch* roared away from the satellites. He flipped the cover off a red button to his right, jabbing the button without hesitation.

The ring of jamming satellites exploded in succession, the shock waves scattering debris throughout planetary orbit. The scout rocked as the waves overtook the ship, careening it toward the dreadnaught he had skimmed earlier. Dawson tugged on the controls, righting the ship seconds before impact. He rotated the scout, flying belly-to-belly underneath the dreadnaught and his shields flared as they scraped the shields of the larger ship. The scout pulled away.

The channels read clear and Dawson tried his message again. "All units, this is Lieutenant Mark Dawson, fugitive retrieval. Parliament is under attack. All units converge and apprehend escaped prisoners. All units, Parliament is under attack!"

"What are you doing?" Secretary Terra demanded, staring at the officer. "I gave you no order to fire!"

"Lieutenant Derez works for me," Dari explained. She crossed the room and drew one of Angel's pistols from the Officer's belt. Without preamble or warning, she shot her politician husband in the abdomen. The man collapsed next to a desk, grasping his stomach as he fell. He propped himself up, watching as a red stain spread across his grey suit.

"What?" he cried. His breathing came in ragged gasps. "Why?"

Angel looked away from the politician as she heard Dawson's transmitted message. Jake heard it too and turned to see Derez touching his ear. The Lieutenant leaned forward and whispered into Dari Terra's ear. The woman nodded and turned to her ex-husband.

"Jake, dear. The jammers you put in orbit have been destroyed," she mocked. She shook her head sadly. "Reinforcements are enroute to secure this building and re-capture you."

She squatted a meter in front of Jake. She pointed

to the bleeding politician "Dante had nothing to do with this," she smiled. "I put the bounty on your head."

The words hit Jake like a sack of bricks. He saw her laugh at his pain. He tried to speak, but the words would not come.

"You want to know why?" she asked. Jake nodded blankly. "Simple. I wanted more from life than you could offer," she scoffed, then sneered at her ex-husband. Venom filled her voice. "I learned to hate you over the years. You were never home. And when you were, all you wanted to know is if I would fly around in that broken-down freighter." She paused before shaking her head, "I never had any intention of flying around in that dump of a freighter. I wanted out.

"Then I met Dante at a fundraiser. He was charming and gave me a taste of a life I had only dreamed of." Dari's voice faded as she remembered and recited her path. "Dinner parties, influence, privilege. My biggest fear was you would return and ruin it all.

"Then I met the man who would become my mentor," she continued, a satisfied grin on her face. "He opened up other doors. Doors that Dante could not, or would not, open. Desmond told me that one day I could be Chancellor, but warned me that your existence could destroy everything.

"The Sergeant, the man who arrested you, remember him?" She paused as Jake numbly nodded. "He ran the security detail for Desmond. Desmond told me that he wanted a way back to Cla'nix to run a rather lucrative smuggling business, and I wanted you gone. For a small percentage of his profits, he vowed to make that happen."

She stared down at Jake, disgust in her eyes. "Desmond got me close to Dante. The Sergeant had you arrested," she continued. "I confessed to Dante that you were an abusive louse and he made arrangements with your lawyer. The one you fired, remember?"

Jake nodded.

"I knew you would declare your innocence and protest any deal. I knew you, Jake. Once the trial was over, the Sergeant escorted you to Cla'nix. Everyone won."

"But the baby?" Jake asked.

Dari threw her head back, laughing loudly. "There was no baby." She moved closer to her ex-husband, squatting to look him in the eye. "I sat home, alone, for eight years, wasting my life away waiting on you to come home. I wanted you to feel what I felt: distraught, humiliated," she paused, "devastated, and alone.

"I made up that story to haunt you, in what I thought would be your final days. I had no idea you would find friends," she nodded toward Angel. "Or learn how to fight...to survive." She laughed again. "The ironic thing is, if you had shown those qualities to me then, we might still be married."

"This isn't you, Pamela," Jake croaked. "No one could change this much in such a short time."

"Never underestimate a scorned woman." She stood and walked back to stand beside Derez. Dari faced Dante, still lying on the floor, and addressed him directly. "With your death, at the hands of my ex-husband, I will be positioned to take the next step." She paused, a content smile occupied her lips. "The sympathy vote alone will propel me to the Senate."

She pointed her pistol at the bleeding politician. He held up a bloody hand in protest, a look of terror on his face. He opened his mouth to scream. Terra shot him in the chest without a thought and tossed the weapon aside.

She crossed her arms and turned to face Jake. She rubbed her chin thoughtfully. "Now, which one of you dies first?"

Mark Dawson pushed the throttle forward and fought the bucking scout as it raced across the cloudless sky. He watched as the capitol city took shape on the distant horizon; the wagon wheel layout distinct against the surrounding green grasslands. The Scout *Overwatch* shuddered with atmospheric turbulence and warning klaxons began sounding as the heat shields stressed. Mark tapped the throttle again, ensuring he was at full power.

Other contrails filled the sky as a dozen other ships—fighters and pickets mostly—converged on the center of the wagon wheel. He heard the frantic voices of officers over the comm as they demanded more speed. Ground units informed command they were minutes away.

"Which one of you dies first?" the Secretary's widow asked.

"Stall her!" Dawson commanded. "I am two minutes out."

He ignored the computer warning that his approach vector and speed were inconsistent with a safe landing. The Parliament building loomed ahead, growing larger by the second. Dawson pulled back on the throttle, applying the retro boosters at full power. His harness retracted, holding him firmly in his chair as the ship bucked. The groan of metal filled the ship from the stress of the high-speed descent and braking maneuver.

"Why all this trouble?" he heard Jake ask through the comm. "Why not just divorce me?"

The metal fatigue groan grew shrill, followed by the sheering of metal as the communications array ripped from the ship. His secure frequency died. "Damnit!" he yelled and pulled the nose of the scout skyward, bringing the landing thrusters online. The *Overwatch* bucked and more metal shrieked with strain. The ship shimmied as the port stabilizer ripped free.

Warning lights flashed and klaxons blared. The controls died and he lost control. The scout touched the pad on top of the building, skipped skyward, and plummeted back to the roof, crashing onto the top of Parliament.

"Why all this trouble?" Jake asked. "Why not just

divorce me?"

"A divorce was too simple, Jake," she replied. "With you around, you could still cause trouble. Desmond always said one wrong interview, or spoken word, can derail a campaign. So you see, you had to go." Her voice turned cold. "Besides, I learned to hate you over the years, and I wanted to see you abandoned, suffering. Just like you left me."

She shook her head, dismissing the conversation. "Kill the girl first," she told Derez.

Lieutenant Derez raised the rifle, his finger whitening on the trigger. The roar of engines filled the air, followed by a massive impact. The building shuddered. Furniture toppled and windows shattered from the collision. The TSA Officer ducked as the ceiling cracked, raining dust and debris down on him.

"What the hell was that?" Dari asked, shielding her eyes and face from the dust storm raining down.

"Reinforcements," Derez reported. "A ship just landed upstairs. A scout." The ceiling groaned and a section of the roof caved in behind them, filling the room with dust, and smoke. Sunlight streamed through the hole, fighting through the dust to cast light on Jake and Angel. All four of them averted their eyes, coughing from the dusty haze in the room.

Derez kept the rifle trained on the two fugitives. He placed his left hand on his headset, listening. "Ground units have arrived," he reported. "A dozen squads will be here any minute."

Dari nodded. "We are out of time," she said with a cough. She waved a hand at Jake and Angel. "Kill them."

Dawson groaned and shook his head to clear the fog.

The ship lay in shambles around him. The controls took turns spitting sparks as several small fires burned, threatening to suffocate him with smoke. He tapped his harness release and felt the pressure release from his chest. He slumped, gasping for air in the thick smoke. He felt heat from behind him and turned to see the hatch to the main fuselage blocked by fire. He dropped to the floor and pounded the emergency exit button underneath his chair.

The bottom hatch of the cockpit slid open and he tumbled out, smacking the mangled tarmac hard. He lay there for a moment, listening to the hiss of the ship as it died. He climbed unsteadily to his feet, looking skyward as contrails filled the sky converging on his location. Sirens filled the city, growing louder as the TSA reinforcements closed in on Parliament. He drew his weapon and staggered toward the landing pad entrance to the building.

He heard the creak of the building and hurried off the roof. The initial impact point, weakened by the crashing scout, dropped to the floor below. Dawson leaped over the hole, landing awkwardly and felt his ankle give. He pushed the pain from his mind and hobbled through the main doors into the building.

The elevators were nonfunctional and he headed

for the stairs. He took them two at a time. He stumbled and caught himself before tumbling down to the next level. Pain burned in his leg and each step sent a shock through his system. He paused, staring at his ankle. *Not broken*, he mused, and continued down the stairs.

Fire-scorched debris and bodies littered the floor. Overturned tables, broken windows and laser impact points dominated Dawson's vision. He heard groans of the wounded and the stench of charred flesh and burned walls assaulted his nostrils. He limped forward, heading for the office side of the wing as fast as he could. Echoing footfalls announced more reinforcements and he turned to see a dozen armored officers exit the stairwell from the second floor. The squad formed into teams and ran toward the offices. He waved them forward.

"Lieutenant Dawson, Special Activities Branch," Mark identified himself. "Get in there and secure those offices."

The squad of troops flashed passed, stacked up outside the reception area door, and breached the heavy oak door in seconds. Mark followed, limping despite the pain. He made it to the door as he heard a chorus of "Clear." He entered the reception area, his eyes scanning the room.

Dari Terra sat on the floor, knees drawn to her chest and arms around her legs. She rocked back and forth, sobbing. A large TSA Officer stood behind her, a rifle cradled in his arms. The woman's dress was torn, her hair disheveled. Dust covered everything. Secretary Terra lay nearby, blood slowly soaking the rich carpet from his wounds. Dawson's gaze continued around the room, resting on a spot to the left of the door.

Jake and Angel lay dead, their bodies slumped against the wall, Angel's head resting on Jake's shoulder. Each sported a scorch mark in the center of their chest, courtesy of a single laser bolt. Dawson saw Jake also exhibited wounds to his shoulder and leg. He slowly rotated his head, staring at the Lieutenant standing over Dari Terra. Rage replaced the grief and he took a step toward the Officer.

The team leader of the reinforcements intervened, reporting to Dawson with a crisp salute. "Lieutenant Dawson?" he asked.

Mark offered a nod.

"Sir, it's over."

The Jake Cutter Conspiracy

Epilogue

Mark Dawson stood quietly in his dress uniform, studying the TSA Medal of Valor in his right hand. He rolled the medal over, and back again, the medal reflecting the bright sunshine of Heroz. He stood on the bank of the river that ran along the edge of Heroz City. Behind him sat the debris of the demolished house that had once belonged to Jake Cutter and his wife, Pamela. Dawson closed his eyes, fighting back the tears.

With his left hand, he pulled a necklace from underneath his dress shirt. Angel's necklace. Dawson rubbed the pendent of complex knots between his fingers offering a silent prayer to his friends.

The official report, filed by Lieutenant Junior Grade David Derez, told the tale of a pair of escaped convicts and their assassination of Secretary of Commerce Dante Terra. The two sacrificed a freighter to draw security forces away from Parliament. They then stormed the building, killing a squad of guards, the Secretary, and attempted to kill the Secretary's wife before Derez arrived and killed the fugitives. Derez was given a medal and promoted to Lieutenant.

The official report, filed by Lieutenant Junior Grade Mark Dawson, told of his finding the jammers, destroying them, and then sacrificing his own ship in an effort to save the Secretary. Despite arriving too late, his heroic finding of the jammers earned him the Medal of Valor, a promotion to Lieutenant, and his choice of assignment.

Dawson shook his head, knowing both reports were not worth the electrons they were written with. He replaced the necklace, dropping it underneath his shirt, wishing that his ship had survived long enough to retrieve the recordings of Terra. Unfortunately, the ship and all of its contents were deemed a total loss. Nothing could be salvaged.

He looked across the river and saw the image of Dari Terra on the hundreds of billboards throughout the city. He pulled a communicator from his belt and tuned it to the news frequency.

"...and my thanks to the brave men, women, and beings that came to my rescue," Dari Terra's voice said. The woman on the billboards was dressed in black, her left arm in a matching sling. Even at this distance, Mark saw that her hair and make-up were meticulous.

"I pledge to carry on my late husband's work," she continued. "His Senate campaign will now become my campaign. I will run in his honor." Thunderous applause erupted from whatever group she addressed. She broke down, tears streaming down her face. "I know that's what he would have wanted..."

Dawson turned off the communicator, returning it to his belt. He pulled a crumpled piece of paper from his pocket. Smoothing it out, he read it again, wondering for the thousandth time if he made the right decision.

LIEUTENANT MARK DAWSON, the paper read, YOU ARE HEREBY ASSIGNED TO THE TRI-SYSTEM AUTHORITY SPECIAL OPERATIONS COMMAND. REPORT IMMEDIATELY TO TRAINING REGIMENT RITMAR, KORRIEN SECTOR.

He crumbled the paper and placed it in his pocket again. He stared at the medal in his hand. "I swear that I will make this right," he said to the medal. "Your deaths will be avenged."

He threw the medal into the flowing river, turned, and walked away.

The Adventure Continues in

Acknowledgments

Thank you Dimitri Walker for the awesome cover art. You, as always, outdid yourself!
paintingsbydimitri.com

Thanks Dimitri, Amaris, and Cheryl for beta reading the book. Your comments and suggestions keep me straight, and that is no easy task!

Thanks to Gene for working tirelessly to ensure the graphics turned out perfect.

And thanks to my family (Trina, George, and Logan) for your untiring support.

About the Author

With a face for radio and a voice for silent movies, writing was his only recourse.

Award Winning Author R. Kyle Hannah is a self-professed geek and lover of all things sci-fi. He began writing in high school as an outlet for an overactive imagination. Those humble beginnings, combined with real life experiences from a 29-year career in the Army, have spawned a half-dozen full-length adventures and short stories.

"Reminiscent of Arthur C. Clark" is how Writer's Digest describes his first novel *To Aid and Protect*.

His *TIME ASSASSINS* Trilogy (*Time Assassins, Assassin's Gambit, & Assassin's End*) has met great praise from authors and readers alike. The series is a time travel adventure that chronicles futuristic assassins who travel back in time and rewrite alternate timelines into our history. The trilogy features a Pinnacle Book Achievement Award Winner and an Amazon Best Seller.

His next trilogy (*The Tri-System Authority - The Jake Cutter Conspiracy*, *The Tri-System Authority - The Reign of Terra,* and *The Tri-System Authority: Tales from the Busty Ostrich*) are slated for release in 2018 and 2019.

Kyle has several other projects in the works, including *The Coven, Harvest Day, Atlantis Falling*, and a screenplay adaptation of his first novel, *To Aid and Protect.*

He is married, with two children, and lives in the suburbs of Birmingham, Alabama.

He has many convention appearances scheduled throughout the year. You can find his schedule on his website: www.rkylehannah.com.

You can find him:
On FACEBOOK at www.facebook.com/rkylehannahwriter
On Twitter @rkhannah
On Instagram rkylehannah
On the web at www.rkylehannah.com

58254632R00207

Made in the USA
Columbia, SC
19 May 2019